# Bachelorette

# #1

# Bachelorette #1

## Jennifer O'Connell

NEW AMERICAN LIBRARY

New American Library
Published by New American Library, a division of
Penguin Group (USA) Inc., 375 Hudson Street,
New York, New York 10014, U.S.A.
Penguin Books Ltd, 80 Strand,
London WC2R 0RL, England
Penguin Books Australia Ltd, 250 Camberwell Road,
Camberwell, Victoria 3124, Australia
Penguin Books Canada Ltd, 10 Alcorn Avenue,
Toronto, Ontario, Canada M4V 3B2
Penguin Books (N.Z.) Ltd, Cnr Rosedale and Airborne Roads,
Albany, Auckland 1310, New Zealand

Penguin Books Ltd, Registered Offices:
80 Strand, London WC2R 0RL, England

First published by New American Library,
a division of Penguin Group (USA) Inc.

First Printing, August 2003
10   9   8   7   6   5   4   3   2   1

 REGISTERED TRADEMARK—MARCA REGISTRADA

LIBRARY OF CONGRESS CATALOGING-IN-PUBLICATION DATA:

O'Connell, Jennifer L.
Bachelorette number one / Jennifer L. O'Connell.
p.   cm.
ISBN 0-451-21098-0
1. Reality television programs—Fiction.   2. Dating (Social customs)—Fiction.   3. Women
journalists—Fiction.   4. Married women—Fiction.   I. Title: Bachelorette number I.   II. Title.

PS3615.C65B33   2003
813'.6—dc21            2003046401

Set in Centaur MT
Designed by Ginger Legato
Printed in the United States of America

PUBLISHER'S NOTE
This is a work of fiction. Names, characters, places, and incidents either are the product of the author's
imagination or are used fictitiously, and any resemblance to actual persons, living or dead, business
establishments, events, or locales is entirely coincidental.

BOOKS ARE AVAILABLE AT QUANTITY DISCOUNTS WHEN USED TO PROMOTE PRODUCTS OR SERVICES. FOR
INFORMATION PLEASE WRITE TO PREMIUM MARKETING DIVISION, PENGUIN GROUP (USA) INC., 375 HUDSON
STREET, NEW YORK, NEW YORK 10014.

*For John, Carleigh, and Tanner—finally,*
*a real reason to have a party.*

# ACKNOWLEDGMENTS

Many thanks to my amazing agent, Kristin Nelson, who made this so much fun, and to Genny Ostertag and everyone at NAL. I owe a heartfelt debt of gratitude to Grace Bulger, who was there in the beginning to send Sarah on her way, Debbie Baptiste for her tireless editing and enthusiasm, and Vicki King, whose daily e-mails and willingness to read and re-read Sarah's story helped me keep my sense of humor and sanity. To all my friends who provided their feedback and support, and lived through this process with me—Vangie Deane (finally, I get to prove you wrong), Juliet Vestal, Kari Fazio, Kate Healy, Lisa Novak, Tracy Smith, Amy Carden, and Lisa Pedicone. And members of the Barrington Writers Workshop for their willingness to help. Thanks Mom, Dad, and Michael, because I love you. And a special thanks to my husband, John, whose love and support and poolside suggestions helped make *Bachelorette #1* possible.

# 1

"So that's your assignment." Suzanne slid her fashionable granny glasses down her nose and looked at me over thin pewter rims. "Should you choose to accept it."

I took a deep breath and contemplated what she'd just asked me to do. Go undercover. Like I was James Bond or something.

"I'm a married thirty-four-year-old woman—and a mother," I reminded her, just to make sure Suzanne knew exactly what she was dealing with. "The women on that show can't be a day past twenty-five."

I didn't mention that they were also usually blonder, thinner, better dressed, and about as effervescent as Alka-Seltzer.

"That's not a problem." Suzanne swung her Jimmy Choo stiletto heels off her desk and leaned in close to the intercom button.

"Jody, send them in."

The double mahogany doors to Suzanne's office flew open and a train of what could have passed for circus performers strutted in. An oily-headed bald man dressed in black from head to toe. An ungodly tall, dark woman whose foot-long Tootsie Roll of a neck was wrapped in so many gold chokers she obviously subscribed to the Mr. T school of jewelry theory. And a pair of androgynous twins with Clorox-white crew cuts—brother and sister, I thought, but wouldn't put money on it—who were dressed identically in acid-washed overalls and batik tank tops.

"Sarah, this is the team who will be getting you in fighting form. They're the best." Suzanne gestured to the head of the line. "Rolf, master hairstylist, will turn that mousy brown ponytail of yours into a headful of chunky golden highlights Jennifer Aniston would envy. Suma, goddess of facial contouring, and makeup artist to the stars, will eradicate those sunspots and humorless laugh lines and give you a complexion even a baby's ass couldn't lay claim to. And with Toni and Teri, fashion stylists extraordinaire, you can kiss your spittle-stained T-shirts good-bye and say hello to this season's hottest styles."

Suzanne swiped her index finger against the tip of her tongue and made a little hissing sound that I was sure was supposed to show how hot I'd be by the time they were done with me, but instead sounded like my current wardrobe going up in flames.

How did she expect me to pass for a young, single woman desperate enough to go on national TV and vie for the Stag? I couldn't even stomach the show's first season. Although from its ratings, you would have thought the entire country had a personal stake in whether Chad chose Charlotte, the Southwest flight attendant, or Veronica, the actress/waitress from LA. I can only guess that Nielsen boxes are strategically placed in households where naughty viewers are tied to their Barcaloungers and forced to watch mind-numbing shows like *The Stag* as punishment.

"See? You're in good hands—you won't have any trouble fitting in with the rest of the girls," Suzanne assured me.

"But they're bimbos." I could have added, *and I'm not*, but I figured that went without saying.

"It's a great assignment, Sarah." Suzanne raised her eyebrows and waited for my answer. "We love your work, and I'd hate to have to give the article to someone else."

"Suzanne, I appreciate the effort, but don't I have to fill out an application and tell them all about me? Don't they ask for a birth certificate or something?" I wasn't quite sure how exactly the magazine planned to get away with this.

"Don't you worry about that." She grinned at me and tipped her head to the side like she was keeping a fabulous secret. "Just leave that to us."

On the train ride home I laughed out loud. Me, on *The Stag*? How would I explain that in the Wellesley alumnae magazine: *Sarah Divine Holmes, '90, recently appeared on* The Stag, *trading in her Phi Beta Kappa membership for a bikini, a vacant stare, and the opportunity to humiliate herself on national TV.*

*Femme* magazine wanted me to describe what went on when the TV cameras weren't rolling—the cattiness, the ruthless competition, the degrading process that each woman went through just so she could be chosen by the Stag at the end of eight episodes.

"It's an exposé that looks at how single women have been reduced to parading in front of an eligible man like livestock," Suzanne had told me. "And we think you're just the prime grade-A writer for the job."

All I had to do was make it through two auditions and I'd be on prime-time television sucking in my stomach and sticking out my tits like all the other women. The only thing missing was the cowbell.

It was ludicrous. Besides, I probably wouldn't even get past the first round of auditions, which would be even more embarrassing than making it onto the show in the first place.

Even before I got married, I wasn't the poster child for a cute and perky single life. I'd been in grad school only a few weeks when I met Jack. He was a second-year law student, which doesn't exactly support a lifestyle of late nights and fun. Mostly we'd study in the library, order pizza, and drink a six-pack of whatever was on sale at the liquor store. Then again, I did manage to convince him to huddle behind the stacks a few times and let me get into his briefs, and I don't mean the legal ones. So it'd been years since I actually had to seduce a man, but it wasn't as if I'd never done it before.

Some part of me wanted to see how I would do. Could brains and a quick sense of humor beat a killer twenty-something rack? I could be a competitor—after all, how many of those twinkies had been through twenty-seven hours of labor? Without drugs?

By the time the train reached my stop, I'd convinced myself I might actually have a shot at being in the final group of one hundred women presented to the Stag. Forget the fact that I was currently driving a Volvo wagon, the uninspired car choice of suburban moms everywhere. With Suzanne's team of experts, how could I go wrong? I hadn't let myself go since having a baby, like so many women do. In fact, I was in pretty decent shape, really. Although Jack and I were doing the horizontal mambo less since Katie was born, it was more a matter of free time than lack of interest. He still seemed to appreciate my curves. Maybe I could give all the Hooters waitresses and weathergirl wannabes a run for their money—after all, I knew a few tricks too. It took more than saline implants to brainstorm article ideas and put together a shopping list for the week while listening for the baby and making sure Jack's manly urges were satisfied.

By the time I slipped my key in the front door and dropped my briefcase on the foyer bench, I had convinced myself that I could be on the show—that I could be one of the twenty-four finalists. The assignment had even started to sound pretty good to me. Bringing down a show that insults the intelligence of women could be fun. And the fact that I'd get to do it in sunny southern California didn't hurt. We all have our price.

I kicked off my loafers and headed for the kitchen. I was usually greeted by the sound of baby Keds hoofing it around our hardwood floors. But this afternoon our house was silent except for the white noise of a TV coming from the back of the house.

"Marta?"

Our baby-sitter was perched on a stool at the breakfast bar, her orange velour pants stretched like a second skin across her ample Polish rear end. From my vantage point she resembled a very ripe peach.

"Oh, Mrs. Holmes, Bo, he leaving Miss Hope again." She clutched a tattered tissue to her clammy chest. "And Miss Hope, she don't know who she is, think she the Queen of Zimbiba."

Marta was a serious *Days of Our Lives* fan. She even named her cats Marlena and Victor, the latter being the feisty tabby who appeared on her doorstep and apparently dared Marta to turn him away.

"The baby, she sleeping." Marta pointed a finger toward the ceiling, just in case I didn't know where Katie's room was located. "It go good today?"

"You could say that—they want me for an assignment." I took Marta's elbow and helped her down from the stool, where her toes dangled a good four inches from the terra-cotta floor.

"Let me know when you start. I be here." She took the rolled-up twenty-dollar bill from my hand, stuffed it in the pocket of her natty cardigan sweater, and waddled toward the door.

I flipped off the trials and tribulations of Salem's citizens, opened the sliding glass door for some fresh air, and reached for the sippy cups sitting in the sink. As I stood at the sink sudsing up a milk-weary Elmo cup with macaroni and cheese crusted over its spout, the stale refrigeration of the air-conditioning mingled with the smell of fresh grass clippings, courtesy of this morning's visit from the lawn service. It reminded me of summer camp, and the fact that the landscaper's bill had been sitting on Jack's desk for days waiting for a stamp.

As I stacked the clean cups in the dish rack, I listened for sounds like an animal lying in wait, anticipating a ringing phone or Katie's cries, ready to jump into action. When the last drip of water squeezed from the faucet and landed in the empty sink I heard it—the silence. Not the presence of noise, but the absence of it. I had a quiet moment to myself. There were no article deadlines pending, no child who needed feeding or changing, and no husband who needed my undivided attention because he couldn't find the TV clicker, which he swore he left right on the coffee table in plain view.

I brushed my pruned hands against the terry-cloth towel

hanging on the cabinet knob and felt unnerved. What could I do? Since moving out of the city three years ago, there was always something to do, always someone to take care of. First it was my job at the agency and the endless client demands. Then our house, a fixer-upper that consumed nights and weekends for months and put me on a first-name basis with the guys at Home Depot. A few months later I quit my job to go freelance, and then Katie came along—an entirely different kind of undertaking that changed our lives in one seemingly innocent moment.

I wandered from room to room in search of the things I used to spend time on when I was alone, before I amassed the titles of wife and mother and my days became part of the public domain. I ended up collecting stray toys, trying to kill time until Katie woke up or Jack got home from court. I noticed things that used to be important to me, things that at one point could keep me up at night or on the phone with contractors for hours. The pristine white dental molding around the fireplace that still showed traces of the gluey Barney stickers Katie thought were the perfect compliment to our décor. The plush Pottery Barn couches that once offered luxurious comfort and now collected raisins and Cheerios between their cushions, swallowing up an entire sippy cup for weeks before I'd discover the lumpy milk or sour juice. And my office, with its built-in bookshelves and bulletin boards intended to keep me organized and efficient but that instead collected Dr. Seuss books and scraps of paper with crayon scrawls.

My carefully planned house. My professionally planned career. It all went out the window when Katie was born, and I hadn't quite figured out how to put it back together.

I'd organized the toys, rearranged our CDs in alphabetical order, and was in the kitchen contemplating taking some chicken breasts out of the freezer for dinner when Katie's soft murmurings started the monitor lights flashing. I decided to forgo the barbequed chicken in favor of take-out Chinese and headed upstairs to see Katie.

Katie and I were crouching on the floor in her room, playing

Duck Duck Goose with her collection of stuffed animals, when I heard the electric garage door begin its grinding ascent. Soon after, Jack's keys jingled and then landed with a thud on the kitchen counter.

"We're up here," I called out.

Jack swept into the room a few moments later. "Hello, ladies."

"Da-da!" Katie squealed, propelling herself against his knee-caps.

He hoisted our babbling daughter onto his shoulders, grabbed my hand, and led us downstairs for a cold beer and a replay of our days.

Jack's tie already hung loosely around his starched collar, his stark white shirt creased like morning sheets. Every day he left our house tucked in and buttoned up, clothed in the pinstriped uniform of the adult working male. And every evening he returned to us at the end of another inning, expecting me to play the role of the encouraging coach. I'd ask Jack about his day and he'd trip the release valve, letting his day unravel until I was smothered by it. Of course, he always asked me how my day went, but I knew it was more out of courtesy than true curiosity. It was his sense of spousal obligation more than the expectation that I'd have anything out of the ordinary to share with him.

Tonight I didn't wait for him to ask me about my day. Before he could regale me with stories of smarmy defense attorneys and the deteriorating legal system, I brought up my meeting with Suzanne.

"That show's like the old *Dating Game*, isn't it?" he asked, unbuttoning his cuffs and rolling up his shirtsleeves.

"Not exactly. It's the one where the guy eliminates the women until he ends up proposing to one."

Jack nodded slowly, as if he vaguely remembered seeing an episode while flipping channels one night.

"And Suzanne wants you to pose as one of the women?"

He pulled the refrigerator door open and reached inside.

"A hen—they call them hens."

"You're going to be a *hen*?" His laugh echoed against the fridge's insulated walls.

"You know the chances of my actually making it on the show are pretty slim," I admitted quickly, looking away.

He grabbed a cold beer off the shelf and twisted off the cap.

"I don't know about that." Jack rubbed his chin and squinted at me. "Let's see, maybe the Laurie Partridge ponytail has to go, but with the right haircut and a few highlights..." He circled around me, taking sips of his beer. "Tall, nice legs, no sign of postpregnancy stretch marks, sweet ass. Yep, that rockin' babe I knew in law school is still in there; she's just hidden underneath all those Adidas running pants and T-shirts you think look so sporty."

"Yeah, well, the day you wear more than your paint-stained Princeton sweatshirt around the house and those Levi's with the crotch falling out is the day I'll dress up to sit at a computer while our child dribbles apple juice down my legs."

"Hey, I was just saying I thought you could make it on the show if you gave it some effort." He reached into the cupboard and pulled out a bag of Doritos. "So, what's the deal? How does one get on a television show filled with horny single women?"

"I have to go through two auditions," I explained. "The first one is regional, and if I make it to the next round they videotape me and send it to the Stag."

"And if he likes you?"

"Then I'm on the show. I'd spend five weeks in California— assuming I made it through each of the candle ceremonies without being cut."

Jack washed down a handful of chips with his beer.

"It could mean five weeks away from you and Katie, you know." I looked at our drooling toddler, who was happily seated on the tile floor banging a wooden spoon against her daddy's leg.

"We'll survive, Sarah. I'm sure Marta wouldn't mind the extra hours. Anyway, sounds like a great assignment. Suzanne's sure outdone herself this time."

"Have you ever seen the show? I may have to kiss the guy."

Jack shrugged. Did he think I wouldn't make it past the first audition? Of course I would. I was still a professional, and it was my job. Suzanne was depending on me. The Stag was going to fall over himself rushing to light my candle every week.

"Tongue or no tongue?" he asked, wrinkling his forehead in feigned concern and then laughing at me. "We'll cross that bridge if we come to it. It's not like you're going to sleep with the guy or anything. Besides, how many of those women can say they have this waiting for them when they get back?"

He struck a bodybuilder's pose, his arms bent into right angles with clenched fists. He tried valiantly to keep a straight face, a deflated Arnold Schwarzenegger in a Brooks Brothers suit.

"Lovely." I slapped him on the stomach, and he doubled over in mock pain.

"Seriously, it's fine with me." Jack watched as I sorted through the mail on the counter. He bit his bottom lip and squinted his right eye, a look of concentration I'd seen many times as he prepared for an especially important day in court.

"What?" I stopped flipping the pages of a J. Crew catalog.

"Nothing. I was just wondering why they picked you." He must have realized how that sounded because he quickly added, "I mean, you're a great writer, but you're not exactly the type of woman who'd go on a show like that."

"Tell me about it. Me and a bunch of bubbleheaded girls who think it's okay to take five weeks off from work to compete for a man and suffer public displays of desperation—all for their fifteen minutes of fame."

"That attitude won't win you any friends."

"I'm not there to make friends; I'm there to write a story."

I told him all about Suzanne's grand plan to make me over into the consummate single girl—sweet, coy, and sexy as hell. She wanted to meet next week to start going over the rules of engagement— literally. I was going to learn how to snare the Stag in a web of intrigue, sex appeal, and good old-fashioned feminine wiles. Suzanne said she expected me to get all the way to the final candle ceremony, where the Stag decides which woman he'll ask to be his wife. But I suspected she really just hoped I'd make it far enough to get a juicy story.

"I guess I'll tell her to go ahead and schedule the makeover."

"Sounds like an interesting experiment," Jack admitted. "Beats that article on pelvic inflammatory disease."

I shrugged and turned back to the catalog, as if I were truly a candidate for cotton-twill hip huggers and a sheer peasant blouse.

That night as Jack softly snored next to me, I lay in the dark, running my hand across my stomach for the telltale signs of motherhood. Suzanne thought I could pass for a hen, but she'd never seen me naked. Not that I planned on disrobing in front of the Stag, or anyone else on TV for that matter, but I knew the series included getaways for the Stag and a chosen lady, and many of those trips involved hot tubs and late night dips in kidney-shaped pools.

Suzanne's age-reducing makeover would take care of my outside, but I still had some work to do on the inside. I'd have to dig pretty deep to remember what it was like to seduce the opposite sex. I was going to be up against some hard-core husband hunters—women who placed landing a husband above everything else in their lives. Didn't they know there was more to life than snagging a guy, getting married, and having babies? Didn't they want more? What ever happened to focusing on your career, using your education, and collaborating with other women instead of competing against them? The more I thought about it the more ridiculous these women became—they were willing to be called hens, for God's sake!

Even though I hated to admit it, Jack was right. I had to go into this thing with a better attitude. Pessimism wouldn't go over well with the producers, who were probably already on the lookout for radical feminists trying to make a statement.

I had two weeks before the first audition, and getting rejected in round one just wasn't an option. There wouldn't be much interest in an article about a woman who couldn't make it past the regional cattle call. I didn't want to screw up the assignment—or look like the biggest loser in the televised mating game since Darva Conger.

I wanted the story. I wanted to show everyone I could make it to the final round. And, truth be told, I wanted that damn makeover.

# 2

$\mathscr{F}emme$'s receptionist recognized me as soon as I entered the office. I hoped it was simply because she recognized me and not because they told her to be on the lookout for someone who seemed in desperate need of a makeover.

"They're waiting for you in the studio." She pointed a long finger down the hall.

Behind a plain door marked STUDIO, I found Suzanne and my makeover team. It seemed that everyone brought an assistant, and someone to assist the assistant. Apparently I needed a lot of help.

"Sarah! Our blank canvas is here! Ready for your transformation?" Suzanne rose from a black leather chair that, with its shiny steel foot pedal and swivel base, resembled something out of a salon. She was surrounded by rolling carts filled with enough hair products and makeup to keep a beauty queen well preserved for decades. Racks of clothes were stationed around the room in front of large panes of mirrored glass dotted with lightbulbs.

"As ready as I'll ever be."

Rolf stepped toward me and led me by my elbow to the chair.

"This way, darling; we have a lot of work to do."

Like a crack SWAT team, Rolf, Suma, Toni, and Teri, along

with their entourage of ultratrendy assistants, sprang into action. The room filled with pulsating techno music that, had I not known we were in *Femme*'s offices, would have suggested we were throwing a midnight rage complete with a staff of freaky pierced men and women wielding blow-dryers and makeup brushes.

As Rolf tugged at my hair, his right-hand man—if you can call someone with a beard wearing a plaid kilt and pink braids a man—mixed a concoction of bleaches and toners that I hoped would give me a natural look. Judging from my team of experts, *natural* didn't seem to be part of their vocabulary.

"You're not going to do anything too radical, are you?" I asked cautiously, the noxious fumes of the bleach already making my eyes water.

Rolf dropped my hair and perched his thick hands on his hips.

"Honey, we're here to make you into a hen. It doesn't get more radical."

The petite girl kneeling at my feet exchanged an aggravated look with the equally petite girl fondling my hands.

"When's the last time you had a pedicure?" she asked, cracking her gum and exposing her pierced tongue.

"Maybe a year ago?" I answered, wondering if my feet were as repulsive as she obviously thought they were. It's not like I had fungus or anything.

"Do you need another pumice stone?" her manicuring partner asked, ignoring my answer.

"Sandpaper is more like it."

"I'm a mom," I quickly added, hoping that would shed some light on my cracked heels. "I don't have time for pedicures."

"Eight?" Toni asked, appearing in front of me, with a stack of clothes folded over his/her arms, the formerly Cloroxed crew cut now a brilliant shade of green.

"No, one, she's eighteen months." Did I really look old enough to have eight kids?

"I meant a size eight." Toni let out a sigh and rolled his/her eyes in Teri's direction. "You're a size eight, right?"

"Oh. Yeah."

Toni joined Teri back by the clothing racks. Low-slung pants, racer-back tanks, microminis with a fringe of beading—what were they thinking? I couldn't see the labels, but they were obviously the type of designer clothes I'd never buy myself. They fingered the hanging outfits and every once in a while pulled out a shirt or dress and then changed their minds and put it back.

I watched in horror as Teri pulled out a hideous pair of Capri pants, and then felt relieved when he/she put them back on the rack.

"Not with her hips," Toni muttered, and continued sorting through the clothes. Apparently leopard-print Capri pants were fine. It was my hips that were the problem.

I was starting to doubt that this crew of misfits could deliver on their mission. I wasn't a blank canvas to them. I was an aging oil painting.

A plate of doughnuts circled the room, and my mouth watered. With my hands and feet in the process of being beautified, I was in no position to make a grab for them.

"Rolf, can you pass me a doughnut, please?" I asked politely, hoping the hair artist didn't think passing a glazed doughnut was beneath him.

He bent near my ear and kept his voice low. "Honey, I don't think that's a good idea." He tipped his head toward the clothing racks. "Let's try to keep it a size eight, okay?"

"Come on, gang," Suzanne yelled above the thumping music, clapping her hands to get everyone's attention. "We have a job to do this morning. Our strategy meeting is at one o'clock, and I want this hen ready to take the Stag by storm."

The eclectic group nodded in agreement and turned to me as if sizing up the exhausting work ahead of them.

"And you." Suzanne walked over and set down a glass of water with a straw. "You just enjoy yourself. You're in the best hands in the industry. Come to my office when you're done."

An hour later my hair was standing on end, separated by bleach and an entire roll of Reynolds Wrap. My smooth feet were moisturized, my red toenails twinkled under the studio lights, and my fingernails were perfectly shaped into half moons. We were making progress.

"Come with us," instructed Toni, turning his/her back on me and marching over to Teri.

I stood facing a mirror with my tinfoiled head and watched as their assistants held up outfit after outfit in front of me while Toni and Teri provided their expert opinions.

"No."

"No."

"No."

"Absolutely not."

"Are you kidding me?"

"Maybe."

Eventually the racks were empty and we had three piles of clothes: a heaping mound of nos, a stack of maybes, and one very select group of yeses.

"Sarah, it's time," Rolf called to me. I left Toni and Teri and returned gratefully to my black leather throne.

Shampoo. Conditioner. The flying blades of scissors. A few slices with a razor. The whir of a blow-dryer. And finally, a spritz of hair spray.

"Can I see?" I asked hopefully. Could a haircut and a few highlights really make that much of a difference?

Ignoring me, Rolf stepped back and examined his work. He smiled and turned to Suma.

"Your turn."

Suma stepped into place, took my chin in her hands, and began shouting orders. "Look up." "Look down." "Pucker." "Pout." As she wielded her tools with a surgeon's precision, tweezers plucked, brushes swept, and pencils lined.

I closed my eyes and hoped she knew what she was doing. The small crystals dotting the corners of her eyes didn't give me much faith that I'd end up looking like anything other than a circus performer.

"Toni! Teri! She's all yours."

Before I could catch a glimpse of the new me in a mirror I was escorted into a makeshift dressing room and handed the stack of yeses.

The twins didn't try to put me in the trendy hip huggers and bell-bottoms all the single and free-to-mingle were poured into these days. Instead they selected outfits that flattered every curve, highlighted every slim inch, and discreetly covered areas that Britney Spears lovingly exposed to the world. From blue jeans to little black dresses, they were right on the money.

Finally, after Toni and Teri approved everything from my underwear to the belts holding up my pants, I emerged from the dressing area fully dressed.

For the first time since I'd entered the studio, the room fell silent.

"Cue the music!" Rolf called to his assistant.

The familiar beats of my childhood rang through the studio's speakers. Rolf's kilted assistant shook his hips from side to side, mimicking the drum's strong rhythm. "The Eye of the Tiger." Nothing announced a life-altering makeover like a little Survivor.

"Can I look now?" I asked Toni and Teri. If nothing else, today I'd learned that obedience was the golden rule of getting made over.

"Be our guest."

An assistant wheeled over a mirror and turned me toward it.

"Well?" Rolf asked, his hands clasped together in anticipation.

I stared into the mirror and couldn't muster up the words to answer.

"Do you like it?"

"Like it?" I smiled at the amazing woman before me. "Like it? I love it."

"This is fantastic!" Suzanne was perched on the corner of her assistant's desk waiting for me. "I knew you'd look great. Let's go."

She hopped off the desk and led me toward the conference room.

I followed her petite figure down the hall, passing poster-size blowups of past magazine covers. A few of my previous articles were promoted on the covers, brief lines that succinctly summarized four pages of copy. Women's topics were my specialty, everything from political issues to achieving the ultimate orgasm. My latest assignment was somewhere in the middle. Feminists were railing against the concept of women competing for the opportunity to marry the Stag, but women were also the show's biggest fans.

As Suzanne's pencil-thin arms flung open the heavy frosted-glass doors, all conversation screeched to a dead halt. She strode over to the head of the table and stood there like a long black line—knee-high suede boots under a straight, slim tube of a skirt, a wide, corseted belt accentuating her boyish hips, and a tight sleeveless black turtleneck, all capped off by her trademark jet-black Mia Farrow pixie haircut.

"This is a strategy meeting, folks," Suzanne barked to the six people seated at the long conference table. She tossed her hand in my direction. "You all know Sarah."

"Hi, guys." I gave a little wave to the group, but my friendly gesture was met with silence and wide eyes. They were staring at me. Me! And not because I had this morning's cream cheese on my face.

"I can't believe how amazing you look," a woman from Promotion finally sputtered.

I smiled and pretended I just threw on any old thing I had in my closet, when in fact Toni and Teri had marked every outfit and accessory with color-coded labels and instructions. My closet would look like a rack of Garanimals.

I pulled a leather chair out from the table and took a seat. I could get used to this reaction.

Suzanne passed around fluorescent-colored Post-it notes and Magic Markers and then stood back, giving us our marching orders. "Now, let's get to work and snag this Stag."

We spent the rest of the afternoon figuring out how I should play my hand. Did the Stag want an equal or did he want his ego stroked? Did he want someone to have fun with or did he want to settle down and play family man? Outdoorsy, natural women, or sophisticated, high-maintenance ladies? Outgoing or quiet? Book smart or street smart?

After a while it became obvious that he could want anything—we knew nothing about him. But what we did know—that he was willing to go on national TV to find a wife—didn't exactly give us hope. He was supposed to be intelligent, good-looking, successful, and personable—basically, the catch of a lifetime. But couldn't a guy like that get a girlfriend the old-fashioned way, by getting her drunk in a bar? In any case, we decided that the first two auditions were more about what was in my bra than what was in my head. The team promised that if I smiled, flipped my hair, and didn't come across as some bunny-boiling psychotic-stalker type, à la Glenn Close, then I'd be a shoo-in.

Six hours after I arrived in the studio, Suzanne's team had worked their magic and set me loose. As I walked out onto Michigan Avenue I felt lighter, and it wasn't just my new hair color. It was the way the material of my black crepe pants draped around my legs and made each stride seem longer and leaner. The way my silky cream blouse slipped along my shoulders and opened to expose a hint of cleavage and a short necklace of chunky gold coins (the cleavage courtesy of the latest in water-filled bra technology). With each footstep, the heels of my strappy pumps clicked on the sidewalk and announced my presence. The new and improved Sarah Holmes had arrived.

The usual chain of cabs loitered in front of *Femme*'s building. Ordinarily I'd thankfully fall into the backseat of one of them, the worn vinyl rubbed dull and smelling vaguely of artificial pine and stale tobacco. I'd watch from behind a pane of glass as the car slid along the city blocks toward the train station. But today was no ordinary day.

Instead of catching a cab I decided to walk, to test out the new me and see how she fit. As I passed my reflection mirrored in the window of a Starbucks, I glimpsed a woman who reminded me of the person I was at twenty-six. A PR professional who used to walk down these same streets on her way to meet clients. She looked sure of herself, with the confident stride of a woman ready to grab the world by the balls and take what she wanted instead of waiting for someone to give it to her. I couldn't help smiling at myself. It was nice to get reacquainted.

I glanced up at the Chicago skyline, and for the first time in years actually missed living in the city. When we moved to the North Shore three years ago, I was looking forward to owning our first house—the space, the yard, the free parking. At that point Jack and I wanted to start a family, and it made sense to make the big move. We were outgrowing our two-bedroom condo in Lincoln Park, and since I was going to begin freelancing, I really needed a home office.

Besides, moving to the 'burbs had always been part of the plan. I was supposed to keep ascending the ranks at the PR agency until Jack made partner at his firm. Then I'd quit and begin establishing myself as a freelance writer so that when baby number one arrived, I could have a flexible work schedule. Jack and I had logically thought out the whole thing, and so far it was all going according to schedule.

But now, as I passed my reflection in towering columns of glass and steel, I remembered what it was like to be part of the crowds that stood on a busy street corner waiting for the buses and taxis to pass by in clouds of exhaust. To be part of all the action that took place every day in every building, and the crowd's palpable energy—investment bankers closing million-dollar deals, ad whizzes creating campaigns and slogans that become part of the American vernacular, traders buying and selling soybeans and wheat the way I shopped for groceries. When I sat in my office at home, the only energy I could feel was the content of Katie's expanding diapers.

As I approached the Ogilvie train station, a well-dressed businessman politely stepped aside and let me enter the revolving door ahead of him. Inside the cavernous station an announcement for my train crackled over the loudspeaker, and I bolted for the escalator—not an easy feat in four-inch Manolo Blahniks.

"Excuse me," a man huffed behind me, his briefcase smacking against his thigh as he attempted to keep up. "Are you running away from me?"

I quickly turned toward the voice, a cascade of blond highlights flying over my shoulder and landing across my right eye like a forties movie star.

It was the three-piece-suited guy from the revolving door.

"Nope, just trying to catch my train," I explained as we both took long strides up the shimmying escalator, straddling two steps at a time.

"Please tell me you're not happily married," he jokingly pleaded, a broad grin spreading across his tanned face and crinkling the corners of his eyes.

Before I could stop it, an equally charming grin made its way across my lips.

" 'Fraid so." I held up my hand and showed him the twinkling diamond on my finger. "And a baby, too."

"I figured as much, but I thought I'd take a chance." He stopped trying to keep up with me, and fell back as I walked on alone.

"Hey," I called over my shoulder in his direction, the *click-clack* of my heels echoing as I skipped toward track six. "Thanks. You made my day." Feminism be damned!

"And now, ladies and gentlemen," I announced in my best Don Pardo voice. "She hails from Chicago, enjoys tuna melts with the crust cut off and chocolate milkshakes for breakfast, here she is, Bachelorette Number One!" I took a step out from behind the dining room doorway, and struck a pose normally better suited for models on *The Price is Right*.

"Wow." Jack stopped in his tracks and let his eyes wash over the new me.

"I'm assuming that means you like the hen in me?" I asked, enjoying the look on his face.

"Like it? If I'd known that having you try to score a younger guy was going to turn you into this, I'd have dropped you off at the local community college myself."

I shook my hair like one of Charlie's Angels, letting all the layers fall into place around my newly found cheekbones. Rolf had really lived up to his reputation. He turned my shapeless, grown-out bob into chunks of blond that looked so natural it was as if I'd spent a summer hanging out on *Baywatch*. Fortunately, despite all my years of sun worship and spring breaks broiling in baby oil, Suma had been able to accomplish just the opposite. Despite her own heavy-handed lip pencil and kohl-rimmed eyes, Suma had managed to naturally enhance what I'd forgotten was there to begin with—deep green eyes, subtly arched brows, high cheeks with a hint of rosy glow.

"Nice outfit." Jack reached for my hand and spun me around like Ginger Rogers. "And what's in the outfit is even nicer."

"It's amazing, isn't it? Every woman should get to do what I did today."

"Okay, now I'm a little worried." Jack loosened his tie with a single finger, Rodney Dangerfield style. "You really look hot."

"I thought you said it didn't bother you."

"It didn't; I just forgot what it was like to come home to a woman who looked more like a girlfriend than a wife."

I had to admit, I'd forgotten what it was like myself.

After I obsessed over my audition outfit for two weeks—it was one thing to look hot, but it was another to look like I was on leave from the Mustang Ranch—the moment of truth had arrived. I entered what appeared to be a warehouse on the west side of the city and was corralled into an auditorium with about two hundred other women. All shapes and sizes from as far away as Nebraska and as close as Indiana sat in movie theater–style seating while the show's producers explained the process. They passed out our applications and asked us to examine them for accuracy prior to our personal interviews. Each of us would be called into a private room to meet and talk with the producers, after which we'd return to our seats and wait to find out if we'd been selected to be part of the final group presented to the Stag. They were taking only twenty-five finalists from each of the four regional auditions. The Stag would choose the final twenty-four hens to appear on the show.

While I waited to be called for my interview I reviewed the application that Suzanne's staff had prepared. I was using my maiden name, Sarah Divine, and other slight variations on the truth. I'd still attended Wellesley, although my graduation date was altered, but they left off my years in graduate school. I was from Chicago, but I was unmarried and childless. My profession was listed as *public relations associate*, and not *freelance writer hired to infiltrate your show and expose all the ugly ways you demean and degrade women.*

To say the interview was brief is like saying Everest is a good-size bunny hill. Two men and a woman examined me from head to toe, making notes on yellow legal pads they balanced on their laps. A tall, gangly man with John Lennon glasses, a salt-and-pepper goatee, and a graying ponytail seemed to be the one in charge.

"Can you turn to the side, doll?"

"Like this?" I stood facing the wall as the three of them got a good look at my Mega Bra profile.

"Very nice." Ponytail man nodded appreciatively and elbowed the woman to his right. She scribbled something on her notepad, which I hoped was a scathing letter of resignation and feminist manifesto, but was more likely a guess at my measurements.

The woman asked if everything on my application was true,

and told me they'd be calling references and conducting a criminal check if I advanced to the next round. After waiting to see if I would break down and admit I was a cross-dressing crack addict who stashed dead bodies in my basement walls, they thanked me and I left.

Back in my seat, I watched the other potential hens and took mental note of the scene around me. A few of the women chatted with one another, making friendly conversation to kill time, I imagined. For the most part they were exactly what Suzanne had expected: perky young things in clingy tops and pants slung so low I could make out a fuchsia thong peeking over a waistband or, even more horrifying, the beginning of someone's butt crack as nothing came between a girl and her Calvins. When had panty lines become the latest social scourge?

"Dr. Shapiro?"

A girl in the row in front of me was kneeling on her seat, her chin resting on the stiff backrest as she waited for my answer.

"Excuse me?"

"Your boobs." She pointed to my chest, as if I didn't know where my boobs were. "Did you go to Dr. Shapiro?"

"Um, no. It's a Mega Bra."

"Really?" She leaned over her seat for a closer inspection. "That's amazing. They look great."

"Thanks." I crossed my arms, afraid she might reach out and cop a feel.

"I'm Bess Brewster, but my friends call me Bebe."

"Nice to meet you, Bebe. I'm Sarah Divine."

"I can't believe how many girls are here," Bebe observed, sitting back on her seat but keeping her upper body twisted toward me. "It's very brave, don't you think?"

"Brave?"

"Sure. You gotta figure most of us are going home today without getting picked. And even if you make it on the show, the chances of actually making it through till the end is, like, one in a million."

Obviously Bebe wasn't an accountant.

"Actually, the chances are one in twenty-four if you make it on the show," I corrected her. "So why are you here, Bebe? Looking for love?"

"That'd be great, but I just want to make it onto the show. Did you see what happened to Charlotte after she lost to Veronica last season? Offers up the ying-yang—I heard she's landed her own sitcom and a book deal, not to mention the *Playboy* spread and all those parties in LA. Who needs a Stag when you're famous?"

"Apparently not Charlotte," I answered, wishing I could pull out my notebook and jot down our conversation. Bebe was writing my article for me right here.

"Oh, hey, I know that girl over there." Bebe waved to a blond bombshell across the room. "I'm going to run over and say hi. See you later!"

For the next two hours I watched women nervously touch up their lipstick and spritz enough hair spray to single-handedly deplete the ozone over Chicago, until finally the producers ambled back onto the dark stage. Ponytail man stepped forward to the microphone.

"Girls, can I have some quiet, please? Thank you for your time today," he began in a tone that sounded more put-out than thankful. "I'm going to read the names of the contestants who will move on to the next round. If your name is called you will be receiving a phone call to schedule the filming of your video. After reviewing the videos the Stag will make his final selections."

He said it all very matter-of-factly, as if he were explaining how to change a tire.

A wave of anticipation swept around the room as women sat up a little taller in their seats and peered over the heads of the competition in front of them.

The young woman seated to the man's right handed him a piece of paper with the lucky names. I placed my hand on my stomach, which was starting to feel like I was on a roller coaster poised to plunge into oblivion. I was actually nervous. And I hated myself for it.

One by one the winners were called. After a round of bouncy names peppered with more Tiffanys, Ashleys, and Brittanys than a porn-house marquee, I heard "Sarah Divine" and my ears stopped working. I didn't hear another name he called. Suzanne's team had been right—the first audition was a breeze.

Five minutes later, the group of producers started to file off the stage, and I finally exhaled. I made it. Me, Sarah Divine Holmes, suburban wife, mother, and part-time writer, still had it going on. Suzanne would be ecstatic—she was one step closer to getting her article. I was supposed to call her immediately with my news. I stood up to leave and came face-to-face with the devastation around me. The majority of seats were filled by women sunk down in their chairs like deflated balloons. Heads hung low and shoulders slumped forward in defeat. It wasn't pretty.

As we shuffled out into the bright afternoon sun a few women burst into tears, but most of the crowd walked along quietly, reluctantly accepting a pamphlet at the door for the Last Chance Internet dating service.

"Hey, Sarah!"

I turned and saw Bebe rushing toward me.

"We made it! Can you believe it?" she gushed, barely able to keep herself from bouncing up and down. "We're going to make a video!" She wrapped her arms around me and squealed.

I instinctively returned her hug, my own excitement getting the better of me.

I was one step closer to becoming a hen. Thank God for the Mega Bra.

A few days later I received a call from the show and was scheduled to make my video at a local studio. After consulting with Suzanne and her team, and once again ensconced in my trusty Mega Bra, I was ready to be captured on film.

I reclined on a white leather couch while a team of lighting experts made me feel about as glamorous as a rotisserie chicken—I needed softer light, heavier makeup, and more reflective panels than a solar-powered submarine. As the crew filmed, the director asked me questions off-camera—why should the Stag choose me? What was my idea of the perfect guy? How did I feel about sex?

"Sex?"

"Yeah, sex," he repeated.

"I'm for it?" I ventured, realizing too late that my answer could come back to haunt me someday. I'd possibly given my daughter all the ammunition she'd need when, as a teenager, she'd remind me that I'd said I was strongly in favor of sex. I hoped that little pearl of wisdom landed on the cutting-room floor.

The following week I waited every day for the mailman to deliver the news. Each time I saw his little white truck pull up to our mailbox I raced down the front walk with a mix of hopeful anticipation and dread. It was like waiting for my college acceptance letters all over again.

When I finally discovered the thin white envelope in the pile of grocery-store circulars and bills, I almost couldn't pick it up. I let it sit on the kitchen counter while I tried to figure out whether it looked like a rejection or an invitation. Was a simple white envelope good or bad? After almost an hour of tormenting myself I picked up the letter and held it in my hand, turning the envelope over and over for some clue. I don't know what I was expecting, maybe an express package or flowers. Something more romantic than an envelope labeled PERSONAL AND CONFIDENTIAL. It just didn't seem to do the moment justice.

Finally I tore open the envelope, unfolded the letter, and nearly screamed when I read the first word: *Congratulations!*

"Yes," I hissed, pumping my hand in the air like a football player. "Katie, Mommy did it. I did it!"

I turned toward Katie, sitting quietly in her high chair squishing yogurt in her ears, and guilt shot through me like a lightning bolt.

I was happy to be going away. I couldn't wait to write the article. What kind of mother would take an assignment that made her leave her baby for weeks on end? Katie was too young to know her mom was tarting it up in California with the Stag, but she was definitely old enough to know that Mommy had deserted her—was I going to be shelling out big bucks to a therapist when she was sixteen?

I had to call Jack.

As I waited for his secretary to put me through, I attempted to scrape the yogurt out of Katie's ears, which only resulted in screaming as Jack got on the line.

"I made it."

"Made what?" he asked, distracted by the sound of papers shuffling in the background.

"The show. I'm going to be on *The Stag.*"

"That's incredible," he answered slowly as the shuffling stopped.

Did he mean *incredible great* or *incredible unbelievable?*

"I know." It was *incredible great.* "I leave next Saturday."

"Wow. I just can't believe it."

*Believe it, buddy,* I wanted to say but didn't.

"I'll call Marta and set everything up. Are you sure you and Katie are going to be all right? It's not too late for me to tell Suzanne I can't do it," I offered, caught in my own tug-of-war between wanting to go on the show and the guilt I'd suffer being away from Katie.

"We'll be fine. Don't worry," Jack assured me. "How hard could it be?"

He was about to find out.


"Mommy's going on a trip," I told Katie when I rocked her to sleep that night. Katie's room was dark except for the yellow glow cast from her

Cow Jumped Over the Moon nightlight. She nestled in my arms rest-
lessly at first, but settled to the rhythmic sways of the rocking chair.

Even though I knew I was going, I still didn't know how long
I'd be gone. I'd have only one chance to put Suzanne's makeover to the
test before the Stag had an opportunity to nix me at the first candle
ceremony. In the worst-case scenario I'd have the audition and two days'
worth of material for my article.

Although five weeks wasn't a long time in the grand scheme of
things, it seemed like an eternity when I thought about leaving Katie. I
leaned down, buried my nose in the fine blond hair on her head, and inhaled her sweet baby smell.

"Mommy will send you pretty postcards, and call you all the
time," I whispered near Katie's crescent-shaped ear as we rocked in the
darkened room. "And Daddy and Marta will take good care of you."

Her little tummy was rising and falling as she sucked her
thumb. My assurances must have been a relief. She was out like a light.

# 3

"*What* if someone recognizes me and calls the show?" It was beginning to hit me that I was going to expose a major network's most popular show as nationally televised pimping. My flight left the next day, and I was starting to get nervous.

Suzanne placed her manicured hand on my shoulder and held me firmly. For such a skinny thing she sure had a strong grip.

"Sarah, the show is taped. By the time the first episode airs and the article is published, it will be too late. We'll be interviewed on every morning show around, and *The Stag* will get more publicity than the network ever imagined. There's nothing to worry about. Just memorize every single detail on your application." She dropped her hand and moved back until she was looking me straight in the eyes. "You can do this. I wouldn't have asked you if I didn't think you'd do the best job."

I appreciated her faith in me, but she wasn't the one going away to play make-believe, pretending to be someone else—or at least a younger, better imitation of herself.

"Job number one is gaining the trust of a few hens, becoming their best buddy. I want our readers to see the desperation in their faces, feel their lips quiver as they explain their fear of being alone. Then I want to know what makes a grown man think he can actually have a relationship with a woman who'd do this. God knows he's probably just some aspiring actor or showbiz wanna-be who thinks he's the next Tom Cruise. And the producers . . . they'll be harder, but try to find out what they really think of their pathetic little three-ring circus."

I scribbled notes in my spiral binder as Suzanne rattled off her vision of the end product. But the story itself was the least of my worries. I pretty much knew what I was going to write. I wasn't expecting to be surprised by the actual experience—there couldn't be too many rocket scientists clamoring for a proposal from the Stag.

I checked my watch and realized I was going to miss my train if I didn't get going. It was time to leave Suzanne and any uncertainty behind.

"I've got it. I know what the magazine's looking for; I'm sure you won't be disappointed."

I stood up and reached under my chair for my briefcase.

"I know I won't. So how's Jack with all of this?" she asked as I packed up my notebook and PalmPilot.

"He says he's fine with it, but I don't think the reality of the situation has sunk in."

"Well, wait until he can tell everyone at work his wife was a hen."

I doubted many of the lawyers in Jack's firm even watched the show. The secretaries, maybe.

"Somehow I don't think his partners will be that impressed. If it doesn't mean he can increase his billable hours, I could be on *That's Incredible* with our dinner plates in my bottom lip. They wouldn't care."

"I don't know; the idea of twenty-four hotties dueling it out gets some guys going." Suzanne had a mischievous grin on her face, probably picturing an orgy of hens and a huge spike in circulation.

"You've obviously never spent much time in a law firm."

"Thank God." Suzanne dramatically threw her head back and

pretended to wipe her brow with the back of her hand. "Anyway, good luck."

She patted me on the back as I walked out the door.

"Thanks." I'd need it.

Katie sat in a suitcase on the floor placing the inside straps over her chubby legs like a seat belt. A steady stream of snot made its way across her cheek every time she'd wipe her runny nose with the back of her hand. My futile attempts to give her a tissue had resulted in a nest of Kleenex shreds at the bottom of the suitcase.

I was trying to organize my new wardrobe into the larger suitcase on the bed, squeezing water bras and slenderizing undergarments between cocktail dresses and tank tops and palazzo pants. My new wardrobe was arranged on the comforter in piles, enough outfits to last five weeks and suit activities ranging from a game of tennis to a night of ballroom dancing.

"Sweetie pie, don't chew on that." I removed the luggage tag from Katie's prying fingers. She sneezed on my hand, leaving me with a fistful of runny mucus. I'd been pretending that she wasn't really sick, and that my going away had nothing to do with her cold. She'd slept most of the afternoon for Marta, which I thought was a sign she might be getting better. I was wrong. Now I wasn't just a selfish mommy leaving her child behind while I did my job; I was verging on negligent as well.

Katie's cold was going to throw a monkey wrench into the night I'd planned—a night that included some family time with Katie before Jack and I had a little adult fun of our own. Toni and Teri had picked out a few lacy underthings that I wanted to preview for Jack. We hadn't had sex in almost two weeks, since I'd become a finalist, but I'd be damned if I was going away for five weeks without getting laid first.

My new *haircut* was a little surprise for Jack. Suzanne had suggested it, and even booked me an appointment with the wax nazis, a duo of sisters famed for their no-holds-barred Brazilian bikini lines. Odds were that if I made it past the first episode I'd have to don some form of a bathing suit. The twins had selected a triangle-topped two-piece with a navy-and-white nautical thing going on, as well as some hot pink—and-yellow tropical numbers with underwires and padding. One look at the high legs and I had to agree with Suzanne. All it took was ten minutes to rip just about every pubic hair screaming from its roots and leave stunned, silky-smooth skin in its place.

After a trio of sneezes practically knocked Katie over, I ended up tossing the clothes haphazardly into the suitcases and calling it quits. They had irons in California, and they definitely had a concierge at the Ritz.

It was time to move on to dinner. Marta had picked up everything on my grocery list, and I had some culinary skills to hone in the kitchen.

I chopped onions, sliced potatoes, and peeled carrots—all the wifely duties I typically managed to avoid, thanks to Jack's unpredictable schedule. I kept checking back with the cookbook I was using, an old Julia Child hardcover my mom gave me when I got engaged and she was still under the impression I'd evolve into a domestic goddess.

After an hour I tossed the vegetables, two cups of wine, a can of chicken stock, and some chicken breasts into a large pot, as the recipe instructed. And then I crossed my fingers. I'd left the wine bottle next to the stove, still plenty full. I reached out, uncorked the bottle, and poured a river of red into the pot. I figured if the two cups of wine the recipe called for were good, then half a bottle must be an absolute culinary delight—or would at least give us a good buzz.

After a few minutes, the smell of coq au vin wafted through the house, the woodsy aroma of burgundy mingling with onions and rosemary. One foot in the door and Jack would know this was no ordinary night.

When I told Jack I was planning a special evening, he said he thought I was making a much bigger deal out of this than it was. I'd be gone five weeks, tops. He'd had trials that lasted months and required him to leave before I was up and to stay at the office way into the late hours of the night. During those cases we barely saw each other except when he was either crawling into bed or crawling out. It was the same sort of thing, he thought.

But I thought it was a big deal, leaving him and Katie for so long. He promised he'd make it home early so we could enjoy a special dinner tonight before we got down to business.

Katie was in her high chair grabbing fistfuls of peas from her tray, and I was lighting the candles on the dining room table when the phone rang. It was Jack. I knew what he was going to say even before the words were out of his mouth.

"I'm sorry; I know it's your last night," he apologized, sounding as disappointed as I felt. "The defense came up with a last-minute motion to dismiss—on a fucking Friday night."

I could hear him slamming his desk drawers shut in the background.

"I'll be home by nine. Promise."

It was almost six-thirty.

"Fine." I had trouble working up much sympathy for him. "I'll be here."

"Sarah, I said I was sorry."

I muttered something about it being all right, and hung up.

Phase one of my evening was shot to hell. On to phase two.

By eight o'clock I had Katie bathed, filled with medicine, and all set for bed. She sat in my lap while I read books, her stubby fingers stabbing at the pages as she pointed to Pooh and Piglet and Tigger. I wondered if she realized that beginning tomorrow, Marta or her daddy would be making the silly sounds of Tigger bouncing on his tail. And I'd be at the Ritz-Carlton in Laguna Niguel. Preparing to come on to a strange man.

I rocked Katie until she fell asleep, her stuffy nose making a little whistling sound as she breathed.

On my way back to the kitchen to clean up, I checked myself in the hall mirror. Still looking good. Onward.

The kitchen smelled amazing, and it almost seemed a shame to be packing away such a delicious—and rare—meal into my dishwasher-warped Tupperware. Jack didn't get to see my pretty meal, but at least he'd have leftovers all weekend. After the food was packed away and the kitchen was scrubbed of any last vestiges of my gourmet cooking, I grabbed the bottle of remaining wine and went to the living room to wait.

And wait. It seemed I was always the one doing the waiting these days. Waiting for Jack to come home from work. Waiting for him to call to let me know what time he'd be home. Waiting for his hello kiss, for a hug, or just a look that said the things we seemed to be too busy to say anymore.

When Jack considered quitting law school halfway through his second year, I couldn't imagine what else he'd do. I'd been in grad school five months, surrounded by other aspiring writers and journalists and future lawyers and business leaders, and I wasn't quite ready to embrace the idea of dating someone who wanted to give that up to play in a band. Sure, it was cool having a boyfriend in a band, as long as he was also in law school.

Not that Jack really intended to play in a band the rest of his life. He just thought it was a way to make money while he figured out what he wanted to do next. But I knew his indifference toward law school was probably the result of cramming for final exams and jockeying with classmates for the best summer associate positions and clerkships. After a six-pack of Heineken and a marathon session on my futon, he agreed with me. But he still had another year and a half to go before graduating, and then years of toiling as an associate before making partner. He wanted to be sure I'd stick it out with him. *Will you wait for me?* he'd asked, as if he were asking me to make a sacrifice. I assured him I would.

And so I continued to wait.

Tomorrow the tables would be turned, and it would be Jack waiting for my phone calls from California, waiting to find out what I was doing and who I was doing it with. We'd see how he liked it.

I was standing in front of the stereo waiting for the final Van Morrison song to end, my hand ready to flip the off button, when Jack's headlights lit up the room as his car turned in to our driveway.

I knew his routine by heart. He'd come in through the kitchen door, throw his keys on the counter, and riffle through the mail. On cue, the familiar jingle of car keys landed on the granite and annoyed the hell out of me.

"You're late."

"I know. I'm sorry." He came up behind me and wrapped his arms around my waist. "Mmm, it smells good in here."

"That was your dinner."

"I'm starving." He rubbed his stomach. "How was your day?"

"Oh, the usual." I broke away from his hold and took a few steps back. "I had a meeting in the city with my editor, I had to pack for my assignment, I had research to finish, and Katie's all stuffed-up and screamed every time I walked out of the room. Thanks for asking."

I crossed my arms over my chest and Jack let out a sigh.

"Is this how you want to spend our last night together? Arguing?"

"No. I would just like you to acknowledge that you blew it." Again.

"I said I was sorry. It's not like I didn't want to be here." Jack took off his suit jacket and threw it over the armchair. "It's a Friday night for me, too. I'd like to be home with my family instead of holed up in a library reading legal rulings. I have a job."

"You act like I'm going on some Vegas junket for a few weeks. I have a job, too, remember?"

Jack walked up to me and took my face in his hands.

"I'm sorry. I want to be with you tonight. I'm going to miss you."

Jack looked at me with exhausted eyes, a week in court and late nights taking their toll. I brushed my hand along his cheek, feeling the shadow of a beard that was already reappearing.

The clock on the mantel started chiming. It was ten o'clock.

"Let's go upstairs," I suggested, taking his hand and leading the way.

"What about your dinner?"

"We're going straight to dessert."

Although I couldn't wait to get Jack naked, I let him slowly help me undress. I savored his soft touch, the way his thick fingers gently unbuttoned my pants and slipped them over my hips, letting his hands linger along my skin.

I could tell that Jack was impressed when he discovered the ivory lace La Perla bra and panties Toni and Teri had picked out. Not that he had time to tell me. He had me out of them in two seconds flat.

A hint of this morning's aftershave still clung to Jack's warm skin and reminded me of the old days, before he made partner and Katie came along. When we'd kiss good-bye in the mornings and then find our way back to bed.

I slid my tongue along his collarbone, inhaling him deep into my lungs and letting his salty taste coat my mouth. I remembered when he didn't wear cologne. I used to watch him play at bars in Evanston. He'd smell like stale smoke and taste like cheap beer. Watching him on-stage, his fingers sliding effortlessly up and down the neck of his electric guitar, bending strings that I'd pretend were my naked body under his skillful touch, I couldn't wait to be alone with him—the way he'd close his eyes and hang his head during his solos with an intensity I couldn't wait to unleash in bed.

Now when he took clients out to dinner and came home stinking of cigar smoke and scotch, he knew to take a shower before slipping between the sheets with me. At twenty-six it was sexy; now it was just gross.

We kissed deeply and pressed our bodies together so urgently that I was afraid we'd get ahead of ourselves. I wanted this to last.

"Is that Katie?" I whispered as Jack's lips lingered on my neck.

"Ignore her. She'll go back to sleep."

I tried to concentrate on Jack's fingers as they worked their way up my thigh. I buried my head in the threadlike hairs on his chest and hoped the rapid beating of his heart would drown out Katie's whimpers. Nothing worked. As a mother, I just wasn't biologically equipped to ignore a crying child.

"I can't do this while she's in there crying," I told him.

"Fine." Jack rolled off me. "I'll get her."

I pulled the sheets and comforter up around my neck and watched Jack wrap himself in a robe. Even the thick terry cloth couldn't hide the tent that was pitched between Jack's thighs as he walked away.

While I waited for Jack, I watched the red glow of the numbers on the alarm clock: 10:23. In less than twelve hours I'd be in the air, on my way to the Stag. It didn't seem possible.

"She's okay." Jack dropped his robe on the floor and crawled into bed with me.

"Did you give her Huggy Bear?"

"I gave her all the animals off her shelf."

"Does she have Huggy Bear?" I asked again. "She won't sleep without him."

"I don't know. She's fine. She stopped crying."

I listened. The house was silent again.

"Are you sure you're gonna be okay without me?" I asked, looking for reassurance that my sick daughter wouldn't suffocate from the sniffles in my absence.

Jack didn't answer. He was already working his way down my stomach, his tongue gliding slowly past my belly button, toward the land of no return.

"Well, are you?" I asked again.

He stopped abruptly and looked up at me. "Sarah, will you please give it a rest?"

How does one respond to that question when your husband is two inches away from bringing you infinite pleasure? *No, I'm a total bitch who needs an answer?*

I closed my eyes and let Jack go to work.

# 4

$\mathcal{A}$ driver met me at my gate in terminal two of John Wayne Airport and whisked me to the Ritz-Carlton. Not a bad way to start an assignment. It sure beat the commuter train.

When the bellboy let me into my room, I was instantly immersed in luxury. Dark wood framed the elegantly appointed room, from the crown molding hugging every curve of the ceiling to the paneled doors hiding a fully stocked bar. The king-size bed was flanked by ornately carved night tables and topped off with a thick upholstered headboard that accented the heavy floral drapes and jewel-colored fabrics adorning the furniture. No toys, no snot, no annoyingly late husband. Who needed the Stag? I was already in love.

Nestled between the decorative chintz pillows on the bed, I found a welcome packet, complete with fruit basket and complementary grooming supplies. I was expected to be in the Pacific meeting room at eight A.M. sharp tomorrow for a continental breakfast and orientation. Then I was free to explore the amenities of the hotel and prepare for the evening's cocktail party until four o'clock, when the limos were scheduled to pick us up and bring us to the Stag.

After unpacking and leaving a message at home for Jack to let him know I arrived safely, I ventured downstairs to check out the hotel.

Guests were mingling in the lobby, carrying tennis rackets and beach totes and shopping bags. I looked around for uncoupled women who might be checking in for *The Stag*, but they didn't exactly show up with a big red H on their chests. As long as she wasn't wearing a wedding ring, carrying a baby, or over thirty, any of the women could have passed for a hen.

After taking a cruise around the pool, I decided to go back to my room, order room service, and prepare some notes for the article. On my way through the marbled lobby I took a detour through the hotel gift shop. The rack of postcards displayed picture-perfect waves, pristine sandy beaches, and orange sunsets. I fingered a few cards until I found one showing a view from the hotel's pool area down to the beach. Although the pool area I visited was filled with sunbathers and swimmers, the photo on the card showed an empty, serene pool, leading to a deserted beach. I contemplated sending it to Jack and Katie. But they were probably at home sweltering in the August Chicago heat. Why rub it in?

At eight o'clock the next morning I was seated in an uncomfortable metal chair between two blond twenty-somethings, waiting to listen to an aging Hollywood producer impart his television wisdom.

The gray-ponytail guy from my Chicago interview stood at the head of the room rustling papers. The Pacific room was the type typically used for business meetings. The walls were paneled and hinged every four feet so they could fold up and open to the adjoining rooms. Although every effort was made to avoid the clichéd sterility of a hotel banquet facility, including tasteful chandeliers and gold-embossed geometric shapes on the paneling, the room wasn't exactly welcoming. There were some things even the Ritz-Carlton couldn't change.

Ponytail man cleared his throat and stepped up to the podium.

"Good morning, ladies. I'm Arnie Silverman, one of the

show's producers. I'd like to welcome you and let you know that we are all excited to start another season of *The Stag*." He removed his glasses and turned toward a severe-looking woman on his left, pointing to her with the frames. "My wife, Sloane, and I know you probably have some questions, which I hope we'll cover for you this morning. Please turn in your booklet to page one."

The flutter of pages turning filled the room as twenty-four hens found page one.

"There are a few things you should know before tonight's cocktail reception."

I glanced around at the other women, trying to catch someone's reaction to Arnie, our fearless leader. Everybody stared straight-faced ahead, listening intently. Like military recruits preparing for battle.

Arnie began reading off the list of show protocol.

"You can be filmed at all times. Twenty-four hours a day, seven days a week. There may be hidden cameras. As you already know, the use or possession of recording devices, cameras, and laptop computers is prohibited. The use of mobile phones is highly discouraged, however we understand that they can be useful in emergency situations. Their use should be limited to your room, and in no case should be brought along on dates or outings." He looked at us over his glasses to make sure we were all listening and then continued reading. "While at the Ritz, you are not to tell anyone not associated with the show why you are here, or discuss your activities. Those of you who make it through the third candle ceremony will be moved to a secluded bungalow for the remainder of the taping. You must live, participate, and cooperate with the other individuals and the producers during the taping of the program. Foul language is discouraged and will be removed from the tapes when the show is aired. Although you are being filmed, you should act as normally as possible. Dates should reflect typical 'date behavior.' Kissing, fondling, and sexual acts will be edited to meet standards and practices requirements. In other words, we won't show your boobs—no matter how much you want us to!" The hens laughed politely. I hated them already—the hens and the producers.

Arnie finished reading and placed the booklet on the podium. He turned to Sloane as if waiting for her approval and then continued. "Take some time to review the rest of the pamphlet. There are other important things you should know that I'm not going to go through in detail. I would like to point out, however, that page five covers excessive hotel charges beyond those that are reasonable and customary to your stay here. Page seven explains how we'll handle any property damages and recovery of costs—so if you're considering taking out your frustrations on the hotel's furniture after a candle ceremony, you might want to review the section on legal liability. And finally, pages nine through eleven outline sanctioned versus unsanctioned visits with the Stag."

Arnie stopped talking and let the long hand of the law, or at least the deep pockets of the network's legal team, put the fear of God in his audience. I glanced around at the crowd and didn't see anyone who appeared defiant and capable of taking Arnie on—just as I figured, not a law degree in the room.

"Those are the important things. You can review the rest of the booklet at your leisure. Go, have fun. We'll see you in the lobby at four o'clock."

As the rest of the women stood to leave, I stayed in my seat, sizing up this season's crop of hens. Not much different from the women from the Chicago audition, just a little more mainstream, with fewer tattoos and piercings.

I noticed a familiar-looking head of blond curls taking up the rear of the exiting hen parade and waved.

"Sarah!" Bebe waved back and pointed to the hallway.

I made my way down the aisle and found Bebe waiting for me by the ladies'-room door.

"Isn't this great? We both made it! You'll have to forgive me if

I neglect you now that we're here. I need all the on-camera shots I can get. You understand, don't you?"

"Sure, I understand, airtime and all."

"Exactly. Man, I just can't get over those things." Bebe placed a palm on my left boob and squeezed. "They even feel natural."

At four o'clock on the button, all twenty-four of the hens met in the hotel lobby and were escorted, one by one, into black stretch limousines. I caught brief glimpses of the women before they ducked behind tinted windows and drove away. They were better-looking than your average crowd, but they seemed normal enough—or at least as normal as women who were about to pursue a strange man and have the entire event taped for national TV.

I was decked out in the midnight-blue dress Toni and Teri had insisted would set me apart from the predictable numbers the other women would be wearing. They were right.

Unlike my dress, the uniform for the night appeared to be little black or red cocktail dresses that exposed tanned shoulders, jutting collarbones, and cleavage that could moonlight as the continental divide. The women left little to the imagination, with short and tight being the preferred fashion statement.

My Toni-and-Teri selection accentuated my legs with a subtle flare of soft chiffon overlay falling midthigh. The spaghetti straps, which were more the width of fetuccini, fell about five inches before they met the front of my dress and gently sloped into a vee neckline that suggested I had more to offer than met the eye. Suzanne and her team wanted me to look different enough to attract the Stag's attention, but not come across as too obvious. To pique the Stag's interest and leave him wanting more. I think the last time I felt that elegant without the justice pronouncing me husband and wife was when I belted out "Sweet Child o' Mine" and toasted college graduation at a seniors' dinner dance.

Twenty-four limousines lined up along a thin beachside street waiting to unload their passengers. Every two minutes one of the limos ambled up the circular driveway leading to the cliffside bachelor pad that was the Stag's temporary living quarters. We were instructed to carefully exit the cars, making sure not to give the camera a muff shot up our skirts, and walk like beauty contestants toward the front door. The Stag would be waiting for us, where we would greet him in a friendly manner; either a hug or kiss on the cheek would do.

After what seemed like hours of watching the sea grass blow outside the car window, my driver slowly turned onto the gravel driveway. I felt an unexpected rush of adrenaline pulse through my body. Out of habit I kept sliding my thumb along the palm of my left hand, feeling for the familiar rings that usually adorned my finger. But the rings weren't there, just smooth, empty skin announcing that I was available. Even the pale circle of skin that remained untouched by the summer sun blended in, thanks to a daily dose of self-tanner. I felt strangely vulnerable, naked. But there was no time for insecurity. It was showtime.

When the driver opened my car door, I was greeted by a blinding white light that not only startled me, it made me see stars. I wanted to rub my eyes, but I didn't want to smudge my mascara. This was TV, after all. Once I was able to refocus I saw the cameraman zooming in on me. I peered down the stone walkway toward the front door, where a man in a navy pin-striped suit waited for me fifteen feet away—an absolutely gorgeous guy who appeared to be as perfect as the producers had promised.

The Stag's name was Chris Masters. Stanford undergrad. Harvard MBA. Avid sailor and skier. Newspaper publisher whose family owned a string of papers throughout the northwest, not to mention the fledgling papers he was buying up throughout the country. He was twenty-eight years old, six-foot-one, and had a wide grin, chiseled cheekbones, and brown eyes. And he still had all his hair.

"Hi, I'm Sarah." I held out my hand and immediately regretted it—I was shaking! And was that my lotion or was my palm actually sweaty?

"Hi, Sarah. I'm Chris. It's nice to meet you." He flashed me a broad smile as a camera pulled in closer to film us.

"Move along," the director hissed at me from behind Chris, interrupting what felt like an inordinately long and lingering handshake. Was the Stag reluctant to let my hand go? Or was my palm so sweaty our hands were stuck together?

I released my grip and followed the director's orders, continuing through the front doors to wait among the other women. More cameramen, the director, and a few assistants were stationed around the living room. They were all outfitted in sleek black headsets with microphones. The presence of elegantly dressed women was ignored as they strategically positioned themselves to film the Stag's entrance.

I spotted Bebe seated on the arm of the couch, her legs carefully crossed as she practiced poses for the camera. The other women watched her intently, and a couple even took her cue and tried out a few poses of their own. They all seemed so self-possessed, so sure of themselves and determined, yet when a new hen entered the room they slid their eyes toward the door to size up the newcomer with the strategic intent of war generals.

As the last hen joined us in the sunken living room, we waited for Chris. The host was interviewing him behind the large, weathered, barnlike front doors, a mere ten feet from where we stood.

All of a sudden the camera crew scurried into place, the front doors opened, and the Stag stepped into view—a slightly nervous king surveying his harem.

The cocktail reception was scheduled to last two hours, during which we were all supposed to mingle and get to know one another. That worked for me. After all, I was trying to learn what on earth would make a woman go on *The Stag*. I needed a few women who'd loosened their tongues with cocktails to start giving me the story I was here to get.

I selected a flute of champagne and strawberries from a silver tray on the coffee table and wandered around the living room. The décor was both masculine and homey, like a combination of an upscale ski cabin with a beachside cottage. Distressed wood tables were softened with candles and large, shallow glass bowls that held water and floating votives, and chenille throws were draped casually over the backs of chocolate leather chairs. For a reality show, it sure beat being stranded on a deserted island eating crawly critters.

"Weird, huh?"

"Very," I answered, turning to the woman on my left, who was stuffed into a strapless black cocktail dress. "I'm Sarah."

"I'm Iris."

"Where are you from, Iris?"

"The bucolic state of New Jersey." She let out a laugh and I smiled.

"What do you do?"

Iris hesitated, carefully choosing her words. "You could say I was in the information business. I'm between jobs right now."

"Sorry about that. Tough economy, isn't it?" Poor girl. She'd probably spent her last dime on that black satin sausage skin.

"Yeah, something like that." Iris looked around nervously. "I'm going to go find the bathroom before I pee myself. I'll see you around."

I watched Iris weave her way through the crowd of hens. The women appeared to be carrying on friendly enough conversations with one another, but I noticed that each hen was acutely aware of the competition. Eyes darted around the room, scoping out the women who posed the greatest threat and tallying up the minutes they spent talking to the Stag. They eyed the Stag with the painful hunger of an anorexic eyeing a plate of sweets, calculating the minutes with Chris like they were computing calories, starved for his attention. Every time he moved on to a new girl, with a camera leading and trailing every move, the crowd seemed to breathe a collective sigh of relief, thankful he didn't fall on his knees and declare the show over—he'd found the woman of his dreams.

Whenever a camera neared a group of women, hair was flipped, lips were glossed with a flick of the tongue, and forced laughter broke through the polite conversations. There was as much flirting with the camera as there was with the Stag.

Three women leaned against the imposing grand piano, waiting their turn. This was my opportunity—my very own focus group.

"Hi, I'm Sarah Divine," I said, stepping toward the group.

"Hi, there," a willowy redhead with a Southern lilt replied. "I'm Holly Simpson from Memphis. And this here's Vanessa and Dorothy."

I nodded at the other two women who held up their champagne glasses in a mock toast. Vanessa, the tanner, taller, and more exotic-looking of the two, gave me a bored nod and looked away. Dorothy, with her short, full wedge of hair and compact body, actually resembled Dorothy Hamill—a resemblance I'm sure I wasn't the first to notice.

"This house is beautiful, isn't it?" I asked, hoping to get the ball rolling. There wasn't a whole lot of talking going on. Just a lot of visual daggers flying across the room at whomever was lucky enough to be talking to the Stag at that moment.

"He's not so bad, either," Vanessa answered, not taking her eyes off the Stag. She wore a sleeveless scarlet dress resembling a kimono, its shimmering satiny material creating highlights and shadows where her body's curves demanded to be heard under the tight row of buttons and high neck. There was something both sexy and standoffish about Vanessa, like a belly dancer who beckons you nearer to her with bared skin and skilled moves and then hides her face behind sheer scarves so that she's not completely exposed. Of course, comparing Vanessa to a belly dancer would actually require her to have a belly—and if there was one thing made clear by her geisha-girl getup, it was that Vanessa's belly was as flat and tight as her smile.

"So where are you from? What do you do? Why are you here?" Holly quizzed me.

Vanessa and Dorothy watched, waiting to size me up.

"I'm from Chicago and work in PR."

"And why are you here?" Holly repeated.

"Probably the same reason you're all here." Wasn't I supposed to be asking the questions?

"Because men are dogs," Vanessa deadpanned.

Holly and Dorothy turned to her, looks of concern crossing their faces.

"And I've been their chew toy way too long," Vanessa added.

I let out a laugh, and Holly and Dorothy reluctantly joined me.

With the ice broken, I listened as the three women told me their stories. Vanessa was a real estate agent from Washington, DC. She'd been engaged to a former client, an older man she'd met when he was looking for a place in Georgetown—his wife was awarded their Potomac farm as part of their divorce settlement. The day after he closed on his new town house he broke up with Vanessa, admitting that he'd really just wanted to reduce the commission cost on the sale. He saved himself ten grand and cost Vanessa seven months of her time.

Dorothy was a chef from Atlanta. She worked nights, a schedule not conducive to meeting or dating men. The men who did ask her out always suggested she cook dinner for them—she said that was like asking a dentist out for a free root canal on Friday night.

And Holly worked at a Victoria's Secret store in Memphis.

"You can bet the Stag will have quite a treat if he takes me away for the night." She winked at us as a blush spread across her freckled face.

I couldn't quite picture the twangy Southern redhead with Nicole Kidman ringlets as a G-string-clad seductress, but I'd take her word for it.

"Oh, look." Holly grabbed Vanessa's bronzed arm and started bouncing up and down. "It's him. He's coming over here! Can you see my thong through this dress?"

I slipped away before Holly could ask me if her nipples showed.

As I walked, I felt the Stag's eyes on me. The room was thick with the desperation of single women who obviously felt they were without options. I knew I couldn't suck up to him to the same degree. I had a sudden, daring thought and took the risk. With the most confident, uninterested gait I could muster, I walked right on out of the room.

Out on the slate terrace an early-evening breeze was rustling the palm trees surrounding the patio. The Stag was put up in his own bachelor pad complete with hot tub, swimming pool, and stone-lined cliff walk leading to the beach. A fear of water would not go over well in this situation.

The back of the house was encased in glass. French doors ran the length of the living room and opened up to a terrace that stepped down to the pool. Beyond the pool a stone wall lined the property where the land fell off into the sea.

In the glow of the footlights surrounding the tropical landscape, I tried to figure out what, if anything, I'd just learned. Vanessa was cynical. Dorothy was hopeful. And Holly was calculating. The only thing they appeared to have in common was the fact that they were relying on the Stag to renew their faith in men.

"Nice view." A deep voice drifted over my shoulder.

I turned to find the Stag standing behind me, his eyes intently watching the fiery pink sun slide into the ocean. Score one for the old lady.

"Why are you out here alone?" he asked, turning his attention away from the horizon.

"I could ask you the same thing."

"Oh, yeah." He shrugged and avoided looking directly at me. "I told the camera crew I had to use the men's room, and they parted like the Red Sea. Just needed a breather."

"I'm Sarah," I introduced myself, and held out a hand.

"I remember. I'm Chris." He shook my hand firmly and looked over his shoulder. On the other side of the French doors twenty-three pairs of mascaraed eyes were anxiously scanning the room, their antennae on high alert.

"It's a little overwhelming in there. I didn't really know what to expect." Chris ran a large, solid hand through his hair.

I knew this was my opportunity to grill him, to find out what would make a guy go on a five-week hunt for a wife. The journalist in me had to be gagged, because tonight the goal was to make it through the ceremony without getting cut. My patience would be rewarded with a candle and one more week to get inside the heads of the hens—I was sure there was lots of elbow room in there.

"I know what you mean; we're all a little new at this." I smiled at him and he seemed to relax.

"I guess I should be getting back. Only an hour left to thin the herd." He let out a nervous laugh. "Sorry, that sounded bad."

Yep. It did. Strike one for the Stag.

"That's okay. I know what you meant."

"No, it was obnoxious. I hope you don't think I'm an asshole."

"How could I already conclude you're an asshole? I figure that will take two conversations, at least."

He cocked his head and looked like he was trying to figure out a response.

"I'm just kidding," I told him, and couldn't help but laugh at the poor guy. Maybe he wasn't a jerk after all.

Chris smiled, and I noticed a small dimple in his left cheek, a very endearing dimple.

"Well, I hope we get to have that second conversation, to test your theory. Maybe I'll be the exception to the rule."

Chris started walking back toward the house, his figure casting a long shadow on the terrace as he neared the door.

"Hey, Sarah," he turned around and called back to me. "It was nice meeting you." He waved and, as he opened the terrace door, was swallowed up into bright lights and a crowd of clucking hens.

"Very nice, Sarah," a voice commented appraisingly.

I turned toward a darkened corner of the yard, where Arnie and a cameraman emerged from the shadows.

"Where'd you come from?" Was Arnie spying on me?

"I watched Chris follow you out here. We went out the side door," Arnie told me, motioning for the cameraman to head back inside. "Of course, the 'asshole' comment will have to be edited out, but, all in all, nice job." Arnie shot me a thumbs up.

"You were watching? And listening?"

Arnie pointed to the planters and trees. "Mikes. Everywhere."

Everywhere?

Arnie started walking back toward the house as I stood there like an idiot.

"Sarah, watch the language," he called without bothering to turn and look at me. "This is prime time, remember."

I'd remember. Now that I'd fallen victim to Arnie's commando tactics, how could I forget?

# 5

"*L*adies?" A French-accented man stepped into the room and waited for us to quiet down. He was model-perfect, with chiseled features, dark hair gelled into place, and a thin build that was way more pretty-boy than ruggedly handsome like the Stag. "I am Pierre, your host for this season's journey toward love."

He made his way across the room and stood beside Chris.

"Chris will now retreat to his study," Pierre announced. "When he returns, the candle ceremony will begin."

Our eyes trailed Chris as he followed the host down a long tiled hallway lined with what appeared to be Native American renditions of copulating animals, and disappeared around a corner.

From watching tapes of the show, I knew what was going on back there. Chris and the host were doing a postmortem, talking about which women he liked and who rubbed him the wrong way. He also had framed pictures of each of us to look at, to jog his memory in case he couldn't recall all the scintillating conversations he'd managed to have.

While Chris was in his study determining our fate, we waited like prisoners preparing for the electric chair. All around the room women were doing one of two things—either trying too hard to act like they didn't care, or wringing their hands and promising the powers that be if they were picked they'd never, ever do another bad thing as long as they lived.

I sat alongside Vanessa, Dorothy, and Holly on a leather couch facing the creamy marble fireplace. Even though it wasn't below sixty outside, a low flame fluttered on an artificial log for added effect.

As a camera was pointed in my direction I sat up a little straighter. If the camera added ten pounds, I figured slouching on camera must add at least twenty. Besides, no audience would root for a hunchbacked hen.

"So what do you think?" I asked the three women.

"I think if he picks that twit over there he needs his head examined." Vanessa pointed to the corner of the room where a group of women stood huddling around a blonde blowing her nose into a tissue. The camera was eating it up, practically sticking the lens up the girl's nostrils. The women took turns patting her on the back and muttering positive thoughts, taking advantage of the opportunity to look like team players. No one seemed to underestimate the power of winning the audience over, even though the show wouldn't air for another four months.

But even as they told the crier that she would definitely be picked, each of them kept stealing glances down the hallway.

"See that one over there?" Holly gestured discreetly toward a woman standing alone. She had long, shiny black hair that she used like a veil to shade one eye and drape over her shoulder like a pashmina shawl. "That's Claudia. Don't turn your back on her. I hear she's willing to do anything to win."

"How on earth do you know that already?"

Holly shrugged, helping the slim lacy strap of her nightie-style dress slip off her shoulder. She let it hang there, not bothering to replace it, and didn't take her eyes off of Claudia.

I'd have to find time to talk with Claudia. If what Holly was saying was true, she'd make great copy.

"What if you aren't chosen?" I asked, turning toward Vanessa.

"At least my streak won't be broken."

"Oh, don't be so morose," Holly scolded her, taking a break from her Claudia watch. "If I'm not selected then he obviously didn't get a chance to know the real me. He'd be making a big mistake."

"Holly, you talked with the guy for all of seven minutes," I reminded her.

"Yes, but when you know, you know."

"All I know is that I asked for an extended leave to come out here for five weeks, and if I end up flying back to Atlanta after two days then I'll look like a total loser," Dorothy told us, and then fell silent. "Look."

Across the room women were falling into place as the show's host started to pass out small vanilla-scented candles to the women. When he got to our couch we all stood up and joined the other hens in forming a half circle around the circumference of the room.

"Ladies, should Chris choose to light your candle and you accept his gesture, you may stay. Those of you who choose not to stay will indicate this by blowing out your candle. Those who choose to leave, and those of you not selected, will exit through the front door and return to the hotel, where you will pack up and check out immediately."

Boy, this was romantic. I've had yeast infections that were more forgiving.

Holly jabbed me in the ribs with her elbow, signaling that Chris was on his way. He stopped near the grand piano, where the host presented him with a very large, red tapered pillar candle. I wondered if anyone else thought that candle resembled a huge fiery penis.

Chris cleared his throat and prepared to address us as a group for the first time.

I spotted the director whispering into his headset, calling his troops into action. Immediately a camera zoomed in on Chris. They were probably trying to catch the sincerity in his face, make the Stag the good guy. Last season the Stag was always the good guy. They showed shot after shot of women crying, talking behind each other's backs, and plotting to win, but the Stag was always the good guy.

"I just wanted to say how much I enjoyed meeting each one of you. This hasn't been easy for me, and I hope that no one's feelings will be hurt."

It wasn't easy for him? He had no idea what these girls were going through, placing their entire future in his hands, probably already reciting *Mrs. Chris Masters* in their heads over and over. He had it easy; all he had to do was pluck a few women from the crowd and go to bed knowing that fifteen women were still working themselves into a lather over him. The women who weren't picked got to hang their heads and go home branded unlovable.

Nonetheless, the hens murmured in somewhat over-the-top compassion for his profound inner struggle.

Chris took a deep breath and started toward the circle. Every time he took a step near us Holly let out a little gasp. I hoped she wasn't going to pass out. Although it might be good material for the article.

His first picks weren't a surprise—Samantha, a bouncy blonde from Santa Barbara, the dreaded Claudia, several other thin, generic beauties, and a few women who actually appeared human. Finally, after lighting the candles of two openly ecstatic hens, he hesitated in front of me. After briefly making eye contact, Chris tipped his candle until its flame caught the wick of my own vanilla-scented Stag magnet. I stared back, silently thanking that endearing little dimple. I was in.

Relief trickled through me. I let out a thankful sigh and watched in horror as my flame flickered and gasped for air, verging on extinction. Chris had started walking away, but abruptly stopped, watching me with an expression that was a cross between curiosity and disbelief. Twenty three women were gaping at me, wide-eyed. The cameras' lenses were poised on me, and even the director's mouth hung open as he waited to see what I'd do next. I quickly cupped my hand around my candle, protecting the flame from any more thoughtless breaths. It stayed lit. I smiled reassuringly at Chris and he continued on to the next girl.

When the moment of truth was over there were nine hens holding dark candles. One of them was a steaming Bebe.

The cameramen focused on the host as he stepped into position beside Chris.

Pierre nudged Chris aside and placed his hands flamboyantly on his thin French hips. "Don't mean to be a bitch, but you're blocking my light," Pierre whined in a nasal New York accent. "Makeup! I'm beginning to glow!"

We all watched in shock as, before our eyes, Pierre, the suave French host, turned into a queen from Queens. Suzanne was going to love this!

The director hung his head in his hands as a harried woman rushed up to Pierre and powdered his brow.

"Rolling!" the director shouted. The makeup woman ducked out of the picture and the dashing Pierre once again surfaced.

"The fifteen hens who remain will spend the next week getting to know Chris better before he once again must choose between you. Those of you who weren't chosen this evening, will you please exit?"

As eight other disappointed hens prepared to leave, one livid Bebe marched straight up to Arnie.

"This is a mistake! You can't ditch me. The cameras love me! I'm better than any of them—my God, those aren't even her boobs!" Bebe pointed an angry finger at me. Me! The one woman I was vaguely acquainted with before arriving in California had just outed my Mega Bra. All the eyes in the room were riveted to my bodacious curves. I crossed my arms and pretended to be fascinated by the weave of the Oriental carpet.

Arnie threw his arm around Bebe and escorted her hastily toward the door. I could swear I heard Holly snicker.

A few of the remaining hens consoled the rejected girls with hugs and brief kisses that landed more often in the air than on their cheeks—or at least, they did as long as the cameras were watching. Everyone tried to remain gracious, congratulating the hens who held flaming candles and emoting about the departure of others as if they were long-lost sisters instead of near-total strangers. I'd hoped to talk with a few of the women who were leaving, but they were quickly sent outside with two cameramen to film the humiliating moment in real time. I didn't get a chance to talk with them before they were sent away, and Suzanne wouldn't like that.

When the front door had closed for the last time and the heavy brass lock clicked shut, Pierre pushed on.

"Ladies, a toast!" He held up a glass of bubbly as tuxedoed waiters appeared with trays of champagne and handed glasses to the remaining hens. "To our Stag and our hens. May you discover true love."

We had five days before the next candle ceremony. I held my glass up in the air and then thankfully downed the entire contents.

While the rejected hens took the walk of shame to their waiting cars, the rest of us blew out our candles.

"Oh, I'm so excited," Holly gushed. "I can't believe the Stag chose all of us."

"The boy obviously has taste." Vanessa bristled a little as Holly tried to hug her.

I couldn't believe I was selected, that I'd passed for a woman who would really be excited about the idea of picking my spouse off a TV show—or more accurately, having my spouse pick me. I'd fooled them all, although I swear I caught a retreating hen looking over at me, pointing me out to Sloane as if to say, *Her, the fake blonde by the couch— what's she still doing there?*

The host poured everyone a round of champagne and encouraged us to mingle with Chris before stomping off to the terrace for a cigarette.

With only fifteen women left it was easier to keep tabs on people, and it seemed everyone was keeping tabs on Chris. I watched as he took each woman aside for a personal visit. During these encounters, heads tilted with interest, hair was tossed over shoulders, and the lucky woman hung on his every word. It was a scene right out of a high school gymnasium dance. The only thing missing was the Thompson Twins playing in the background.

He always seemed to be making the women laugh, and I wondered if he used the same line on everyone. I'd have to compare notes with the other girls.

"Hey." Chris appeared beside me just as I was stuffing a cheese cube in my mouth.

I nodded and pointed to my bulging cheek.

He placed his hand on my shoulder and leaned me in toward him as his hand covered the microphone discreetly clipped to his lapel. "I guess you'll get to put that asshole theory to the test," he practically whispered.

I swallowed my cube and took a sip of champagne to wash it down.

"Then you'd better hope this doesn't count as conversation number two," I whispered back playfully, impressed with my ability to think up such a witty response on the spot. He had to love that.

We were standing there, grinning at each other and feeling a little impressed with our own quick humor, when the host announced it was time for Chris to leave. He led Chris down the hall, and they vanished.

I'd made it. Not the most encouraging display of candle savvy, but the Stag liked me. I couldn't wait to tell Suzanne. I had to call Jack. I was going to be in California for another week.

Back in my hotel room, there was indistinguishable babble on the other end of the line, peppered with a few words I actually understood— *Mommy, Da-da,* and *juice.* As I lay on my bed surrounded by Ritz-Carlton finery, Katie's small voice seemed foreign and far away. Far removed from me.

"Did you get all that?" Jack asked, taking the phone back.

"Enough of it. How's she feeling?"

"A little better. How're you doing?"

"Good. I'm sorry I'm calling so late. I glanced around the room, suspicious of any plant or decoration that could be concealing a microphone. I cupped my hand over the mouthpiece of my mobile phone and lowered my voice. "I just wanted to talk to you guys."

"Not a big deal. I'm sorry about Friday night," he said, his voice becoming soft.

"I know. Me too." I reached for my wallet and slipped out a picture of Katie and Jack. Had I really just left them yesterday? "I miss you guys," I whispered.

"We miss you. But that's exciting, another week. Suzanne must be ecstatic."

"She will be when she gets the voice mail."

"So are you getting what you need for the article?"

"I haven't spent much time with the women yet, but I think this week I'll be able to talk with them more. So far it's pretty much what we expected." I glanced at the clock on the night table and saw it was getting late. "Katie should be getting to bed, and I should be going. I've got to do some writing in my journal, I mean," I added, eying a suspicious-looking ice bucket on my bar.

"Yeah, sure, your *journal*. What's on tap this week? Lap dancing?" he joked.

"Nothing as nefarious as that. Just some day trips to help us get acquainted with the Stag and everyone else. I'll be thinking of you guys back home."

"We'll be thinking of you, too. I love you."

"I love you, too," I told him, feeling lonely for the first time since I'd arrived in California. "Tell Katie I love her and give her a big kiss from me."

I held on to the phone after the line went dead, and then reluctantly snapped my phone shut.

Between orientation, getting ready for the cocktail party, and meeting the other women, I hadn't thought about anything except the Stag all day. It was as if the only thing that mattered were getting my candle lit. But now that I'd won myself another week, there was work to do.

After inspecting the ice bucket and planters to confirm that my room wasn't bugged, I grabbed my notebook and got myself comfortable at the desk. Unlike the other articles I'd written for *Femme*, I couldn't interview my subjects with a pen and paper in my hand. This assignment relied on recounting conversations and events hours after they'd taken place. I intended to sit down every night and get everything down on paper as soon as possible, before I forgot.

I needed to get my thoughts together to start figuring out where this story was going. Where to begin? In one respect I understood the motivation of the women more than the Stag. Him, I didn't quite get.

Chris Masters. He was charming, and good-looking if you went for that all-American jock/successful businessman sort of thing. Okay, who didn't? So the guy seemed perfect—I'd give him that. But then why come on the show? You'd think he'd have his pick of women off-camera as well as on.

I expected him to be a little smoother, more suave, almost verging on smarmy. But he wasn't slick and definitely didn't come across as a player, used to lobbing lines at women like softballs. Sometimes he even seemed uncomfortable being the center of attention. Then again, he was only twenty-eight. Maybe that was something men gained with age. Like penile dysfunction.

The women were pretty much what I expected. Not one was larger than a size six, their teeth were straight, their skin was clear, and every hair was in place. They were right out of *Friends*. From what I'd seen so far, the women were trying really hard to put their best feet forward—I didn't see one woman scratch her nose or pick at a wedgie the entire night. Not that I was sticking my finger up my nose for all to see, but at least I had an excuse for my picture-perfect demeanor. Getting cut meant my article was over. You'd think the other women would want the Stag to choose them for who they really were, not some imitation of a Barbie doll who'd taken a class with Emily Post.

For two hours everyone was just too good to be true. But I guess that's the way everyone is in the beginning.

When Jack and I met, I wasn't exactly bitching at him for being late. And he had been late. Our first date was a Saturday afternoon Northwestern football game, and I waited for him outside the stadium gate for twenty minutes before he came running up, out of breath, apologizing. He'd forgotten his wallet and had to go all the way back to his apartment to find it. His cheeks were flushed and his breath was steaming in the cold autumn air, and he just looked so cute I shrugged and told him it wasn't a big deal.

For a year, when we weren't studying or in class, we were together. He didn't take for granted that I loved to spend my Saturdays watching college football, and I never complained when he failed to replace the empty toilet paper roll if he used the last sheet. We peacefully coexisted in a state of mutually agreed-upon ignorance—we knew the flaws were there; we just weren't in any rush to find them.

In fact, the cocktail party hadn't been so different from any first meeting, although the pretense was more out in the open—and the camera crew caught it all on film.

# 6

$\mathcal{I}$ awoke the next morning with the California sun streaming in through my balcony window. I loved Jack the most in the mornings—when I reached over, my body still heavy with sleep and the residue of dissolving dreams, and felt his spot next to me cool to my touch and vacant. In those early hours after feeding Katie, I wished he were there to share a cup of coffee from the thin, fragile cups and saucers we received for our wedding and kept stored away in the dining room cabinet for special occasions. I pictured us seated around the table on the terrace, our hands folded together on the table next to a tray of flaky croissants, like a couple out of a Ralph Lauren ad. But then, little by little it happened—a pair of boxers discarded haphazardly next to the hamper, a wet towel crumpled on the bathroom floor, crumbs from his morning toast littering the kitchen counter like grains of sand, grating on me, buffing away those morning feelings until the only thing left was raw skin. And all before nine o'clock.

Here at the Ritz those same morning feelings began to rise to the surface, but they were held at bay by the foreign surroundings, the strange bed and unfamiliar room that held no memories of Jack and therefore no desire to reclaim what had been lost.

This morning we were all meeting the producers downstairs

for breakfast before being loaded into a bus and shuttled to Disneyland like a third-grade field trip. Our dance card was full all week long. Tomorrow they planned a pool party at Chris's house, then a sunset sail in the Pacific Ocean on Wednesday, and finally a trail ride through the mountains on Thursday. A few bonding exercises before Chris whittled the group down yet again.

At the front of the bus Arnie and Sloane stood up and faced us. They had to be in their early fifties, but apparently that was news to Arnie and Sloane. I'd recognized Arnie's skeletal build and silver ponytail from my audition in Chicago, but I was personally introduced to Sloane for the first time in the hotel lobby.

Sloane wasn't exactly a mother figure for the hens. Her severe bob was dyed a solid black sheet, without a single highlight or subtle wave to suggest that she was anything but all business. Blunt bangs cut across a Botoxed forehead that remained serene and crease-free even while she animatedly shouted four-letter expletives and bossed around the cameramen and crew.

"Ladies," Arnie shouted down the aisle for our attention.

A round of shushing followed, as the women tried to get one another to stop talking and pay attention to our fearless leader.

"Ladies, Chris will be waiting for us when we get to Disneyland," Arnie explained, his gravelly voice resonating throughout the bus. "But it's your job to figure out where he is."

Whispers bubbled up again as the group tried to decipher what he meant.

Arnie held on to the tops of the seat backs and started making his way down the aisle toward the center of the bus. With his cowboy boots, Wrangler jeans, and suede blazer, Arnie obviously hadn't realized that the *Urban Cowboy* thing fizzled out almost twenty years ago. Although Sloane didn't share Arnie's sartorial interest in the Wild West, she herself was a victim of eighties film fashion, with her Annie Hall–inspired tie, waistcoat, man's shirt, and flowing cuffed pants.

As the bus turned a corner Arnie gripped an upholstered headrest for dear life before regaining his balance and composure.

"This is a way for you all to get to know one another, and enjoy a little game of '*Find the Stag*' in the process." He glanced back at Sloane, who was chewing on a pencil and examining a clipboard. "There are no winners here, so just have fun. The goal is to enjoy yourselves and learn more about Chris. He was given free access to Disneyland's resources and told to pick something or somewhere that best reflects his personality. When we arrive you'll be dropped off at the park's entrance, and the rest is up to you."

All around me women began speculating where Chris would be and strategizing how to be the first one there. But while castles and Space Mountain were catching the imagination of the others, a lump was settling in my throat.

Dorothy reached over the seat and tapped me on the shoulder.

"Hey, what's wrong?" she asked softly, ignoring the frenzy around her.

I shrugged. "Nothing, just nervous, I guess," I managed to say with a weak smile.

"Well, you have nothing to be nervous about. I've been to Disney World lots of times; this can't be too different. I'll help you figure out where to go."

I remained silent, afraid that opening my mouth would dislodge the tears that were building in strength as I tried to fight them back.

"Hey, Sarah, it's okay. Don't worry; I'm here if you need me."

She squeezed my shoulder reassuringly before turning around and joining the other women mapping out their treasure hunt.

I couldn't tell her that it wasn't nerves that were bothering me. It was guilt.

I hadn't been to Disney World since I was eight, and the plan was not to go until Katie was old enough to go on most of the rides.

We'd planned for a family trip. Instead here I was about to see all of Katie's favorite characters, not to mention swirling cones of cotton candy and ice-cream sundaes. She would have loved it.

"He's got to be in Cinderella's castle. He is our Prince Charming, after all," Iris suggested.

"The Indiana Jones ride," Samantha recommended. "Because he's our dashing hero."

It went on and on like this until I thought someone would say the Dumbo ride because Chris had big ears. The sole cameraman on the bus shot the entire thing, making sure the hens' inane suggestions were indelibly captured on film for public viewing.

Once the vocal guessing had died down, nobody actually divulged where they planned to start. So when the bus pulled up to the entrance and we all took our place between the front gates, I had no idea where anyone was going. I'd hoped to follow some of the women, but as soon as Arnie said, "Go," everyone headed off in a different direction. At first the group of women tried to act calm, walking at a regular pace beside one another, but all it took was an eager Holly to turn the walk into a brisk stride, a head of red curls bouncing behind her, and the group made a mad dash for the Stag.

Not one determined Stag-seeker even noticed the scenery around us. They missed the passengers waiting at the turn-of-the-century station for a ride on the steam-powered train. They didn't stop to look in the windows of the old-fashioned stores lining both sides of an artificial Main Street. With determined faces and eyes focused straight ahead, they didn't even see the man-made mountains and rotating rides high above. The women were oblivious to the fact that they were in a land of make-believe.

I hung back, watching the group disperse like mercury, starting in one big clump and breaking up into smaller subsets until they were just individual blurs running away, a team of cameramen trailing behind them.

I didn't have a plan to find the Stag. But I did have an agenda. I wanted to find a present for Katie. Maybe I could assuage my guilt with gifts.

I found what I was looking for in the Toontown five-and-dime: a plush Tigger with a corkscrew tail, just right for bouncing and Katie's tiny grasp. With my Tigger in hand, I set off to find some of the other hens. I figured I'd start in Fantasyland—it sounded like the ideal place to find a bunch of women looking for the perfect man.

As I passed Donald Duck's boat, the *Miss Daisy*, a friendly furry creature waved furiously in my direction.

"Hello, there," Pooh called out, greeting me with a soft hand. The person in the oversize costume tried to sound authentic, but his imitation sounded more like a southern Scooby-Doo than Katie's beloved Pooh.

"Hi, Pooh."

"What are you doing here all by yourself?" Pooh asked, his black saucer eyes staring at me.

"Just walking around, exploring."

"Then why do you look so sad?"

"Because it would probably be a lot more fun with a kid who appreciated all of this." I pointed to the rides around us.

"That's sweet."

"Yeah, that's me. A real sweetie."

Pooh's belly shook as he laughed.

"How do you like living here, Pooh? They treat you okay?"

"The food's good, but Mickey's ego can sometimes be a drag. Can you keep a secret?" Pooh raised his large felt paws and started to reach for his neck as if to strangle himself.

That was all I needed, to bear witness to a suicidal Pooh in front of hundreds of children.

I reached out to stop him, but I was too late. Pooh's head was no longer attached to his body. As the velvety black nose and black glass eyes fell forward toward me I furiously looked around for unsuspecting children. The unveiling of Pooh and the crushing of childhood dreams—this was the sort of moment parents sued over.

When I saw the coast was clear, I turned my attention back to Pooh and my hands shot up to cover my open mouth, because in his place I found a very large-bellied, yellow-pawed Chris.

"Oh, my God," I finally managed to say when I composed myself. "What are you doing dressed up like Pooh? Do you have any idea how many women are puking their guts out on Space Mountain looking for you?"

"Actually, I thought it would be more fun to wander around and watch everyone. There must be six girls hanging out by Cinderella's castle like they're waiting for a bus or something." Chris let out a very un-Pooh-like laugh. "It's kinda surreal."

Chris held Pooh's head under his arm while we talked, and fast-thinking parents directed their children away from us.

"So I'm the big winner," I declared.

"Didn't Arnie tell you there were no winners?"

"Sure, but I figured he was just being nice. Without a winner, what's the point?"

Chris seemed to like my answer. He nodded his head and grinned.

"You're quite the competitor, Sarah Divine. That should make it interesting." He took Pooh's head out from under his arm and started to lift it above his shoulders. "Well, I'd better go and give some of the other girls a chance to meet the silly old bear."

Chris slipped the Pooh head on and started to wobble away. I didn't even notice we'd been under surveillance until two people started trailing behind Pooh's stubby tail.

A cameraman. And the boom operator holding a long pole with a microphone attached.

The director stepped out from behind a lamppost and shot me a thumbs-up before following the Pooh parade.

Our entire conversation had been filmed. And recorded. And

I'd just come across as a hypercompetitive hen. Next time I'd have to be more careful.

With my Tigger doll in hand, I made my way toward Critter Country in search of some hens. But as much as I tried to enjoy the walk around the park, I couldn't shake the feeling that behind every garbage can or food stand there was a *Stag* crew member lurking with a camera just waiting to catch me with toilet paper on my shoe.

As the final drop of Splash Mountain came into view, I thought I spotted a familiar head of dark hair flying downward into a spray of water. I stopped to watch the log and its riders slowly unload, hoping it was who I thought it was.

"Claudia!" I called out, waving at the waterlogged beauty as she wrung out her hair.

She spotted me and made her way over, leaving a trail of wet footprints.

"What are you doing on Splash Mountain?" I asked.

"Holly told me she heard Chris was on the ride."

"Holly told you?"

"Yeah. He must have left, because I've been up and down that thing four times and he's nowhere in sight." She pulled her sneaker off and emptied the water onto the pavement.

Of course he wasn't. Holly had no clue where Chris was, and if she did she certainly wouldn't share that knowledge with Claudia.

I, on the other hand, did know where Chris was—or at least that he was dressed as a life-size Pooh.

"Kinda wet, huh?"

Claudia shrugged. "Yeah. Holly said if I sat in the front of the log I'd barely get a splash. I guess she meant the back."

Nope. Looking at Claudia's matted hair and limp outfit, I decided Holly definitely meant the front.

"If Holly knew where Chris was, why do you think she didn't come here herself?" I asked.

Claudia nodded her head slowly as the lightbulb went on.

"You know, my friends warned me about hens like her. You're right. I should have known better. She was all too eager to help."

I couldn't let Holly get away with misleading Claudia. After all, what did I care if someone else found Chris? It wasn't like I was actually competing for him.

"You know, I don't think Chris is actually on a ride. I thought I heard Arnie say he was dressed up as Pooh."

"Pooh? Like the bear?"

"Yep."

Claudia looked at me skeptically. "How do I know you're not misleading me, too?"

"Just trust me, Claudia. Besides, you've got nothing to lose. You're already soaking wet."

"If you're pulling my leg, Sarah, I'll remember this."

"I'm not pulling your leg."

Claudia started to walk away in search of Pooh.

"Hey, Claudia!" I called after her.

She turned back toward me. "Yeah?"

I pointed to her shoe.

She smiled at me, bent down to remove the trailing toilet paper, and continued on her way.

The phone was ringing on the other end, and although I wanted to talk to Jack and Katie, I didn't really feel like going over my day at Disneyland. I wanted to hear their voices, but now that I was back in my hotel room I felt awkward. How could I describe talking to Pooh and discovering it was Chris? Even though I thought it showed Chris had a twisted sense of humor, no matter how I explained it, Jack would think Chris was a fool. And even though I knew it sounded strange, picturing Chris in that big-bellied body made me smile. He looked so silly, and he didn't even care.

"Hey, it's me," I greeted Jack when he answered after four rings.

"Hey, you. What's going on in the land of sunshine and the stud?"

"It's the Stag, and not much." I hoped he didn't ask me to elaborate.

"So where'd you go today? Will I be jealous?"

"Disneyland," I admitted.

"No way. Katie would have loved that."

"I know. I got her a stuffed Tigger. Can I talk to her?"

"Hey, Katie, Mommy got you a Tigger!" he yelled across the room. "She's in our bathtub. I figured she'd like the added space. I filled the tub with bubble bath and turned on the jets, but judging from her hysterical screams, she's not quite ready for a whirlpool." He let out a laugh and I heard Katie squealing in the background. "You should see her. She's got suds all over her chin like Santa Claus."

Jack was giving Katie a bath? Considering he was hardly ever home in time to give her a bath I thought he just assumed kids always smelled like Mr. Bubble.

"Did you have any trouble leaving work today? Did they give you a hard time?"

"Actually, no. I'm not sure anyone even noticed. I've got my laptop. I'll do some work after she's in bed."

"So you guys are surviving without me?" I asked, feeling a mix of relief and annoyance.

"We're fine. I'd better go. She's going to start throwing suds all over the floor in a second."

"Well, I love you. Tell Katie I love her."

"We love you, too. Bye-bye."

I don't know what I'd felt guilty about; they were doing just fine without me. Figured. Jack was supposed to be floundering, finally appreciating the finer points of caring for our child. And I'd thought Katie would be inconsolable in my absence, clutching like a life preserver the picture of me I'd placed on her dresser. Instead they were giggling like a dip in the tub was a day at the circus.

And Jack didn't even care that I went to Disneyland with Chris—well, that we all went to Disneyland with him, that is. I didn't have to explain how a guy in a Pooh costume could look so cute. And I don't mean cartoon-character cute. I mean cute like the kind of guy you'd fall for.

# 7

$\mathcal{I}$f Chris had enjoyed watching us run around Disneyland searching for him, he was beside himself with joy as he surveyed fifteen attractive women parading around half-naked at Tuesday's pool party.

As the cameras panned toward Chris, women piled hot dogs and hamburgers on their plates, scooped out large spoonfuls of potato salad and cole slaw, and grabbed fistfuls of chocolate-chip cookies for dessert. But when the lenses were focused in their direction, the over-filled plates were pushed aside and bowls of chips were passed over in favor of watermelon and grapes. Nobody wanted to be the skinny girl who could eat anything and not gain an inch. And nobody wanted to appear to have an eating disorder. Neither of those were very good for viewer sympathy.

Besides, who needed to get a sesame seed stuck in her teeth just when the lens pulled in for a close-up? There was plenty of time for eating when the cameras weren't rolling.

One by one we were pulled aside for on-camera interviews, poignant little moments in which we were expected to confess our inse-curities and secret thoughts.

When my turn came, the director asked me what I thought of the other girls. I scanned the pool scene around me, in which not one single woman was actually in the pool. Instead, they lay on lounges, their concave stomachs creating hollows beneath bikini tops bursting with pride. What did I think of the other girls? I thought they made me look like a lard-ass.

"I think we're developing very strong friendships," I told the blinking camera as convincingly as possible. "This is a unique situation and it's bringing us closer every day."

I half expected the director to start laughing, but he just nodded and waved his hand, indicating I should continue talking.

"I suppose we're all competing for the Stag, but I think we all share a common bond."

I had run out of things to say, but the director waited for me to continue so I babbled on. "We share the same hopes and dreams," I added, figuring that was the end of it. How much more could I drag out such an inane line of questioning?

"And what are those hopes and dreams?" he asked, while the camera continued to film.

I just hoped I stayed on the show long enough to finish the article, and dreamed of the day I could leave the Stag behind.

But the director was waiting for my answer like Bob Barker interviewing a beauty contestant.

"Um, world peace?" I stammered.

The director yelled cut and dismissed me, but not before giving me a little advice. "The audience wants to see who you really are, Sarah," he told me. "Show 'em a little skin."

My sarong never left my hips during my interview. And it wasn't leaving them, if I had anything to say about it. Holly, on the other hand, had no problem stripping down.

"What's wrong, Sarah? Don't like the sun?" Holly asked as I sat on a lounge chair watching the girls compete for Chris's attention.

"Just waiting for someone to go in the pool. Aren't you hot? You're not even sweating."

"I come prepared," she assured me with a wink.

"How, other than being freakishly thin?" Vanessa asked under her breath.

"The best in waterproof makeup," Holly confided, ignoring Vanessa's remark. "You want to borrow some? I brought it with me."

I could feel the perspiration dripping between my boobs and settling in my belly button. All I needed was a nice close-up of that on film. "Well, I'm sweating my ass off. Sure, where is it?"

I followed Holly into the house and returned ready for a cool dip. I made sure Chris was occupied with a coven of hens, quickly shed my sarong, and made a hasty retreat into the shallow end. The water felt refreshing after frying on the deck of Chris's pool.

"Aren't you guys coming in?" I called to Holly and Vanessa, pointing my toes and floating, doing my best Esther Williams impersonation. "It feels so nice."

I waved good-bye and dove under, the water cooling my face as I swam toward the deep end. When I resurfaced gulping for air, I wasn't alone.

"Hey, there!" Chris greeted me, droplets of water sliding off his bare shoulders as he treaded water. His cheerful expression quickly changed. "Oh, my God, what's wrong?"

"What?"

"Your face." He reached out and ran a finger along my cheek. "You're all muddy or something."

He held up his hand. It was black. Like mascara—mascara that wasn't waterproof.

"You're dripping into the pool. You need a towel."

When Holly saw Chris retrieving me a towel instead of running away, she rushed over and helped me out of the pool. "Sarah, I'm so sorry! I must have brought the wrong makeup. Can you ever forgive me?"

I took the towel from Chris and wiped my face, leaving inklike stains on the terry cloth.

"Really, Sarah, it was an accident. You believe me, don't you?" Holly pleaded, looking like she meant it.

I wanted to push her skinny little ass into the pool, but I couldn't let her get the best of me. Not if I wanted to get my story. I couldn't afford to have any enemies if I wanted to get Suzanne the inside scoop. But Holly had better watch her step. Even I had my limits.

"Sure, Holly. No problem." I smiled sweetly but stared coldly into her baby blues and hoped she got the message—one more attempt to undermine me and she was going down.

After my mascara meltdown, the rest of the afternoon was boring by comparison. Nobody dunked her head underwater and surfaced with a George Washington unicurl framing her face. There were no cannonballs or belly flops. It was all very well behaved. Like a G-rated party at the Playboy mansion.

Wednesday's sailing adventure was a little more challenging thanks to heavy winds that were great for picking up speed but wreacked havoc on the hens' carefully coiffed hair. As the hens and the camera crew clung to the deck for dear life, Chris worked the sails like a former member of the America's Cup team (which, we found out, he actually was).

On Thursday Chris traded in his swashbuckling Hugh Hefner role for that of the Lone Ranger. While the hens were placed on plain old brown and caramel-colored horses for a little beachside horseback riding, the director had Chris saddle up on a white stallion.

Dorothy looked cautiously at her horse as a production assistant held out his hands to give her a lift into the saddle.

"I've never been riding," she admitted, backing away.

"It's easy. Stick with me," Samantha offered from atop her dappled mare. With her blond hair tucked under a tan Stetson and worn cowboy boots securely in her stirrups, Samantha looked completely at home on horseback.

"You'll be fine," I assured Dorothy, trying to steady my own gelding.

"You ride?" Samantha asked hopefully. "I've been riding since I was a little girl. My family has a horse farm in Santa Barbara."

"Actually, only a few times," I said. Samantha looked disappointed, as if she'd thought we'd be riding buddies. "But I love *Mr. Ed!*"

We all followed Chris's lead down the beach. From the way he effortlessly handled his reins, it was obvious he knew his way around horses. Not surprisingly, it didn't take long before Chris and Samantha were galloping along in unison while the rest of us struggled to keep up.

"Howdy. I'm Rose." An athletic brunette moved up in line next to me as I struggled to keep my horse from wading out into the water.

"Hi, I'm Sarah from Chicago," I introduced myself as I tugged on the reins, hoping the city reference would excuse my obvious inexperience on horseback.

"I know. I remember you from the audition."

"You remember me?" Was I that memorable?

"Actually, I remember those." She nodded in unison with my bobbing boobs.

"Yeah, well, I guess after Bebe's revelation, we all know that these have a little help from Mega Bra. I'm sorry. I don't recall seeing you in Chicago."

"I'm not surprised." She didn't seem at all offended at my lack of recognition. "No nose ring. No heaving breasts. I think they picked me because I represent 'everywoman'—maybe they needed someone who actually looked like she used the Toilet Duck the show's sponsors are pitching."

"So, everywoman, what brings you here?" I asked, glad I had someone normal to talk to as I tried to show my four-hooved friend who was boss.

"Oh, probably a story you've heard a million times before. I've been going out with the same guy for four years. I tell him I want a commitment. He tells me he's not ready to settle down. I break up with him. He comes crawling back a few weeks later saying he can't live without me. Everything's wonderful. I tell him I want a commitment and the vicious cycle starts all over again."

"Yuck. So now you're broken up?"

"For good, as of four weeks ago." Rose looked around and then turned to me with a mischievous grin. "Unless you count the two A.M. booty call I made to him the week before the show."

"But you don't want to get back together with him?"

"He's been getting the milk for free way too long. Time to buy the cow or move on to another pasture."

I'd always hated that comparison, but it certainly did illustrate the point.

"She's a really good rider, isn't she?" Rose pointed to Samantha, who was galloping toward us. As she neared she slowed her horse to a graceful canter.

"Isn't this great?" she gasped, before letting out an ear-piercing "Ye-haw" and taking off back toward the stable.

"That girl's got energy, but she's also got the right idea. I'm heading back, too. You coming?" Rose started to turn her horse around.

"I think I'll keep going and meet you back there in a bit. Old Rusty and I are just getting used to each other."

With Samantha heading back to the stable I knew this was my chance to get Chris alone. I held on tight to my reins and kicked Old Rusty into action. In a few short minutes I'd passed a struggling Holly, who couldn't seem to get her horse to budge from a clump of seaweed, a tanned cheerleader who was reciting cheers for the women and a cameraman who wasn't lucky enough to break free from her pack, and Iris from New Jersey, who had apparently given up on riding her horse and was now walking beside it.

"You look pretty good up there," I called out to Chris as I approached him and prayed my horse wouldn't throw me as I attempted to slow down.

"You don't look so bad yourself."

Old Rusty obeyed and took his place next to Chris's horse as we rode along together. It was only a matter of time before one of the other women caught up to us, so I jumped right into my first line of questioning.

"What possessed you to come on the show?" I asked, breaking the brief silence. "And what do you think of a woman who'd come on the show to find a husband?"

"Hey, what is this? Twenty Questions?"

"Sorry." I quickly backed down. He wasn't likely to open up to someone who came across as a nosy hen. "I just think it's amazing how the show has caught the attention of viewers, and how there were hundreds of women competing for you—before they even knew who you were."

"Well, you were one of them. What possessed you to come on the show?"

An insatiable editor? A desire to expose the Stag? An all-expense-paid vacation to a luxury resort?

"I thought it would be fun."

"Well, there you go. Me, too. Are you having fun?"

"I don't know if *fun* is the word I'd use to describe the burning sensation in my thighs, but then again I've never ridden anything as big as Old Rusty before." As the words escaped my mouth I wished I could grab them and stuff them back in. Once again, the camera was catching me in rare form. *The Stag*'s entire viewing audience would be wondering about the size of things I was accustomed to riding. I hoped Jack wouldn't take that the wrong way.

"Really?" Chris laughed. "Old Rusty could give the rest of us a complex."

As a cameraman ahead of us burst into his own round of hysterics, it seemed the only one in danger of developing a complex on the show was me.

# 8

*B*y the end of the week we were either exhausted, sunburned, sore from the stiff leather saddles, or all three. Friday brought a welcome break from Arnie and Sloane's carnival of camaraderie: a free day to get ourselves prepared for that night's candle ceremony.

Friday morning my eyes didn't even open until nine-thirty. I'd had a dreamless sleep that helped me feel refreshed after a week that was not only physically draining, but mentally grueling as well. Walking around Disneyland, clinging to the railing of a sailboat, and managing to control a horse for three hours was easy compared to observing fourteen women, one man, and two producers while carrying on mundane chitchat with people who were just passing through your life for a few weeks.

I needed today. I needed some time to myself. If I didn't make it past tonight's candle ceremony I had to have a story for Suzanne. So far Holly seemed to fit what I expected from the women. She'd be easy to write about, fulfilling the stereotypical hen role to a T—a seemingly sweet Southern belle who giggled at the sight of the Stag while mumbling nasty remarks about the other women under her breath. Dorothy, on the other hand, wasn't as conventionally pretty as most of the other girls and seemed a little leery of the entire process. She was also the only one who seemed to be extending a hand of friendship to me. Her compact athletic shape with the short and sassy seventies wedge tucked behind her ears made her one of the least intimidating women there. And then there was Samantha, who had the looks, but also had a carefree, fun-loving demeanor. She acted like we were just a bunch of girls at summer camp, and almost seemed surprised when the Stag appeared. Like she'd forgotten why we were all here in the first place. Although Holly had initially pointed out Claudia as the greatest threat to her status as a married woman, Samantha appeared to have the total package. As if a bubbly personality weren't enough, she had a body most of us had seen only in centerfolds.

Holly was definitely where I'd start.

I threw back the covers and grabbed the hotel robe off the back of the desk chair. The heavy curtains had been hiding the morning sun, and when I threw them back to step out onto the balcony, I was greeted by a burst of light. I snatched my sunglasses off the dresser and sat down at the table to write.

No matter how much I'd wanted to dislike Chris, I couldn't. He was just so fucking nice! No matter where we were, he tried to give each hen equal time, and he never showed preference for one person over another or intentionally tried to get a woman jealous. He was like the ambassador for all single men, doing his best to represent his gender to a foreign crowd.

Sure, he was doing a pretty bizarre thing, going on the show. But he didn't seem to be the Hollywood wanna-be Suzanne had thought he'd be. And it wasn't like he picked only the fifteen prettiest women out of the twenty-four we started with—not that any of the fifteen were even remotely unattractive. Was it possible that the Stag was just a decent guy looking for true love?

I smacked my pen on the glass table. What was I thinking? Had the sun fried my brain and the horse shaken all the common sense out of my head? Of course he wasn't looking for true love! It was a damned TV show!

I needed a shower and some breakfast. Fast.

On my way through the lobby toward the restaurant I passed Iris on her way to the pool and caught a glimpse of five hens shoulder-to-shoulder on stools at the bar like a firing line. And it wasn't even noon. I couldn't blame them. A drink sounded good to me, too.

Holly and Claudia flanked the group at either end. Samantha, Dorothy, and Vanessa sat between them, probably keeping the peace.

As I got closer I noticed there wasn't any conversation, just silence as they watched the bartender mix drinks.

"Hey, guys, can I join you?"

Vanessa craned her neck to see who was asking.

"Sure, pull up a stool. Chuck here's showing us all what he learned in mixology school." Vanessa faced the bartender. "What is this yellow thing with the vodka and lemon zest?"

"Electric lemonade."

"Mmm, that was good." Claudia licked her lips in approval and took a sip of her bloody Mary.

Dorothy and Samantha sucked frozen margaritas through short straws, barely stopping long enough to breathe. Holly was daintily sipping a wine spritzer.

"Do you think Arnie and Sloane would consider midmorning binge drinking reasonable and customary expenses?" I asked Vanessa, picking up the long slip of paper that held a running tally of the damage the women had already done to Arnie's expense account.

"I think it's highly reasonable to expect that we'd need to unwind after a week of *Stag* boot camp. And it's customary to unwind with your troop."

"I'll have what she's having." I pointed to Vanessa's electric lemonade.

Vanessa gave me an approving nod. "Good choice."

I thought that once I joined the group, they'd at least make some effort at small talk. I was wrong. Apparently there wasn't going to be any attempt to break the mutually agreed-upon silence.

The bartender placed my juiced-up lemonade on a cocktail napkin and slid it toward me. Still no conversation. I guess we were all just here to drink.

I picked up the chilled glass, gave it one good stir with a swizzle stick, and started chugging. The ice cubes rested against my upper lip, numbing it after just a few sips.

"You guys sure are quiet," I finally pointed out. Master of the obvious.

"We're all talked out." Dorothy picked up her margarita glass and drained the few remaining drops clinging to the bottom. "Four days of small talk is plenty for me."

Samantha nodded in agreement.

Small talk be damned. I needed to get some information.

"So now that Arnie and Sloane aren't breathing down our necks, what do you all really think of Chris?" I ventured, hoping someone would take my bait.

"He sure is good-looking," Holly observed, running her finger slowly along the rim of her wineglass. With her hair loosely gathered on the top of her head and two tendrils framing her face, she looked like an old-fashioned Gibson girl.

"I'm with you there," Samantha agreed. "That Disneyland thing was a little odd, though, don't you think?"

"He kinda made us look like idiots, watching us all run around looking for him while he laughed his ass off under a yellow bear costume." Vanessa reached for the bowl of peanuts on the bar.

"It was Pooh," I reminded her.

"Whatever." Vanessa scooped up a fistful of nuts. "I was waiting at Davy Crockett's Canoes, figuring he's from Seattle, he must be outdoorsy. Who'd have thought a grown man would rather walk around like a fucking kid's cartoon than guide a canoe down a treacherous river? That's just weird."

"I think it's cute," Holly answered, smiling into her glass.

Claudia brought her drink up to her mouth, and then hesitated. "Yeah, well, you're from Memphis; you still think Elvis was abducted by aliens."

It was silent again as we all watched Holly's face become dark.

Claudia looked from side to side and threw her hands up. "What? I was just kidding. It was a joke."

"I'm going to head to the gym," Samantha told us, breaking the tension. "Anyone want to come with me? I'll show you a great new step routine I've been working on."

Claudia nodded and they both hopped off their stools, a little off balance.

"See you tonight," Samantha called back to us cheerily, weaving through the lobby as she held on to Claudia's shoulder.

Once they were safely out of sight Holly finally spoke. "What a bitch."

"Holly, she was joking," Dorothy said, even though I think we all knew Claudia's comment sounded more like a dig than a joke.

"She was not, Dorothy," Holly snapped back, indignant. "I'm not an idiot; I know when someone's putting me down. And by slandering Elvis, no less."

"Anyway, did you get to talk to Chris much, Sarah?" Dorothy asked me, ignoring Holly.

"About as much as anyone else, I guess."

"I don't know about that," Holly interrupted. "Claudia sure seemed to get more than her share of time with Chris."

"So who do you think will make it?" Dorothy turned her attention back to me.

I had to say, Samantha was my odds-on favorite. She was girl-next-door perky, but also sexy in a nonthreatening way. Her shaggy blond hair and watery blue eyes gave her a look of eternal optimism, a look that was buoyed by her unself-conscious laugh that sometimes ended in a snort. She was like the walking bastard child of Meg Ryan and Cameron Diaz.

"I think Samantha has a pretty good shot."

"Yeah, me too."

"Did you know she's an aerobics instructor?" Holly asked us, drawing upon her extensive research into the background of every woman on the show.

"Really?" Vanessa asked. "Can't say I'm too surprised. She looked amazing in a bikini."

"Well, what about me?" Holly piped in. "Do you think I'll make it?"

The three of us hesitated while she looked at us expectantly.

"Hi, ladies," a man's voice greeted us. It was Joe, one of the cameramen. "Forgot this." He held up a black power cord with silver tips.

When Vanessa spotted Arnie loitering in the hallway she didn't look convinced. "Arnie send you over to spy on us? What, no camera?"

Joe laughed nervously. "Actually, the Ritz wouldn't let us have hidden cameras and mikes, fear of lawsuits from guests and all—and we can't shoot you guys in the public areas of the hotel without giving away the show, so Arnie just wanted me to come over here and see if I could convince you to move this little party to a private room in the restaurant."

Vanessa turned around and shook her head deliberately at Arnie. "Tell him we're not moving. Even animals in the zoo get some time to themselves."

Joe shrugged and waved Arnie off.

"Point taken, but Arnie won't be happy. I'll get out of your way. Looks like you're having a better time now than when the cameras are on."

"Join us." Vanessa kicked a chair back with her bare foot. "Have a seat."

"That's okay; I'll stand."

Vanessa shrugged. "Suit yourself."

Joe stood next to Dorothy, who was staring at his legs, which were so tan the hair sparkled like gold filaments against them. Joe could pass for the anti-Stag. Not more than five-foot-eight, he wore nylon surfer shorts and a faded T-shirt that proclaimed, IF IT SWELLS, RIDE IT. With a few days' growth, his beard needed a good shave, but because he was tan and his hair was bleached from the sun, his scruffy beard was more Brad Pitt than homeless surfer dude.

"So how do we compare to last year's crop?" Dorothy asked, her eyes a little glassy and crossed.

"You guys know I can't talk about that." Joe waved the bartender over and ordered a beer.

Holly tossed a copper curl over her shoulder and turned her attention to Joe. "Then tell us about Chris. What's he saying to the host when we're not around?"

"Okay, I can see you ladies just want to pump me for information. You know I could lose my job." He turned to leave.

Dorothy reached out to grab him, almost falling off her stool. "No, wait."

Joe stopped, as if he had any choice, considering Dorothy had two fingers inside the collar of his shirt and was practically pulling it off his shoulder.

"Well, then, just tell us what you think of him," I suggested. Maybe Joe could help me. "From a man's point of view."

He moved back to the bar.

"Actually, he's not a bad guy. Better than last season's Stag. That guy was an asshole." Joe took his beer from the bartender and put a five-dollar bill on the bar. "Chris is cool. I don't know what else to tell you."

"Would you ever go on the show?" I asked him.

Joe was about to take a drink out of his Budweiser bottle, but stopped in midair.

"Me?" He laughed, like I'd made a joke. "I don't think I'm the type of guy they're looking for."

I was about to ask why not, but we all knew the answer. No Stanford. No business school. No family empire. Even if he didn't have the credentials, he certainly had the looks—if not the height.

"I think you'd be a great Stag," Dorothy slurred, smiling so hard her cheeks practically squeezed her eyes shut.

"I think you girls had better get her onto a lounge chair for a little nap." He shifted his eyes in Dorothy's direction, where she'd laid her head on the bar for a rest. "We don't want any hangovers for tonight's candle ceremony."

He was right. In less than four hours we all had to be dressed and ready to begin round three of Operation Stag.

"I'll take her to her room," Vanessa offered.

"That's a good idea. And I'm going to take this to my room." Joe held up his beer. "You're not the only ones with a big night ahead. The crew has to set up before you all arrive, and I don't want to be shooting you out of focus."

We all let our eyes trail Joe as he walked away. His casual swagger was confident but relaxed, the self-assured stride of a guy who didn't have to prove anything to anyone. Joe must have felt our eyes burning a hole in his ass, because he turned around at the elevators and yelled, "Next time take a picture. It lasts longer." He burst out laughing and waved to us as the elevator doors closed.

"He's a real man," Dorothy mused, resting her chin in her hands.

"Yeah, if you mean real scruffy," Holly added with a hint of distaste.

"Let's get her upstairs," Vanessa suggested. "Sarah, will you help me?"

We each threw some money on the bar for a tip and left Holly to sign Arnie's room number on the bill.

"Do you ice skate?" I asked Dorothy over the Muzak seeping through the elevator's stereo system.

"Oh, my God, don't even go there. Do you have any idea how

many times I've been asked that question? It's not like I haven't tried other hairstyles—I have, you know. But I like it short."

"I do too," Vanessa offered, shifting her weight to keep Dorothy upright. "You look great."

"You know, Dorothy Hamill isn't exactly a guy's fantasy. Even if I could lift my leg over my head and spin like a top, I have these thighs to deal with."

"There's nothing wrong with your thighs, Dorothy," Vanessa assured her.

"They're shaped like spark plugs. It's not easy being around cream sauces all day—experimenting with new entrée and dessert ideas requires testing them, you know." She looked to Vanessa and me for understanding.

"Of course it does," I told her.

Dorothy leaned against Vanessa, who did her best to keep our Olympic look-alike from sliding to the ground. Standing together like that, they could have passed for sisters—not because there was any physical resemblance, but because Vanessa appeared to want to take care of Dorothy the way an older sister would look after her younger sibling. Vanessa's austere exterior, like hardened enamel, was a stark contrast to Dorothy's unabashed loquacious confessions.

"I think I need to lie down." Dorothy closed her eyes briefly and let out a sigh. "I'm tired."

"Don't worry. We'll tuck you in, and you can take a little rest before tonight." Vanessa patted Dorothy's wedge of hair.

"Thanks." Dorothy looked up at Vanessa and then over to me. "You guys are great."

The red light on my cell phone was flashing when I got back to my room. It was a message to call Aunt Suzy, Suzanne's code name.

I picked up the phone and dialed *Femme.*

"I was so excited to get your messages; I love the updates," Suzanne gushed. "Sorry I didn't call back sooner; we were closing next month's issue. So how's it going?"

I told her about my week of activities with the girls and Chris.

"Have you been drinking?" she asked, an amused smile in her voice.

"A little. Some of the girls were down at the bar."

"Super. Did they get loaded and give you some good stuff for the article?"

"I'm getting what I need." Sort of.

"How do you think you'll do in tonight's ceremony?"

I walked out onto the balcony and closed the sliding door behind me, still not convinced Arnie hadn't rigged my room for sound. "The Stag didn't pull me to the side and declare his undying love for me while everyone else was bringing the horses into the stable, if that's what you're asking. But I think I have as good a chance as anyone else."

"That's all we can ask for. I'd better run, but we're all rooting for you here, you know."

I knew. And I was rooting for me, too.

# 9

$\mathcal{W}$hen the host gave Chris the go-ahead, it was as if he'd dropped the checkered flag at the Indy 500. Chris sprang from his spot and walked briskly straight ahead, in my direction. Not only was he going to light my candle—he was going to pick me first. I straightened my candle and held it out a few more inches. I didn't want wax dripping on my linen dress. Toni and Teri had warned me it was a bitch to get out. I tried to catch Chris's eye, but he was too focused on where he was heading, right toward me—and two steps to my right. To Rose, the woman next to me.

I inhaled deeply and continued to hold my head high, with a smile plastered on my face and an intense desire to see the candle flare up a good twelve inches and singe off Chris's eyebrows.

He stood before Rose and soon the sole flame in the room became two. Rose's candle flickered in her hand, casting a warm light around her face and reflecting a slight sparkle in her dark eyes. She reached out for Chris and gave him a quick hug, careful not to set his sport jacket on fire. A huge smile made its way across her lips as she returned to her spot in the circle. Next to me. The hen who didn't get picked first.

Although none of us gasped or showed any signs that we were

anything but cool and collected, I knew we were all surprised. Claudia we could understand. The woman was stunning. Or Samantha, with her aerobicized body and playful outlook that could make even the most mundane task sound like a rousing good time. But Rose?

Rose wasn't the sexiest, the prettiest, or even the most outgoing of the group. With her athletic build and a plain brunette bob usually pulled up in barrettes or held back with a headband, she didn't exactly jump out as a contender. Chris surprised us all. A dark horse had entered the race.

One hen down and nine to go.

I watched the girls' faces for signs of fear or the kind of dread that someone holds in the pit of her stomach when she's expecting the worst. But most members of the circle had their game faces on, superficial smiles that showed they were willing but not too eager. Only Holly's veneer offered any sign that betrayed how she really felt. While her freshly glossed lips beautifully framed some of Memphis's best orthodontic work, and her blushed cheeks exposed just a hint of girl-next-door freckles, her right eyelid twitched like a fluorescent lightbulb on the blink.

Even though I didn't believe my future was at stake like most of the other women, I knew my article—not to mention my self-esteem—depended on making it past this ghastly ritual. I stood a little taller and sucked in my stomach. It couldn't hurt.

Samantha, Claudia, Iris, and two twin sisters, Jackie and Josie, were approached by Chris's flaming phallus, and I started to worry. I didn't have the body of Samantha or the mystery of Claudia, but it wasn't like I was a dog. I was every bit as appealing as the remaining women. And even more appealing if you took personality into account. There was no way Chris could choose the cheerleader from the University of Arizona. She had a freaking wildcat mascot tattooed on her ankle, for God's sake. He had to have more sense than that.

Dorothy and Vanessa received the flame next. Although a recipient of the flame tried not to look at the other girls, for fear she would appear to be gloating, Dorothy intentionally caught my eye as Chris moved away from her. Her nap had paid off. There was no sign she'd been slumped over the hotel bar just a few hours ago. She offered me an encouraging little smile as she held her candle. She meant well, but managed only to ratchet up my stress level a notch. By the time Holly stood cradling her lit candle like a newborn, I felt like I was surrounded by a ring of fire. I was going to be burned at the stake of unwanted women.

It finally dawned on me that I wasn't going to get picked. I really wasn't going to make it past the second round. That jerk. The Stanford grad, the moron who made it through Harvard Business School, the idiot who ran a multimillion-dollar business still couldn't get his brains out of his pants long enough to pick a woman who was not only his intellectual equal, but was also a dynamo between the sheets (okay, so there wasn't any recent proof of this, but a guy said that to me once in college and I've chosen to believe him).

Chris eyed the six leftover women while we remained the picture of nonchalance. Finally he took three steps in my direction and stopped. The guy was acting like he was charged with anointing a new pope. It was a game show! Pick already!

A few more steps in my direction, and Chris tipped his candle toward mine. I felt triumphant, like I was holding the Olympic torch. It was the brightest flame I'd ever seen, dancing on my candle wick and proudly announcing that I was desirable after all. I'd known it all along.

The host led the rejected hens from the room, Miss Wildcat Tattoo among them, and the rest of us were bonded together by our status as the chosen ones.

And then there were ten. Four blondes, four brunettes, one redhead. And a writer who had another week to get her story. He was probably just saving the best for last.

I was in the bathroom finishing my makeup the next morning, when I heard three quick raps on my room door. Vanessa and Dorothy were meeting me before we headed downstairs. We had to be in the lobby by eleven A.M. to catch the bus to Chris's house, where we were getting our next assignment. I put down my lip pencil and went to answer the door.

Since the elevator incident, Dorothy, Vanessa, and I had formed a small allegiance to each other—the sort of bond forged between complete strangers trying to survive together even though they know, in the end, the safety raft can hold only one.

"Hey, Sarah," Vanessa greeted me, stepping inside. "Dorothy's going to meet us downstairs. She wanted to give her restaurant a call to check in. She's sweet, isn't she?"

"Yeah, she is," I agreed. "I was just finishing my makeup; take a seat."

Vanessa settled herself onto my bed, tucking her sinewy legs under her like a spider.

"You look pretty today," I called out to her from the bathroom, where I could see her reflected in the mirror. Vanessa's lavender silk pants resembled pajama bottoms, tying at her waist with a drawstring and complementing her formfitting lavender tank top. Her dark hair and features contrasted with the pale lilac color and softened her, like a filter blurring the edges.

"Thanks," she called back, sounding surprised at the compliment. "I know guys don't usually like purple, but I figured, what the hell? I'm the one who's got to wear it."

"What do you think of him? Chris?"

"No comment."

"You're not impressed?"

"Hey, I thought I knew the guy I was engaged to, and I was wrong. There's no way I'm basing my judgment on a dip in the pool and a train ride with Mickey Mouse."

"Pooh," I corrected.

"Whatever. He's off to a pretty good start. Let's see if he can keep it up."

She swung her legs off the bed and moved toward the balcony.

"Who's this?" she asked, holding up a wallet-sized snapshot she found on my night table.

I popped my head out of the bathroom and came face to face with my own carelessness. I had to think fast. What plausible reason did I have for carrying around a picture of a little girl?

"My niece," I answered, and quickly finished lining my lips the way Suma instructed me. I capped the pencil and joined Vanessa.

"She's cute."

"Yeah." I walked over and took the picture of Katie from Vanessa's hand. She was all dressed up in a pink smocked dress for her first birthday. "She is."

I started back into the bathroom and Vanessa followed behind me.

"How old are you?" Vanessa asked, scrutinizing my reflection in the mirror.

"Twenty-six," I answered, and hoped she'd believe me.

"I'm almost thirty," she told me, fishing a lipstick out of her purse.

Thirty. That sounded young to me, but Vanessa made it sound ancient.

"That's not old."

"Yeah, that's easy for you to say."

She pursed her lips and slicked on a coat of the lipstick.

"Let me tell you what you're in for the next four years before you hit the big three-oh and become a social pariah." Vanessa hopped up onto the counter and crossed her legs. "In the next two years all your friends will get engaged and start inviting you to celebrate their nuptials by wearing some hideous dress that only serves to highlight how beautiful they look as they exchange vows with some guy they think will ride them off into the sunset on his white stallion, but who will only end up bursting their bubble when he starts leaving the toilet seat up and forgets the three-year anniversary of the first time they said 'I love you.' Then your friends will all start talking about having babies, and become so obsessed with the idea that you will learn intimate and disturbing details like how often they're examining their cervical mucus and gender-specific sex positions that promise to produce exactly the little girl your friend wants. Most of them will quit their jobs, join play groups, and forget you ever existed except when their husbands are working late, *again*, and they need someone to call to complain that their spouses don't realize how hard it is staying home and raising a baby all day, and, gee, you really need to get together for dinner or something but their social calendar is just so full, maybe next month."

She kicked her beaded sandals off and pulled her legs up onto the counter Indian-style.

Vanessa made it sound like all women became consumed by the changes brought on by marriage and parenthood. You didn't have to change, I wanted to tell her. Jack wasn't exactly the same person he was when we started dating, but I hadn't allowed that to happen to me. Had I?

"You make it sound so horrible; why do you want to be one of them?"

"I don't want to be one of them." She held up my eyelash curler. "Do you really use this thing?"

I nodded.

"Then why are you here?" I asked.

"You want to know why I'm here? I'm here because I've got a great job, I'm financially self-sufficient, I'm attractive, I'm smart, and you'd have thought I was diagnosed with leprosy the way my mother re-acted when that middle-aged dickhead called off the engagement. She thought he was my last hope."

"You're here because of your mom?" Sitting on my counter in her fabulous outfit, telling me what it was like to be her, Vanessa was the picture of a totally put-together woman—completely in control

and sure of herself. Funny how her mom saw only a nuptially challenged bachelorette.

"Yep. She filled out the application, sent them my picture, the
whole thing."

"But you didn't have to go through with it."

"Hey, my younger sister's on her second kid. I figured this was
the least I could do to help my mom hold her head up when she plays
bingo with her church group."

"But you don't strike me as someone who'd need a guy to be
happy."

"I don't need a guy to be happy. I just need to be happy. Unfortunately, I grew up with the bullshit most of us were fed. God forbid I can actually function without a boyfriend or a husband, especially
when my ovaries are shriveling up inside me as we speak. It's now or
never. My mother would prefer it was now."

"So you don't want to win?"

"Hell, yeah, I want to win. But not so I walk away with a ring
on my finger. The only thing I want to leave here with is my dignity and
proof that I could land a guy if I wanted. Then everyone will get off
my back and stop pitying my lonely little existence."

Vanessa felt pressure. I couldn't blame her for that. I'd certainly interviewed enough "experts" on the topic for my assignments,
and *Femme*'s circulation numbers practically depended upon it. With
all the articles about declining female fertility, the shrinking popula-
tion of men, and how a woman over thirty-five has a better chance of
being struck by lightning than getting married, how else was she expected to feel?

When I got pregnant at thirty-two, some people acted like it
was the miracle baby. As if I'd waited one more day to conceive I'd be
giving birth to a three-headed lizard. For the longest time our friends
and family hounded us, making us feel selfish for taking even a few
years to ourselves before committing to a lifetime of parenthood.

Even after I got pregnant, people didn't leave me alone. They asked in hushed tones if I was going to continue working after the baby was born—when what they really wanted to ask was whether I was going to put my selfish needs for professional advancement ahead of my child's basic right to a devoted mommy. I'd tell the overinterested party that the plan was to stay home full-time and write when I could. They'd breathe a sigh of relief, thankful that I wasn't under the contemporary illusion that women could do both—there was hope for society yet.

"Does the dickhead know you're here?" I asked.

"I sure as hell didn't tell him. Let him see me on TV and eat his heart out." Vanessa handed me the tube of mascara. "What about you? Who are you here to piss off?"

"Me?" I opened my eyes wide and swept the mascara wand along my lashes. "I'm not here to piss anybody off."

"Oh, come on. There's got to be some guy you're dying to have turn on the TV and see you, all made up and beautiful, seducing America's most in-demand Stag. Don't we all want to prove that we're a catch, that all those guys we dated didn't appreciate us while they had the chance?"

I thought about Jack's comment. How he'd forgotten what it was like to come home to someone who looked more like a girlfriend than a wife.

"I guess I wouldn't mind if a certain guy saw me and realized what he had," I admitted.

"I figured as much. Anyway, finish up. We've got to meet Dorothy downstairs. The bus leaves for Chris's house in five minutes."

As the hens waited for the host to announce our next mission, we each settled comfortably around the living room in Chris's temporary chairs and sofas. With only ten of us left, the mood had changed slightly. After a week together we'd had time to talk with one another and figure out our place in the group—in the case of Holly and Claudia, that place was as far apart as possible. We'd shared unique experiences and had become, if not exactly friends, at least comfortable acquaintances. The women were willing to open up a little more, let their guard down, and trust that we were all in this together. At least for the time being.

While Arnie and Sloane talked to the director, I decided to make my move for Pierre. Our French-speaking host from Queens could surely add a little spice to the article. As he stood by the terrace door sneaking a smoke, I sidled up next to him.

"Pierre?"

He whipped around to face me, his wrist barely seeming strong enough to support the thin cigarette he had cradled between his fingers. "What do you want?" he spat between pursed lips, all sign of his French accent gone.

"I just thought I'd say hi, considering we've spent so much time together and never really been introduced."

"My contract doesn't say I have to talk to you girls."

"I just thought we might get to know each other."

"Honey, I don't have time for this. Now shoo." He waved his manicured hands at me and returned to his cigarette.

I'd given Pierre his chance to play nice. Now it looked like I'd been given creative license when it came time to reveal the debonair host as gay, nicotine-addicted Pete from Queens.

The camera crew positioned themselves around the room and checked their equipment as we waited. Joe, who had on worn jeans and another faded T-shirt, was on his knees twisting some cords together. Although he'd given us a quick wink when we walked in, there wasn't any other indication that suggested he'd shared a drink with us yesterday. I guess the help wasn't supposed to fraternize with the hens. The viewing public didn't want to see a woman flirting with a plain old Joe.

The director mumbled into his headgear, and pointed a long finger at the cameraman by the front door.

Pierre tossed his cigarette butt into a planter and resumed his position in the front of the room.

"You all completed brief questionnaires when you arrived. Those questionnaires included questions that the Stag thought would give him a better understanding of who you are, and how much the two of you have in common. Out of the ten of you we've selected the three women whose answers most closely matched Chris's, and those women will be going on a date with our Stag this week."

Pierre let the camera zoom in on our faces for a few moments before continuing. "And the three lucky ladies are . . ." He hesitated, trying to draw out the drama. "Rose, Dorothy, and Sarah."

Dorothy and I turned to each other. She shrugged and bit her lip, probably to keep her jaw from dropping to the floor.

I think we were both a little surprised. A lot surprised.

"Sarah, your date is first. Tomorrow Chris will meet you in front of the hotel at eight A.M. You'll find out then where you'll be going for your special day."

I nodded, as if I my agreement mattered.

"Excuse me." Dorothy raised her voice and her hand to get the host's attention.

I don't know that Pierre ever expected to be addressed by anyone other than the Stag, because he looked at Dorothy like she'd breached some sacred protocol. I didn't remember anything in the booklet about not speaking out when the host was talking.

Pierre raised his eyebrows and looked down his nose at her. "Dorothy?"

"Where's Chris?"

"What do you mean?" The host's voice was thin and impatient.

"I mean, where's Chris? Why didn't he tell us this himself?"

Samantha and Vanessa started to nod, and we all diverted our eyes from Dorothy back to Pierre. Like we were following the ball in a riveting tennis match.

"Tell you himself? Because that's my job," the host explained dismissively.

"Well, it's his date," Vanessa piped in, her hands perched defiantly on her slim hips.

"Yes, it is." Pierre scanned the room, probably realizing for the first time that he was outnumbered and on the verge of losing his audience. I was starting to like this spunky crew of hens.

"Hold on." He held up a finger and scurried toward the director. After a few hushed whispers the host took off down the hall.

"What the fuck is he doing?" Vanessa asked the group. The director started chopping at his neck, indicating Vanessa should watch her language.

"Fuck him," she mumbled under her breath, just loud enough for me to hear.

First Dorothy, then Vanessa. The crowd was getting rowdy. It was great.

The sound of heavy footsteps on the tile grabbed our attention, and we turned to find Chris, in shorts and a golf shirt, coming toward us.

"I'm here. I wasn't hiding," he called out, grinning.

"I didn't think you were hiding, I just thought the way we were told about our dates was kinda rude. Shouldn't *you* ask us on a date?" Dorothy went on, not letting Chris off the hook.

"You're absolutely right." He stepped over the camera's cables and stood in front of Dorothy. "Dorothy, would you like to go on a date with me?"

"Well, as long as you asked," Dorothy answered, teasing him.

"And Sarah, Rose. Would you like to go on dates with me?"

"Sure," we answered in unison.

"Then it's all taken care of," Pierre said. "Ladies, there are sandwiches out on the patio for lunch. Why don't we all head out there?" He pushed through the French doors into the warm California afternoon.

A hand grabbed my arm before I could move.

"What was that all about?" Holly hissed in my ear. "She's just trying to put all the attention on her."

"Dorothy?" Our Dorothy? The girl who practically fell asleep with her head on the bar and thought her thighs resembled a car part?

"Of course Dorothy. All that fuss trying to get an edge with Chris. That wasn't fair."

I was about to point out that anyone looking to get an edge with Chris wouldn't be calling him on the carpet about being rude, but instead just shook my head and followed the trail of women onto the patio.

"Sure, what do you care? You've got a date," I heard Holly snarl as she followed behind me.

That's right. I did.

# 10

$\mathcal{T}$he doorman held open the heavy brass-and-glass door leading to the portico, and pointed to a car idling on the paved driveway. Chris was already waiting for me. He looked completely in his element behind the wheel of a cherry-red Porsche 911 convertible.

I tossed my canvas bag over my shoulder and walked in the direction of the purring car. A cameraman was in place to watch me strut toward my date, and I almost felt like he was waiting for me to straddle the hood of the car like a chick in an MTV video.

"Nice wheels." I slid into the soft leather seat beside Chris.

"Too bad it's only ours for the day. You ready?" he asked, slipping a pair of Ray-Bans off his head and shielding his eyes from the early-morning sun.

I nodded.

"You look great." He gave my legs an appreciative nod.

"Oh, this little thing?" I joked, slipping the skirt of my sundress up above my knees.

He laughed at me. Where was I coming up with these lines?

Chris clutched the gearshift and let his foot drop onto the gas pedal. The tires gripped the pavement and we shot off, leaving the

cameraman in a cloud of burning rubber. Whoever said fast cars were a
turn-on had obviously ridden in a Porsche.

I scanned the black leather dashboard for concealed cameras.

"What, no cameras?" I asked, not finding any.

"I told Arnie that if I was driving a Porsche, I was going to
take advantage of it. I convinced him that between the wind and the en-
gine there'd be no way the cameras would catch anything but garbled
voices and me flaunting the speed limit."

"I still get the feeling we're being followed," I told him, pointing at the helicopter hovering over us.

Chris shrugged. "I guess they've got to film something, right?"

"Where are we headed?" I asked into the air rushing by me.

"San Diego," Chris answered, the words blowing by as we sped
down I-5. "The Hotel del Coronado."

Hotel? As in a place with beds? Where people slept? And
had sex?

I removed a chunk of hair that had blown into my mouth and
tried to keep my voice steady. "I thought this was a day trip."

"It is, but we can do whatever we want, play tennis, go swimming, hang out on the beach."

I hoped I didn't look relieved. But I was. It was only the second
week; of course we weren't expected to hunker down in a hotel room
for an afternoon between the sheets. I'd seen the tapes of last season's
show. I knew that part didn't come until much later.

"Did you get to pick who you took on which date?" I asked,
running through the mental list of questions I wanted answered on
this trip.

"Nope. I'm just a passenger on this roller coaster. I only get to
pick who joins me on the ride." Chris turned to me. "Hey, why do you
look so serious? We're going to have a good time, I promise."

Chris laid a hand on my shoulder and I almost jumped. The
pressure was beginning to get to me. How could I have fun when I had
a job to do?

I took a deep breath. I needed to mellow out.

I settled into my soft leather seat, tipped my head back onto the headrest, and decided to let myself enjoy the ride.

Just over an hour later, we crossed the bridge onto the Coronado peninsula, and pulled up to the hotel, a grand old-fashioned resort. The Victorian-era building shone bright white in the southern California sun, while its red-peaked roofs rose and fell around eaved windows and large turrets topped with flags blowing in the breeze. It was amazing, like something out of an old movie.

We were taken to our private villa overlooking the Pacific Ocean. It seemed such a waste to have a place like that and not spend the night—not that I wanted to spend the night with Chris. But the place was beautiful. The villa was flooded with light and echoed the peach and blue hues of the sand and water outside our door. I opened the sliding glass doors connecting the living room with the sun-splashed deck and inhaled the salty air. It would actually have seemed quite romantic, if it weren't for the cameramen jockeying for shots of our every move.

"How did I end up lucky enough to come here?" I asked Chris, closing my eyes and letting the sun warm my face.

Chris walked up and stood at the edge of the deck with me.

"You were the only one who could answer the question about Jimmy James and the Blue Flames. How'd you know that?"

I swallowed hard. It was Jack. I had Jack, and years of listening to Jimi Hendrix, to thank for my date. But I couldn't exactly tell Chris that my husband was a sixties music fanatic.

"My brother."

"Well, he's got good taste in music. I was obsessed with Jimi Hendrix when I was in college. I play the guitar."

*You'll get over it,* I thought. Jack hadn't picked up his guitar in years.

But at least he was a twenty-eight-year-old who didn't think Nirvana was classic music. And he played an instrument. Chris wasn't a one-dimensional Stag poster boy at all. I could see what the other women saw in him. Shit, I could see what *I* saw in him.

"That's cool. Any plans to serenade me on the beach?"

"You never know; there may be a twelve-string in the trunk of the Porsche." He reached his hand out toward my face and I thought he was going to kiss me. But he just brushed some hair off my face and tucked it behind my ear.

Close call. Or was it? Why didn't he try to kiss me?

"So what do you think so far?" I asked, turning back toward the villa. "Is being the Stag all you thought it would be?"

"It's actually not as easy as it appears. Choosing between all the women is hard."

"That's a problem most men wouldn't mind having."

Chris shrugged, grabbed my hand, and led me back into the villa. Was that sweat on my palms, or was it just the humidity?

"So how about a game of tennis?" he suggested, lacing his fingers with mine.

"I didn't bring a racket," I stammered, caught off guard by his warm, soft hand. He was holding my hand!

"Not to worry. The network thinks of everything." He opened a closet next to the front door and pulled out two graphite rackets.

"Okay, but I have to warn you, I was captain of the tennis team in college."

"So you're a ringer?"

"Not really. I haven't played in ages."

Chris looked skeptical. "How long ago is ages?"

"Probably close to ten years."

"But you said you played in college."

Shit, I should have known the guy was quick with numbers.

"Oh, yeah, I was exaggerating. I meant it's been a long time."

"Well, let's see if you remember how to play."

The camera crew headed to the courts ahead of us to set up,

and by the time we arrived you'd have thought it was the U.S. Open. One cameraman was lined up with the net, while two others waited by the baselines to capture our serves. For once I didn't mind the probing lenses. They could even come in handy if we had any questionable calls. Maybe my college tennis coach was into cheesy reality-TV shows. She'd get a kick out of seeing me play.

After a few shaky forehands and lobs that better resembled Little League pop-ups than ground strokes, my body remembered exactly what to do. My serves never faulted, my returns skimmed the net, and my cross-court backhands kissed the tape before skidding past Chris's racket. Not that Chris was a slacker, by any means. His muscled forearms were strong, and once he realized I could hold my own, he didn't hesitate to take me on with full force. We belted the ball over the net, dove for short, dinky shots near the net, and ran breathlessly after long shots with an intensity that was almost sexual.

"Game. Set. Match," I finally declared after a grueling ninety minutes. "Hey, guys, want a shot of me jumping over the net in victory?"

I was enjoying my moment in the spotlight. Finally, a filmed moment I could be proud of.

As we stepped off the court, I thankfully accepted the cup of cold water from Chris's hand. The same hand that I had been holding less than two hours ago. Sweat dripped down my chest into my sports bra. The muscles in my right arm ached, and my thighs burned. I felt great.

"I thought you haven't played in years?" he accused, wiping his red face with a towel.

"I haven't."

"Then what was up with that show out there?"

"Just lucky, I guess."

"Lucky, my ass."

Not only did I remember how to play—I remembered how to win.

"I'm starved. There's a picnic waiting for us on the beach," he told me, refilling his cup from the courtside watercooler.

"Sounds good to me," I agreed.

"Want to go swimming first? To cool off?" he asked.

I nodded.

"You bring your suit?"

"Yep."

He snapped his fingers and smiled at me. "Damn."

After jumping around in the surf like a couple of six-year-olds, we settled onto the beach blanket and dove into the picnic basket. It was a classic picnic—fried chicken, fruit salad, brownies, and lemonade. Not the electric kind.

At last week's pool party the idea of baring my body in a bikini was horrifying. But after working up a sweat and awakening muscles that had been lying dormant, I was exhilarated. I had thrown on my triangle-topped bathing suit with the nautical motif and raced Chris into the waves without any reservations. Even sitting on the beach blanket now with Chris didn't kill my buzz, but I did make sure my stomach didn't hang over my bikini bottoms as I reached for another chicken breast.

"You know what's great about a beach picnic?" Chris asked, holding a chicken breast between his fingers. "You can wash your hands in the ocean."

"True. And, if you need to pee, the world's biggest Porta Potti is at your disposal." I waved my hand toward the water and realized I'd just told the entire camera crew and millions of future *Stag* viewers that I found nothing wrong with fouling our national coastline. Lovely.

"Do girls do that? I thought it was just a guy thing."

"I'll never tell." I put down my chicken and reached for a brownie.

"Want to go for a walk? To those rocks down there?" He pointed to a tall collection of jagged rocks jutting out into the ocean.

"Sure. Can I bring my brownie?"

"Far be it from me to separate a woman from her chocolate."

He started wrapping up the food and putting it back into the basket.

"My mom didn't raise a litterbug," he told me earnestly, and then let out a laugh. "No, really, they asked me to clean up so it doesn't blow all over the beach. My mom did raise someone who follows directions."

We walked side by side up the beach, leaving our footprints to be washed away by the waves. Chris hadn't tried to hold my hand again since we left the villa. Maybe he was bothered that I beat him at tennis.

"Are you mad I won all three sets?"

"Mad? Why would I be mad?" He kicked the sand with his big toe as we walked. "I told you at Disneyland that I like people who're competitive."

Now what? If he wasn't upset that I beat him, then why hadn't he tried to hold my hand again? I couldn't ask him why; then it would look like I wanted him to hold my hand. And I didn't. Did I?

"Just wondering. Some guys get all touchy about stuff like that."

"Well, I'm not one of them. I'm one of those liberated guys who likes getting his ass kicked by a hot chick."

I was a hot chick? Out of anyone else's mouth that would have sounded sexist, and I'd be railing him for being such a Neanderthal. But Chris actually made it sound like a good thing. Or maybe I just wanted to believe him.

"So liberated that you go on a TV show looking for a wife?"

Chris continued walking beside me, but he distanced himself by speeding up and walking a few steps ahead. I'd expected a quick comeback, but instead I got an uncomfortable silence that only seemed magnified by the expanse of sky and water around us.

I'd blown it. I'd gone from hot chick to sarcastic bitch in one minute flat.

"You sure you want to climb on those rocks?" I asked when we reached the jetty.

He ignored my question and stepped up onto a slippery gray stone coated with seaweed. Guess that was my answer.

I was trying to find a rock to climb onto, but all I could find were jagged stones that looked painful to my bare feet.

"Here." Chris reached out a hand and pulled me up onto his rock. It wasn't big enough for both of us to share, and the slimy seaweed wasn't exactly the easiest surface to keep balanced on, so I stepped up to the next one, where I stood eye-to-eye with him.

"Why do you always do that?" he asked, squinting at me.

"Do what?"

"Do that. That glib-little-comeback thing. It's like whenever the conversation makes you uncomfortable you have some smart remark. Like you don't want to have a real conversation with me because then you might actually like me."

"I already like you," I admitted, before I could stop myself.

"Then don't stop yourself from getting to know me. Yes, I'm on the show. Yes, I came on the show to find a woman. But I'm not a misogynist. I'm not looking to score with twenty-four babes—"

"Only one hot chick," I interrupted.

"Well, maybe just one hot chick," he admitted, a grin finally breaking through his frown.

"Now who's being glib?"

"I'm just saying I like you, Sarah." Chris moved in closer until our noses were just inches away and I could see the amber flecks in his otherwise chocolate-brown eyes. "And I hope you feel the same way."

I blinked against the bright sun and before I could open my eyes, his lips were on mine, pushing softly until they parted and our tongues tentatively touched. He tasted like fried chicken and sea salt, and as we kissed I fell toward him, his bare chest and mine pressed together until I could feel the grains of sand that still clung to us from our swim.

"Sarah, I'm falling," he urgently declared, and grabbed me around the waist.

Oh, my God, the guy was falling in love with me!

"What?" I pulled away and Chris slipped backward, his arms reaching toward me to keep from tumbling down into the water.

"I'm falling; the rock is slippery; help me back up." He grabbed my hand and pulled himself back onto the jetty.

"Sorry about that," he apologized, stepping up next to me.

"That's okay," I practically whispered, still tasting him.

"That kiss was nice." He drew me toward him again and wrapped me in his arms.

"Listen, why don't we head back to the blanket?" I suggested, but didn't attempt to leave his hold. "It must be time to go soon."

I could feel Chris glance at his watch behind my back before letting his arms fall to his side.

"It's almost six. How about we go back, watch the sunset, and split a bottle of wine?"

If I could get into trouble on sharp, jagged rocks, what would happen to me on soft, level sand? I looked over his shoulder down the beach, which was almost deserted. Me and Chris, alone on the beach. If you didn't count the camera crew mirroring our every move.

"Sure," I reluctantly agreed.

Chris grabbed my hand and we hopped off the rocks onto the sand and started back toward the blanket.

"Are they going to join us?" I asked, nodding in the direction of two remaining cameramen who tagged along ahead of us like puppies.

"I don't think we have a choice."

A bottle of cabernet was uncorked and waiting for us when we reached the blanket.

"They don't leave anything to chance, do they?" I commented, noticing the deep red rose petals scattered along the blanket's edge. "All that's missing is—"

"The guitar?" Chris guessed, pulling the twelve-string out from under a strategically positioned beach towel.

"The guitar," I repeated before we both burst out laughing.

"At least they stopped short of strolling violins and wandering minstrels."

"The night is young!"

Chris held the guitar and started playing random chords as we watched the sky change colors with the falling sun. I had to admit, I was having an amazing time listening to him and staring into the sunset. It was like something right out of a movie. Including the tender kiss he brushed against my lips when the sky fell dark.

Now I definitely had a hen story for Suzanne. Unfortunately, I'd become one of them—and the opening story was mine.

It was almost midnight by the time Chris dropped me back at the hotel. Jack and Katie would already be in bed. It was too late to call, which was just as well. I wasn't quite ready to share my day with Jack. The ride down to Coronado with the mountains whizzing by in a Porsche-induced blur. My victorious tennis match. The beachside picnic. How could I explain that I had so much fun with the guy I was supposed to be revealing as a philandering jerk?

I reached for my notebook on the desk and scribbled down a few sentences before stopping. Today's date didn't give me the ammunition I needed to slay the Stag. It had turned out to be one of the best dates I had ever gone on.

I crawled into bed, closed my eyes, and tried to forget how much I had enjoyed Chris's kiss. And hoped that in the morning, I'd have something more interesting to write than, *Today I went on a date with a man other than my husband and felt guilty. Not because I betrayed my husband, but because I enjoyed it.*

# 11

"*When's* Dorothy coming back from her date?" Holly asked, fingering the thin gold chain around her neck as she walked about my room inspecting every detail with a trained eye.

"Probably late tonight. The helicopter was picking them up and flying them somewhere."

The first date got a Porsche. The second got a helicopter. If nothing else, the Stag sure got to travel in style.

When my phone rang this morning and woke me up, I thought it would be Chris, calling to say what a great time he'd had yesterday on our date. As I reached for the receiver, I imagined him sitting in his bed, naked except for a pair of plain cotton boxers, the remnants of our date and good-night kiss lingering in his thoughts. But it was only Holly wanting to know if I'd like to go shopping with her.

After we made plans to have her come to my room, the idea of Chris in a pair of boxers refused to leave my imagination. Until I remembered he was probably already dressed and ready to pick up Dorothy for her date. Not eight hours after his Porsche sped away and I floated up to my room still feeling him on my lips.

"So what do you think they're doing on their date, Dorothy

and Chris?" Holly ran her finger along my dresser, as if checking for dust.

I gave her an uninterested shrug, but I wanted to know the answer to that myself. I mean, if Chris could seduce someone like me—and I'd chosen to believe I'd been seduced instead of willing to let his tongue slide into my mouth—then there was no telling what he was capable of getting from another woman.

"How was your date?" Holly asked curtly.

"It was fine." She didn't need to know. Let her squirm.

"I swear, it just isn't fair. I should be in a helicopter right now, flying off to some exotic location." Holly crossed her arms and fell back onto the bed, sulking. "It shoulda been me!"

Two short knocks on my door interrupted Holly's dramatic display of Stag-induced self-pity.

"Can you get that? I ordered us some breakfast. I figured we should shop on a full stomach."

Holly let out a sigh the size of a hot-air balloon, and got up to open the door.

"On the balcony?" the woman from room service asked.

Holly nodded and led her out through the sliding glass doors.

When I finished brushing my teeth and joined Holly on the balcony she was methodically filing her nails between sips of coffee.

"What's that?" Holly asked me, pointing to the notebook I'd left on the table.

"My journal." Lots of people had journals. It sounded plausible.

"Are you writing anything about me?" She stopped filing and waited for my answer.

"Of course not. I just write about what's going on, stuff like that." I waved my hand at her and sat down, pulling the notebook to my side of the table. "It's not a big deal."

"Well, I bet someone would be willing to pay you a pretty penny to write about what goes on here."

Okay, now, that was a little too close to home. I reached for a glass of juice and avoided her stare.

"Why read when you can watch it on TV?"

Holly considered this for a minute. "Because it's exciting. And interesting, even if most people think we're pathetic."

"Do you think it's pathetic?" I asked, taking a sip of my orange juice, which had way too much pulp.

"God, no! I think it's the best thing going. I can't believe it took someone this long to think of it. How many women do you know who get dressed every morning hoping they'll meet some nice-looking man on the bus? And how many women walk into work every day hoping that cute guy in Accounting will ask them out? Or on the weekends they go to the gym and make sure they shower first just in case that attractive blond guy who said hello to them last week is there pumping iron? Here it's all out in the open. We know he's looking for a girl, and he knows we're looking for a guy. It's so much simpler." She reached for the file and resumed sawing her pinkie nail. "And much more efficient, from a time standpoint, that is."

Efficiency in dating. Holly had a point. As long as her point was that choosing a spouse is akin to a shopping trip to Target—and preferring the express checkout.

"So what's it like being in PR?" Holly asked, satisfied with her explanation of the brilliance of the show's concept.

"It's great." Well, at least it *was* great. Working with a creative team. Selling clients on an idea I had in the shower. Going out for client dinners after work.

"What do you do? I've never known anyone in PR before."

I had to think back. It'd been more than two years since I left my job as an account director.

"I help clients promote their products or make people more aware of their company, things like that. We come up with new ways to interact with customers and find opportunities to partner with complementary firms." I thought about my macaroni-and-cheese client who had to explain why their new line of outer space–themed product had rockets that resembled penises, complete with rocket-booster balls, and two-headed space creatures that looked more like a pair of tits than a googly-eyed Martian. "Or sometimes I just perform damage control."

"Wow, that sounds like fun. You must love your job."

"Yeah. I did."

Holly looked at me, confused.

"I mean I do. I do love it," I quickly added.

"Yeah, well, I was never really the career type. I just want the simple things—a husband, some kids, a country club membership." Holly stopped filing her nails and looked up at me. "You know, Chris has loads of money."

"I know his family does."

"Yeah, well, who do you think inherits it all? Besides, he's got to have a trust fund or something."

"So is that why you like Chris? He's loaded?"

"Well, it doesn't hurt," Holly joked.

When she noticed I wasn't laughing she sat up straighter and became more serious. "Chris is exactly what I want in a man. He's good-looking, successful, romantic."

Holly stared into the distance with a dreamy look on her face, the kind of half smile and dazed gaze people get in the dentist chair after inhaling gas. She was probably imagining her prince riding away with her in a horse-drawn carriage. Or at least a Brink's truck.

I noticed she didn't mention anything that even vaguely described Chris as more than a character on TV. Nothing about his sense of humor, which was actually pretty sharp. Or the way he seemed to listen to you when you spoke, like he really wanted to hear what you had to say. She didn't even talk about the fact that he was well educated and intelligent. Holly was only interested in the attractive man who could afford to take her out for expensive candlelit dinners. Chris just fit the profile.

"You know, all the romantic things Chris does are set up by the show. He really doesn't have too much to do with it."

"It doesn't matter. Any man who even wants to do those sorts of things must be romantic."

She left out the part about him wanting to do those things with nine other women, as well.

"So if you make it to the end and he proposes, you'd say yes?"

"Of course!" She threw her head back and laughed. "Wouldn't you?"

"I don't know yet," I answered, looking off toward the ocean as if I were really considering accepting a proposal from a man I met one week ago while my husband and daughter were at home in Chicago. Now, if I didn't have Jack and Katie I still wouldn't know what I'd say, but Chris would definitely be looking pretty good.

"Well, I do. And I know that I will make it to the final candle ceremony, and I know that he'll pick me."

"How do you know that?" Where did this girl get her confidence? I must have had ten years on her, and she made me feel like a novice.

"I can feel it. We were destined to meet."

I frowned and took a bite of my muffin.

"Honey, I know what men want." Holly sat back in her chair and cradled her coffee cup between her hands, shaking her head at me as if she felt sorry that I was so clueless about the opposite sex. "All this talk about wanting an equal, someone who can hold her own. That's garbage. Show me a man and I'll show you someone who wants to come home to a girl who looks nice in a short skirt, has dinner on the table, knows how to give good head, and owes it all to him." She set her cup on the table and resumed filing her nails. "They're really not so complicated, if you know what you're doing."

Holly certainly thought she knew what she was doing.

"Then how come you haven't found anyone yet?" I challenged, watching her gracefully blow on a nail that still had remnants of file dust.

Holly put down the file and looked at me with her mouth

drawn down in pity at the poor, misinformed woman who sat before her. She took a deep breath before continuing, as if I'd need extra time to mentally process what she was about to tell me.

"Because, like I told you, Chris and I were destined to meet. I know what he needs. Don't get me wrong; I'm not naïve. All I'm saying is, a man never left a woman who stroked his ego outside the bedroom, and stroked the rest of him behind closed doors."

Holly was quite versed in the art of male seduction. After all, she did work at Victoria's Secret.

I picked a stool at the far end of the pool bar and ordered an iced tea. I had twenty minutes to kill before Vanessa and Holly were meeting me. Our shopping excursion this morning hadn't resulted in any purchases, but it had made me even more leery of Holly. She couldn't wait to share her thoughts about each of the hens, discreetly leaving out what she thought about me. Vanessa was opinionated and standoffish—no man liked that. Dorothy lacked sex appeal. Iris acted like she was hiding something. Rose was too quiet. Claudia was a raging bitch. If nothing else, I wanted to stay friendly with Holly so I could watch her every move. Who knew what she was capable of as the competition went on?

This afternoon the show was hosting lunch on the terrace for all the women. Everyone, that is, except Dorothy, who was on her date with Chris. Although lunch with the women sounded like a good idea, it was actually a filmed affair intended to provide the background filler for the week's episode. While they showed flashes of me or Dorothy or Rose having a fabulous time with Chris, viewers would also get to see what the other women were up to, which I suspected was supposed to be talking about the missing participants.

At a table toward the other end of the bar, Sloane and Arnie were tucked under an umbrella, deep in conversation. Arnie held a smoldering cigar between his teeth as they talked in low voices. I tried to catch what they were saying but could make out only a few useless words from where I sat. Investigative journalism wasn't my forte, but I'd watched enough *Magnum, PI*s to figure out a simple solution to my logistics problem.

I slid off my stool and walked in their direction, my face buried in a laminated lunch menu. When I reached the bar stool nearest their table I flagged the bartender and leaned in, ordering another iced tea and securing a seat ideal for eavesdropping.

"She's nice to look at, but she won't grab the audience. There's no edge to her," Sloane was telling Arnie.

"She's fine. A little quiet, and she's not a turn-on like Claudia, but Chris sees something in her."

"This isn't a dating game, Arnie; it's a ratings game," Sloane reminded him.

Arnie reached for an ashtray, peeking out from under the umbrella as he stretched a tanned arm across the table.

He caught me watching him and stopped midstretch.

"Hi, there, how's it going?" he asked congenially.

"Fine, just meeting some of the other girls before our lunch."

"That's right, on the terrace. You girls should have fun. The crew is already setting up the equipment."

Sloane tipped back her chair to check out who was on the other end of Arnie's conversation.

"Hello, Sarah. Why don't you join us until the rest of the girls get here?" She patted the cushion on the empty seat next to her.

I grabbed my glass off the bar and went to join them. As I pulled back the chair, its wrought iron legs scraped along the patio like fingers on a chalkboard. Sloane appeared to be wincing, but since her face barely moved, I couldn't really tell.

"So what do you think of Chris?" Arnie asked, puffing on his cigar.

"So far he seems great, but I've only had one date with him."

"That's right; we were quite impressed with your answers on

the quiz. I think Chris was happy." Sloane flashed me a smile that seemed to stretch her taut skin like a tambourine without the clanging symbols.

"What's there not to be happy about? He's got ten women after him." I forced a smile, and Arnie let out a cackling laugh that sent some tobacco airborne in my direction.

Sloane frowned and passed Arnie a linen napkin under the table.

"So, Sarah," Sloane began. "How do you like our Stag?"

"Much improved over last season's pick."

"Yes." She wrinkled her nose, but nothing else. "The last one did turn out to be quite a putz, didn't he?"

"Whatever happened to him?" Arnie asked.

"I heard he's going to be the center square," Sloane told him, stirring her mineral water with a straw.

Poor Chad—nobody had anything nice to say about the guy. Good thing he had that center square.

Arnie shrugged his wiry shoulders and turned his attention back to me.

"So what do you think of the other girls? Anyone you'd like to see off the show?" Arnie winked at me and then grabbed his knee as Sloane kicked him in the shin.

"Anything we can do to make your stay with us more pleasant?" Sloane offered, changing the subject.

"No, this is beautiful. I guess I just have a few questions."

They both waited for me to continue.

"I'm curious. What made you choose me? Or the other girls, for that matter."

"Sarah, we didn't pick you. Chris did," Sloane corrected me.

"Sure, but he only got to see the women you picked from the regionals." I turned toward Arnie. "You were in Chicago. What was your selection criteria?"

Arnie shifted in his chair and looked at Sloane for help. She jumped to his rescue.

"Chris gave us a list of qualities he was looking for in a woman, and we chose the women who best met his requirements."

"But we all seem so different," I told them, thinking about Holly and Vanessa.

"There are some similarities."

"Not the least of which is that you're all nice to look at," Arnie added, before receiving the hairy eyeball from Sloane.

The idea that Holly and I could share anything in common was a little distressing.

"Look, here they come." Arnie pointed across the pool, where Holly, Samantha, and Vanessa were headed toward us.

"Well, you ladies have a wonderful lunch. Sloane and I will be joining you in a bit to see how things are going." Arnie knocked his cigar against the side of the ashtray and kept banging it until an ash fell off.

I stood up and turned my back to leave.

"What do you think Dorothy's up to?" he asked Sloane louder than he had to. He followed his question with cackling laughter. "Gotta given 'em something to talk about at lunch," he said in a low voice, and then started coughing.

Good. Let the guy choke on his Cuban.

"Jesus, Arnie and Sloane are fucking creepy." Vanessa made a sour face as we walked to the terrace restaurant. "The way they watch us like we're specimens or something, always whispering to each other."

"I know, it's like we're their science experiment," Samantha agreed.

I wasn't sure Arnie and Sloane had the brains to be scientists, but they did seem pretty mad.

The camera crew was already in place when we arrived at the terrace restaurant. One large round table was set for nine, with silver-plated chargers serving as the elegant background for peach-and-ivory china. Next to the empty wineglasses, goblets of ice water were already placed at each setting, complete with paper-thin lemon slices garnishing the sweating glasses.

"Ladies, just enjoy yourselves and forget we're here," Joe instructed us.

Sounded easy enough, except that I was constantly peeking into the flower arrangements trying to find the hidden microphones.

When the cameras' red lights flashed on, the table grew quiet. Joe gave us the thumbs-up, but the conversation consisted of Samantha asking me to pass the rolls and Rose apologizing to Claudia for bumping her foot under the table. The weather provided us with barely ten minutes of idle chatter—I mean, it's always sunny; how much can you say? Although the content of our conversation wasn't exactly TV-worthy, the fact that we were being filmed made Holly's Southern accent become even more exaggerated, with more *y'alls* coming out of her mouth than in an episode of *Petticoat Junction*. And Vanessa even remembered to pare down her four-letter words, uncomfortably substituting *gosh darns* and *shoots* for her preferred profanities. The conversation was polite, measured, with words carefully weighed before anyone committed to speaking them out loud. It was like being in a room with politicians.

Finally a waiter showed up to rescue us from ourselves.

"A Cobb salad, please," Holly ordered first.

"Salad." The twins, Jackie and Josie, sang in unison.

"Salad."

"Cheeseburger, medium-rare," I requested and handed my menu to the waiter. Eight pairs of eyes turned to me, the conspicuous carnivore.

"That sounds good," Vanessa agreed, putting down her menu. "I'll have the same."

"A turkey club, please," Rose ordered next.

Not another single green, leafy order was placed. I bet Holly was cursing her Cobb salad.

When the food arrived, we ate, we barely talked, and Arnie and Sloane would probably die of boredom watching the tape. As if we didn't already know how lame we were, the crew started packing up before the hotel staff even cleared our table.

"Where are you going?" Vanessa asked Joe.

"Arnie's on his way to talk with you guys. They've had enough of the lunch."

"How does he know about the lunch? He's not even here."

"I am now," Arnie answered pleasantly, appearing from around the corner. "I was watching from the editing bay, and it was obvious you girls aren't comfortable. Sloane and I were thinking we'd give you a little break."

"Editing bay?" Holly asked, confused.

"Just a little room we have to review the films and see how things are going. Not a big deal," Arnie assured us. "Anyway, you just enjoy yourselves now. We're all leaving."

"So how was your date with him?" Samantha asked once the crew was gone.

"It was nice." I knew they expected to hear more, but I didn't want to share my date. Let them have their own dates. I needed to write about their experiences, not mine—it was already indelibly etched in my brain.

"Nice? Visiting your grandmother is nice. You had a date with America's most eligible bachelor; it couldn't have been just *nice*," Vanessa scolded.

If I told the women how great our date was, how I kicked his ass in tennis and then we had a picnic on the beach and talked—just talked—about things that had nothing to do with mortgages or car repairs or baby-sitters, they'd probably just feel bad.

"It was fine."

"Details."

"He's great. What else can I say? I hope you all have a chance to go on a date with him." I did not! I didn't want anyone else sitting on a beach blanket with Chris while he looked at her as if she was the most interesting person in the world.

"Would you marry him?" Holly asked, maybe figuring this time I'd give a different answer.

"I think you guys are all putting way too much stock in the marriage thing. It's not a cure-all."

"Who's looking for a cure-all?" Claudia methodically folded up her napkin as she spoke. "I'd just like a guy who calls when he says he'll call."

"Sure, but why do you have to sit at home waiting for him? What about your job, your friends, your family?" I asked, getting louder and a little preachy. The least I could do was help them benefit from my wisdom, even if they didn't know it.

Claudia was the only who took me up on my feminist challenge. "I'll start with the job, from which I was laid off when the CEO was indicted for embezzling corporate funds, not the least of which was my 401(k). And as a child of divorce, I can't say my family is exactly the sort Hallmark cards are made for. And friends? Let me ask you. . . ." She was talking to the table, but she looked directly at Holly. "How many of you have exactly gone out of your way to make friends here? Nobody asked me to go shopping this morning." Claudia placed her napkin on the tablecloth in front of her. "I just thought it would be nice to meet a guy who was on my side, someone I could rely on and trust."

I wanted to ask Claudia if she really thought that someone could be accurately selected for her by Arnie and Sloane Silverman, but I stayed quiet. All else being equal, she'd decided to take her chances on love. I had to hand it to her: She was a brave woman. It seemed like everyone else was just taking their chances on the Stag.

"I agree with Claudia." The dark horse had spoken. We all turned toward Rose, who until then had been silently observing our conversation.

"What do mean, you agree?" Vanessa asked.

"I mean this isn't just about finding a husband. It's about meeting someone who's on the same page as you. Someone who has decided that he's ready to take the chance that there's someone out there for him whom he can share his life with." Rose looked around the table at each of us as we let what she'd said sink in.

"Rose, where are you from?" Holly asked, leaning her elbows on the table.

"Saint Louis."

"That would explain the overalls," Holly mumbled out the side of her mouth.

"No, Holly, comfort would explain the overalls," Rose spoke up, choosing not to ignore Holly's comment. "Saint Louis would explain why I have enough manners not to ridicule someone's choice of clothing."

"I just meant . . ." Holly looked around the table for help, but no one offered any. "I thought there were farms in Missouri, that's all."

"There are farms in Missouri; you're right." Rose smiled at Vanessa and passed her the plate of desserts that had arrived. "Cheesecake?"

Vanessa nudged me under the table, and when I glanced up at her, she shrugged and looked impressed.

No wonder Chris chose Rose. There was a lot more to her than met the eye.

Rose took a bite of her apple pie before continuing. "Anyway, so far Chris seems like a great guy, and I'm willing to give him the benefit of the doubt. I've met worse."

"What's the worst thing a guy has ever said to you?" Vanessa asked the table before stabbing a fork into her key lime pie.

Samantha immediately raised her hand like a schoolgirl who thought she knew the right answer. "This one guy and I had liked each other for years. We finally hooked up after this party, and I said, 'So why tonight? How did we end up together tonight?' thinking he'd say something really romantic, of course. Instead he says, 'Well, I guess everybody else just went to bed!'"

The table let out a collective groan before erupting in laughter.

Iris jumped in before anyone else could talk. "I can do that one better. Once, I was hooking up with this guy from Detroit who I wasn't that into, but he'd put the time in, you know?" We all nodded. We'd been there before. "So he says, 'You're really dry; got any K-Y jelly?' And I say no. And a minute later he says, 'It's okay, you're lubin' up, doll!'"

The table screamed in unison and a waiter came running out to us looking concerned. "Everything all right out here?"

"We're fine," I choked between breaths as the other women continued laughing.

He nodded cautiously and retreated back inside the restaurant.

"You can imagine the propositions we get," Josie nodded in Jackie's direction. "One guy actually asked if he could have sex with us in front of a mirror—he'd always wanted to do it with quadruplets!"

Another round of laughter made its way around the table.

"Seriously," I finally managed. "Why are you here?"

The table quieted down before Jackie ventured an answer to my question. "Love would be nice, but I just want a guy whose idea of a date isn't my cooking him dinner. I'm a chef, not a fucking soup kitchen."

Claudia smiled. "Just give me a guy who doesn't flip out when you tell him he has to sleep on the wet spot."

"Oh, please." Iris threw her napkin emphatically on the table before continuing. "All I seem to date are Wall Street putzes who claim to want a real woman but then practically cry out their mommy's name when they come."

Once again we all flew into a fit of giggles, and I crossed my legs and cursed myself for not taking Kegel exercises seriously.

"I'm going to the ladies' room," I whispered to Vanessa, grabbing my purse. I stood up and squeezed my legs together as I pushed my chair in.

"Sarah, are you going to wet your pants?"

"Only if I keep laughing so hard."

"Ew! That's so gross!" Holly made a face and craned her neck to get a better view of my ass. The nosy bitch.

"Well, that's what happens when you give birth to an eight-pound"—I barely caught myself before adding—"kidney stone!"

"Oh, my God." Rose covered her mouth with her hands, feeling my pain. "That's horrible."

Vanessa didn't look convinced. "Seriously?"

The entire table of hens waited for my answer.

"Yeah. I was in a textbook!"

Consolatory murmurings of understanding made their way around the table.

"Go!" Claudia instructed, waving her hands. "We don't want you hurting yourself."

I walked backward toward the restaurant door and then turned and made a dash for the ladies' room, thankful Arnie had told the crew to leave us alone. Considering I'd already practically admitted to peeing in the ocean, the last thing I needed was to have the audience discover I peed on seat cushions as well. I didn't need to become known as the hen who couldn't hold it.

# 12

$\mathcal{I}$t had been three days since my date, and I was sprawled out on a lounge chair by the pool with the rest of the hens. Our terrace lunch had had its uncomfortable moments, but it gave us glimpses inside the women who before then had merely been passengers on the same tour bus. Claudia's declaration of her belief in love, and Rose's display of self-assured confidence, had cast a new light on two hens whom we thought we had pinned down and labeled, and made us even more curious about one another. That lunch had paved the way for a more relaxed get-together, where we were all getting some sun, a good buzz, and taking advantage of the all-expenses-paid amenities before our third candle ceremony sent three more of us packing.

I hadn't seen Chris since he dropped me off Tuesday night, which now felt a little like going from lightning speed to a dead stop. If this was a normal dating situation—and by normal I mean if he didn't have dates with two other women already lined up—I would probably have been sitting by the phone for two days waiting for him to call. But there'd been no call. Or flowers. Or anything to even acknowledge the fact that we'd shared something special. And even though I tried not to think about it, I felt let down. But the fact that Chris couldn't even find the time to dial the hotel allowed me to excuse the way I'd let my guard down and fallen prey to his seduction. He'd given me no choice. Standing next to him, our skin damp from sea spray, our bodies warm and supple from the sun and a wicked game of tennis, what red-blooded woman wouldn't have fallen into the arms of the gorgeous man standing in front of her?

Okay, maybe *seduction* was a bit of an exaggeration. Maybe *swept up in the moment* was a more accurate description of what happened. And as long as I was striving for accuracy, then I'd be omitting a very important detail if I didn't admit that I'd enjoyed our first kiss on the jetty, and that the second kiss on the blanket had been preceded by a little close leaning on my part. After our sunset kiss, Chris lay on his stomach, his head resting in his hand as his muscled forearm held the weight of his body. I was lying on my stomach next to him, my chin resting on my crossed arms as I watched the ocean begin to change color. Our elbows lightly brushed each time one of us reached for our wineglass. When only a small red pool of wine sat in the bottom of my glass, Chris held out the bottle and tipped its neck, waiting for me to place my glass underneath. I leaned into him, my right hand holding out my crystal wineglass like I was offering him a flower, and watched as his eyes neared my own and our lips touched at the moment the camera crew flipped on the overhead spotlights. Our romantic sunset may have been over, but we still had time to share a dip in the hot tub.

"Snap out of it!" Vanessa's voice cut through my daydream. "What are you looking all dreamy about?"

"I wasn't looking all dreamy," I shot back.

"Please, if I waited another minute I thought you'd start moaning."

"You're crazy." I turned away, not bothering to justify Vanessa's observation with excuses. Not that I had any.

"Don't forget, he had two other dates," Vanessa reminded me.

"I wasn't thinking about Chris."

The idea of Chris spending the day with Rose or Dorothy . . . well, I just didn't need to go there.

"Sure you weren't. Where's the damn cabana boy, anyway?" Vanessa asked, propping herself up on her elbows to get a better look around the patio. "This electric lemonade is going down way too easy." She spotted our waiter, flagged him over, and ordered us another round of drinks.

"Hey, Sarah, I know I probably shouldn't ask, but what the hell do you have in there?" Vanessa pointed to my boobs. "Life preservers?"

I tucked my chin into my chest and surveyed the terrain below my neck: two heaping bosoms lovingly tucked into foam cups so perfectly formed they could have been used as soup ladles. Another Toni and Teri attempt to enhance my existing assets. Vanessa was right; they were a little over the top—literally. My boobs were pushed up high and separated into two scoops of flesh.

"A little overkill, huh?"

"Actually, a lot of overkill. You don't need it, you know. What were you thinking?"

What was I thinking? I was thinking Toni and Teri knew what would appeal to the Stag.

"Just enhancing what nature endowed me with, I guess. It looks dumb, doesn't it?"

"No offense, Sarah, but yes. Guys like natural boobs that are soft, not man-made materials."

"Mine aren't real. I had them done when I turned eighteen," Holly piped in, drawing our attention to the sturdy melons tied to her thin frame with the tiniest of triangle tops and what appeared to be a piece of gold yarn. "Guys love 'em."

"Sure they do." Vanessa rolled her eyes and lay back down on her lounge, sipping her full drink from a bent straw.

"So, Dorothy, tell us about your date," Holly instructed, caressing her flat stomach with coconut-scented sun lotion. With her red curls tucked under the shade of a wide-brimmed straw hat and large black sunglasses taking up half of her face, Holly looked like a sun-bathing starlet from the 1950s—if only they'd had gold metallic thong bikinis back then.

"What do you want to know?" Dorothy asked, sucking down the last of her own electric lemonade.

"Everything!" Holly ordered, ecstatic that someone was finally willing to give her the dirt on a date.

"It all began with a helicopter ride up to LA," Dorothy started, and went on to tell us all about her day shopping on Rodeo Drive and her lunch at the Bel Air Hotel. "I got to try on all these outfits at Fred Segal and Giorgio's, and then Chris threw down a credit card and told me to pick one! Then I walked out of the store in my new outfit, hopped in our chauffeured Bentley, and we were taken to the Hollywood Bowl for a private performance by the Los Angeles Symphony. Finally, when we got back to his house around nine, Chris pointed to the sky and when I looked up it was just a blanket of stars. It was so clear out, Chris said it was a perfect night for the hot tub, so we jumped right in."

"No way." I sat up and faced Dorothy, still not believing what I'd just heard. "He said the same thing to me."

"Really?"

"Yeah, but we were at the villa in Coronado."

"Are you sure he said the *same exact thing?*"

I was sure. We'd walked back to the villa after watching the sunset, and as we stepped onto the deck Chris stopped and pointed out what a perfect night it was. Perfect for a dip in the hot tub before head-ing back to the Ritz. At the time it had sounded like a sweet, spur-of-the-moment idea. Now it sounded like a line.

Holly must have known I was rerunning the entire scene in my head, because as she waited for my answer, she watched me with a satis-fied smirk. *See,* that smirk said, *you thought your date was so special, but you're no better than the rest of us.*

"Yep," I confirmed. "I'm sure."

"Hi, guys." Rose waved as she headed toward us with a beach bag slung over her shoulder. "What's going on?"

"Just comparing notes," Vanessa told her, and moved over to give Rose some room on her lounge. "So tell us about your date."

Rose became the unwitting center of attention as we all waited for the details.

"It was great, but not very eventful. We checked out some art galleries, and then had a great dinner down by the water in Malibu— we both had the most amazing lobster risotto. Afterward we went back to his house for a drink. There was champagne chilling in a silver bucket out on the terrace when we got there."

"Did he suggest a dip in the hot tub, by any chance?" Vanessa asked, sparing all of us the gory details of Chris's stargazing routine.

"Yes," Rose answered cautiously, obviously wondering how she knew. "Then we put on our bathing suits and sat in the hot tub drinking champagne. How'd you know that?"

"Our friend Chris certainly does have the moves, doesn't he?" Dorothy reached for a full drink.

"What do you mean?" Rose turned toward her. "Did he do the same thing with you?"

"And with Sarah."

Rose stared wide-eyed at the group of women. "Are you telling me that less than twenty-four hours after swapping spit with you in the hot tub he was playing tonsil hockey with me? In the same vat of hormone-fortified water?"

None of us answered.

"That's kinda gross." Rose shook her head. At first I thought she was going to get angry, but there was an amused look on her face. "That sly dog. He sure knew how to work us, didn't he?"

I'd been worked? That was impossible. All those nice things Chris had said, the way he'd listened to me talk about myself. That couldn't have been rehearsed. Not that I cared; I mean, I was just pretending, right? But if he fed us all the same line about the hot tub, did that mean he told Dorothy and Rose he liked them, too?

I turned toward Dorothy, ready to share her indignation that he'd fed us both a bunch of crap. But she shared Rose's amused grin.

"Gotta hand it to him, though; he's got a great pair of lips," Dorothy said.

"You can say that again," I agreed a little too quickly.

"And he doesn't look so bad in soaking-wet swim trunks, either," Rose added.

"Let's face it," Vanessa piped in. "The guy's hot."

We all nodded in unison.

"A toast." Vanessa stood up and faced our small group.

We held out our glasses in raised salute.

"To Chris—he may be unoriginal, but he sure is hot."

The clink of glasses was drowned out by a round of *Hear, hear*s and laughs as we toasted Chris.

We actually toasted a guy who fed three women the same line just to get us in a hot tub. And forgave him for it because he's hot. Or at least Rose and Dorothy did. They were more forgiving than I was. A perfect night for stargazing in a hot tub, my ass.

Holly started to ask more questions about the dates, but we talked over her and moved on to other topics. It was one thing to make a joke out of it. It was another to keep rubbing in the fact that we all stripped down to thin pieces of Lycra so easily for the Stag.

I sipped my frosty electric lemonade and surveyed the group of nine women who I used to think would provide the material for an exposé on the sad state of single women today. Suzanne and I had been convinced that there'd be more than enough drama and histrionics among the women to write about. But how could I describe the scene before me, where only Holly sat sullenly begrudging us our dates and lack of forthcoming information? If you ignored the fact that we were all on *The Stag*, we could have passed for vacationing friends. But that was a very big *if*. The fact was, we were on *The Stag*. And we were competing for a man—a man who had just been revealed as the jerk I'd thought he'd be. The fact that I had the first date had consoled me, until I realized that even after spending time with me, he still wanted to kiss two other women. And I'd thought we had a great kiss—great kiss*es*. Here I was replaying our day together like a schmaltzy movie montage, when, to him, I was just the date behind curtain number one.

But it wasn't like I was going to write about my date. After all, Suzanne wasn't expecting me to be the subject of the article. Thank God. I was supposed to be writing about the hens—something that I became less and less excited about with each passing day. They hadn't turned out to be as horrible as I'd imagined. In fact, I liked them, if you didn't count Holly, who came the closest to epitomizing Suzanne's view of the women on the show. But the idea of writing about Holly as if she represented the entire group was deceiving. Writing about the three-timing Stag, however, was a different story.

I'd show the Stag for what he was, and not feel the least bit guilty doing it. Hell hath no fury like a woman scorned. Especially when she gets to write about it for a national publication.

Around two-thirty, Holly headed back to her room to get ready for the candle ceremony, and one by one we started packing up, almost reluctantly.

"Man, this is getting to be a drag," Vanessa complained as she and Claudia waited for the check. "I'm sick of all this dressing-up crap, like we're going to the prom or something."

"Tell me about it. Why can't the guy just see us in sweats and T-shirts?" Claudia asked, grabbing a pair of running shorts off the back of her chair. "He can't think we run around in heels and dresses all the time."

Claudia and Vanessa looked in my direction, expecting me to agree. I dropped my head and concentrated on wiping the neck of my suntan lotion bottle with my finger, taking longer than necessary to clean off the single white drip clinging to its side.

They wouldn't get any complaining from me. I liked getting dressed up every day, taking time to carefully apply my makeup and style my hair. The rest of the women were used to putting on trendy pantsuits and feminine skirts for work every morning, but I could do my job without stepping a foot out of my slippers or bothering to comb my hair all day. And while they got to pick out flirty outfits for Saturday-night dates with guys who probably drooled at the sight of them, I had a husband who was too preoccupied to notice any effort short of a complete magazine makeover.

Since arriving in California I cared what I looked like. Not because the cameras were filming us, but because I felt like I was noticing myself again for the first time in years. And I'd be lying if I didn't admit I liked the fact that Chris noticed, too. It was as if I'd put my premarried identity away like a photo in my wallet and had only recently taken her out again to show the world.

"Hey, Dorothy, wait up," I called ahead, grabbing my sarong and beach bag, and hurrying up the patio steps.

"Doesn't it bother you that Chris used the same line on all three of our dates?" I asked once I caught up to her.

"Sure it does. But it's not like we didn't know that was part of the deal." She held the door open for me and I stepped onto the cushioned carpet of the hotel hallway. "Wait a minute." She reached out and took my chin in her hand, looking into my eyes. "You're really upset about it?"

She dropped her hand and followed me inside.

"I'm not *upset* about it. I just think that was shitty of him, that's all."

"Sarah, that's the name of the show. It's called *The Stag*, not *The Monk*."

"I know."

They'd made an entire movie out of Julia Roberts falling in love with a sexy, wealthy man as they strolled along Rodeo Drive, and here Dorothy was managing to keep it all in perspective. It amazed me.

"Did you think he was going to go on the first date, and kiss you and say sweet things, and then go out with us and act like we were buddies from work?"

Maybe.

"I guess in theory I knew, but I didn't think he'd recycle his moves for each of us. Did he play his guitar for you?"

Dorothy shook her head. "He played the guitar?"

I nodded, but didn't go into the details of how he'd had the guitar waiting on the blanket for us when we sat down for our picnic.

"Did he tell you he liked you?"

"No, but we had a good time, so I'm assuming he does." Dorothy stopped walking and put her hand on my shoulder to get my attention. "Hey, Sarah, you can't take this so personally. Yes, it's weird that he kissed all of us, but you gotta figure he's going to end up kissing everyone eventually. Don't be going all Holly on us."

I was being compared to Holly? That was bad.

"Please, smack me if I start acting like that again. Okay?"

Dorothy threw her arm over my shoulders and we started walking toward the bank of elevators.

"Believe me, if you're acting like Holly, it will be my pleasure."

When the elevator doors slid open we were face-to-face with our illustrious producer. I was beginning to wonder about Arnie's impeccable timing—he always seemed to appear at exactly the right moment.

"Sarah, can I talk to you for a minute?" he asked before stepping between me and Dorothy.

I nodded and Dorothy went up without me.

Arnie moved aside and lit a cigar. He let out a breath of smoke before talking.

"I wanted to remind you that you signed a waiver prior to

joining the show. A medical waiver." He stood there puffing on his cigar as if waiting for this reminder to sink in. "And that waiver indicated that the show cannot be held liable for preexisting conditions should you become ill during your stay with us."

He seemed to be waiting for an acknowledgment of this riveting information. "Okay, Arnie."

"Our legal counsel just wanted to make sure you were aware of the situation."

What situation? Why was the show's legal counsel singling me out for this friendly reminder?

Then it hit me.

"What's this all about, Arnie?" I asked, curious to see if he'd admit to the real reason he was suddenly interested in my physical well-being.

"We're aware of your condition, Sarah."

"And what condition would that be?"

"Your kidney stones."

She'd done it again! Holly had probably run to Arnie after our lunch in hopes of getting me kicked off the show.

"And how did you find out?"

"Don't deny it, Sarah." Arnie dangled his cigar in front of his smug face. "We have it on film."

"You what?" I screamed, not believing what I'd just heard.

"We have your admission on film. Now, we're not going to hold it against you—"

"Hold it against me?" I shot back, cutting him off midsentence. "Hold it against me? You lied! You told us you were done filming."

"During orientation you were warned that you could be filmed at any time," he told me, as if reciting from the orientation handbook.

"You hid cameras?"

"And mikes."

I shouldn't have been surprised, but I was. It was bad enough that we let ourselves get caught making out with Chris on camera; now Arnie was screwing us by hidden camera as well.

"Fine, Arnie. Thanks for the warning." I stabbed the elevator button with my finger and waited.

"Don't worry about the close-up on your rear end, Sarah. We'll make sure it's tasteful."

With a short *ding* the elevator doors opened and I took my place inside. "That's mighty big of you, Arnie."

"Hey, we're all in this together, right?"

I gave Arnie a tight smile and let the doors close on him. If we weren't all in this together before, we certainly were now.

When I reached my floor and stepped off the elevator, I could hear the faint ringing of a telephone. By the time I slipped my card key into the door, threw my bag on the ground, and dove across the bed to grab my mobile phone, it was already on its fifth ring.

"Hello?"

"Sarah! I'm so glad I got you. I was afraid I'd have to leave a message." It was Suzanne. "How's it going out there?"

"Good, it's going good." I sat up against the overstuffed pillows and pulled my knees into my chest.

"I just wanted to check in with you and let you know that I'm sending a photographer out," Suzanne told me.

"A photographer?" I rolled over and pulled the pillows over my head, hoping to stifle any conversation from reaching errant mikes.

"Yeah. The article needs some supporting pictures. Nothing posed, of course," she added. "The photographer will pretend to be a hotel guest just shooting the scenery. He'll call you when he gets in tomorrow to work out all the details."

"They're moving us tomorrow. To a private villa somewhere closer to Chris's house."

"Chris?"

"The Stag."

"Oh."

"Tonight's the third candle ceremony, so we're checking out of the hotel. I guess it's easier to film there or something."

With so many of us at the hotel and guests milling around everywhere, the hens hadn't been filmed together that often, unless you counted the prearranged lunch. With only seven women to film starting tomorrow, that would change. Especially with the stakes getting higher with every candle ceremony. At the villa there'd probably be a camera set up full-time to catch the drama as it unfolded.

"Any idea where? I could have someone on the beach with a high-powered lens to catch a little topless sunbathing, maybe?"

I knew the article needed some pictures, but the idea of setting up the girls for shots that would make them look at best foolish, and at worst like sluts, didn't sit right with me. I'd write the article, but I wasn't going to sell out the other girls in the process. Maybe that had sounded fine to me two weeks ago, but now they weren't just nameless, faceless hens. They were Vanessa and Dorothy and Rose and Samantha. Let the magazine use graphics or something.

"Nope. I have no idea where the villa is."

"Okay, hold tight. Let me make a few phone calls; maybe there's someone on the West Coast who can get there tonight. I'll call you back."

After Suzanne hung up, I threw the pillows off my head but I didn't move, stuck between hopping in the shower and getting ready for the candle ceremony, and waiting for Suzanne to call back with a plan—between being a hen and being a writer from Chicago waiting for her editor to call. I couldn't betray the girls. Even though our relationship had been forged under bizarre circumstances, they trusted me. Except for Holly, maybe, we were all in this together.

I swung my legs off the bed and made my way into the shower.

When I stepped out of the tub and grabbed the thick white towel hanging from the rack on the wall, I could see my mobile's red message light blinking. Probably Suzanne, with new plans to get pictures of the hens. She'd be expecting me to return her call right away, but I wasn't in the mood. I had a candle ceremony to get to.

# 13

$\mathcal{T}$he driveway leading to Chris's house was lit on both sides by luminaries. The brown paper bags I used to use to carry my lunch to school in were evenly spaced along the meandering drive, creating an effect similar to footlights as our bus passed between the glowing borders. I couldn't help but wonder if the candles used to illuminate the bags were the same ones the Stag used to determine our fate.

"Hi." Chris held the front door open and greeted each of us as we walked in.

"Hey," I barely mumbled back. My hot shower had provided me with a working angle for the article—skewer the Stag. Show the man behind the camera who traded in honesty for whatever it took to get the girls in a bikini.

"There's some food in the living room." He pointed toward the shrimp and baby quiches sitting on silver platters.

As we stepped down into the living room, the director pulled aside Rose and Claudia, positioning them in front of the camera for an impromptu interview.

Chris closed the front door and came down to join us. Instead of a suit or blazer, he wore a thin butter-yellow cashmere sweater with a crew neck. It wasn't tight, but the soft weave draped down his chest, just barely outlining his well-defined muscles, before it tucked into a pair of navy pants. He looked so nice, standing there watching the host interview Rose, that I almost forgot that I hated him.

"So how were your other dates?" I asked, walking away from the group toward the windows.

"Good," he answered cheerfully, following behind me.

"Nice starry evenings? Just perfect for a dip in the hot tub?" I looked out the window and spotted Chris's offending love puddle.

"Sarah, what's wrong?"

"What could be wrong?" I answered, my back to him and my tone thick with sarcasm.

"It's obvious you're pissed about something."

"What could I be pissed about?" I spun around and faced him.

"I thought we already went through this. If you have something to say, just say it. Don't give me all this sarcastic crap." He almost sounded mad. At me. Imagine!

"You want me to say it, I'll say it. You made me feel like an idiot."

"How?" He folded his arms across his chest and waited for me to answer.

"By making me think you actually liked me. By kissing me and then kissing Dorothy and Rose."

"You're not being fair," he said softly, sounding more hurt than defensive.

"I'm not being fair?" I practically shouted before I noticed the host and camera crew working their way over toward us. I lowered my voice. "What about you?"

"Sarah, think about it. I'm supposed to get to know each of you. Those dates were supposed to give us some time alone. How can I know whether or not we click if we don't get close? And, yes, that means kissing. I'm sorry you felt bad when you heard about my dates with Dorothy and Rose, but you had to know that was going to happen, especially if they were nice. You like Rose and Dorothy; they're great. Just like you're great."

"What about the hot-tub thing?" I wasn't letting him off that easily.

"So I like hot tubs. So California has clear skies and stars. I'm from Seattle, remember? It's not as if I get starry skies every night. I wasn't making that up just to get each of you in a hot tub."

"Yeah, well, it's just gross," I insisted.

"What's gross?"

"The water, for one thing, all those germs," I stammered, starting to sound ridiculous.

"Sarah, I'm starting to think you're a fruitcake."

"I'm a fruitcake?" I jammed my finger into my chest, pointing at the fruitcake. "I thought we had a fun date, and now I feel like I was just one of your warm-water wenches—like our date was just a farce."

Now I was the one sounding defensive.

"It wasn't a farce. And when I kissed you I wasn't just testing the waters. I really wanted to kiss you. I still want to kiss you—even though you seem hell-bent on making me feel like the bad guy here."

The host reached us and tapped Chris on the shoulder.

"We were thinking of starting the ceremony, but if you'd like to continue this little tiff, could you move it onto the terrace? Arnie was thinking the viewers might get bored with so many inside shots." Pierre glanced back at the director and Joe, who were waiting for a signal from him before heading outside.

The candle ceremony! Here I was ripping into Chris mere moments before I'd be standing in front of him with an unlit candle.

"No. We're done." Chris turned away.

I probably should have tried to rectify the situation, tell him it was okay—that I understood the pressure to make out with every girl on the show. But I didn't stop him from leaving, and I didn't tell him it was okay. And for that, I'd probably pay the price.

Suzanne was going to kill me. I was supposed to be nice to the guy, not piss him off. Even considering the whole hot-tub thing, we did have an amazing date. He had to weigh that when deciding, although it took place three days before and I'd been yelling at him not less than five minutes ago.

Pierre clapped his hands, trying to get our attention. "Ladies, you know the drill. Tonight three of you will leave the show. Please keep your candles held out at least four inches from your clothes—last time we almost had a problem with some melting rayon. If everyone's all set, here's your Stag."

But before Chris could move into the host's spot on the carpet, the front doors burst open and three uniformed policemen rushed into the living room wielding their badges.

"Police! No one move!"

Pierre threw his hands in the air and started squealing, "I didn't do it! I swear!"

The director told the cameras to keep rolling and marched over to our unexpected visitors.

"Can I help you?"

A squat, bald Sipowicz look-alike pushed the director aside and scanned the half circle of hens. "Her." He pointed right at Iris.

Sipowicz's two sidekicks nodded and walked straight toward her.

"I did my time! You can't arrest me!" Iris started screaming, grabbing the arms of Claudia and Samantha, who were standing on either side of her. "You can't take me away!"

"What's going on?" Arnie demanded, stepping between Iris and her apprehenders.

"Iris Barnes, you are under arrest for violating parole when you left the state of New Jersey."

Parole? Iris was a criminal?

"Wait a minute. You can't take her away. We're filming a TV show here!"

"Iris Barnes, please step forward."

Iris cowered behind Arnie, but his wiry frame wasn't exactly a deterrent. The cops reached around him and pulled Iris into the center of the room.

"But I'm a white-collar criminal! Who cares if I left New Jersey? Everyone wants to leave New Jersey!"

The cops took Iris by the elbows and led her from the room kicking and screaming.

"Insider trading is a crime, Ms. Barnes, no matter how nice you look in an Armani suit."

"Arnie!" she wailed before the front door closed behind them.

The room was silent for a moment before everyone started talking at once.

The director yelled for Joe to follow them outside and get a shot of the police car pulling away. "And ask if they can put on the siren!" he called after him.

"Did you have any idea?" the hens were asking one another, trying to remember if Iris had dropped any clues—like a penchant for black-and-white-striped prison garb.

"I can't believe it." Dorothy turned to me. "She sure pulled one over on Arnie and Sloane."

I looked around the room for Arnie, who was in a corner of the room surveying the chaos with a huge grin on his face. He didn't seem too upset. In fact, he seemed quite pleased.

"How could this happen?" Dorothy asked.

I had the same question. During the audition I'd been told they were going to perform a criminal check before I'd be let on the show. At the time it seemed logical—ensuring the safety of the hens and all. But now it made even more sense. It wasn't about safety. It was about ratings.

"Ladies! Shush!" Pierre instructed, pushing Chris into his place as the cameras resumed their position.

Chris looked completely dumbstruck.

"Well, go on, silly. Just say what you were going to say before

Starsky and Hutch interrupted." Pierre gave him a pat on the back and stepped away.

"Um, I just wanted to say thanks to the three women who I was lucky enough to have dates with this week. And I want to let everyone know how much fun I've had getting to know you all. Unfortunately, I only get to pick seven women tonight."

Even if he didn't pick you, he managed to make you like him. Why couldn't he just pick a persona and stick with it—loose-lipped, hot-tubbing flyboy or Prince Charming?

Pierre handed Chris his candle and the director started whispering commands into his headset. It was time.

I watched Chris and felt my stomach turn over. Maybe I'd been out of line yelling at him like that. What had I expected? For him to fall for me on his first date and swear off all the other hens? That would have been nice, but then there wouldn't be a show, now, would there? Besides, I had a husband back in Chicago waiting for me.

Who was I to get all pissy?

Chris stood at the front of the room looking at us, his pale cashmere sweater setting off his tan and blending in with the neutral colors around the room. He took a step toward our half circle, his right hand wrapped firmly around the base of the candle while his left hand protected the flame, and prepared to choose a hen.

And he chose me. First.

But instead of moving on to the next candle, Chris didn't leave. He stood there seriously, holding my stare like he was waiting for me to make a decision—he didn't assume anything.

Chris wasn't giving me any wiggle room. If I was that pissed at him, then I had my chance to get off the show. I'd had my time with him and the other girls, and I could leave if I wanted to, probably with enough material to write my article if I had to.

The ball was in my court. The candle was flickering in my hand, challenging me to make a choice.

I'd told Chris how ridiculous I felt and he'd listened. And felt bad about it, not that he should have. Instead of choosing a woman who'd complacently accepted her ranks among the hens, he'd picked someone who was pissy because she wasn't the only one he kissed.

By making me feel singled out, he'd made me want to stay. And not just because I wanted more material for the article. But because I wanted him.

"Thanks."

Chris finally cracked a smile.

"Thank *you*," he replied graciously.

As Chris walked around lighting the candles of the six other women who'd remain—starting with Samantha, then Rose, Claudia, Vanessa, Dorothy, and finally Holly—I felt off balance, and it wasn't my high heels. It was that I couldn't figure out this guy who managed to make me feel special one moment and like the flavor of the day the next. A guy who appeared to fulfill every male stereotype and then turned around and broke the mold. Just when I felt like I knew the lay of the land, he changed it on me. It was like an intimate dance we were both in the process of learning. Every time Chris took a step forward with his left foot, I took a step back with my right. We moved in unison, testing each other with each step and growing more intrigued each time the other person kept up.

It was a dance Jack and I had stopped even before Katie was born. Unlike my unfamiliar but exhilarating tango with Chris, Jack and I thought we knew each other's moves and assumed the other person was in step, without ever checking to see if they'd fallen behind.

But with Chris, I didn't know what he was going to do next. And at that moment, I was having trouble predicting my own moves as well.

After he'd ushered a teary-eyed hen and the twin frowns of Jackie and Josie to the front door, Pierre returned and asked for our attention once more.

"I'd like to introduce you to some of Chris's friends," the host explained, turning toward the three men who were being led into the room behind Chris. "This is Brian, John, and Neil."

The three guys gave us brief smiles when they heard their names and took their places in front of the fireplace.

"This week each of you will be spending some time with Chris's friends, getting to know more about him as they get to learn more about you. Why don't each of you tell us a little about your friendship with Chris?"

The host expected men to talk openly about friendship? I thought this was supposed to be a reality show.

The tallest, a thin blond who kept glancing uncomfortably at the front door, stepped forward.

"I'm Brian," he started, pushing his hands into his pants pockets. "Chris and I were roommates at Stanford. We met freshman year when he set off the dorm's fire alarm trying to heat up leftover nachos on a hot plate. I've lived in New York since graduation, but we still see each other at least twice a year. And we always go out for nachos."

"I'm John. Brian and I live together in New York."

We all paid close attention to John, who was just as good-looking as Chris, only fairer, with dirty blond hair and light gray eyes. Any of the girls would have taken him as a consolation prize in a second. I knew I would.

"I've known Chris since our junior year at Stanford. After graduation we drove cross-country together for a month, during which he locked the keys in the car at a campground in North Dakota, set our tent on fire in Montana, and *accidentally* dropped my wallet off the edge of the Grand Canyon—which he told me was no big deal because I only had six bucks and a condom in it anyway."

The last guy, who was Asian, introduced himself. "I'm Neil. I've known Chris since sixth grade and know all his dirty secrets. I moved back to Seattle last year, so we get to see each other a lot."

"Thank you, guys." Pierre shook their hands, lingering a little longer than necessary with John, and turned his attention reluctantly back to the hens. "Ladies, this week you'll be leaving the hotel and will spend your remaining time here in a private bungalow. But for now, there are hors d'oeuvres on the table and champagne at the bar. Take some time to introduce yourselves to Brian, John, and Neil, and enjoy yourselves."

Chris went over to the guys, where they exchanged some back-slapping and private jokes that produced a round of laughter.

"Hey, Sarah, want to get a drink?" Vanessa asked, maneuvering her way around the ottoman.

"Not yet." I hung back from the group, hoping Chris would come over to me. After moving over to the bar with Brian, John, and Neil, Chris caught me watching him.

"Hey, thanks for not bowing out," he said, coming over and handing me a glass of champagne.

"Well, I guess I was being a little ridiculous, given the circumstances." I tipped my head in the direction of the six women clustered around the hors d'oeuvres with his friends.

"Anyway, I'm glad you said something. Even if it was something bitchy."

"I wasn't being bitchy," I blurted out, almost dribbling champagne down the front of my dress.

"Easy, I was just busting on you. What? You can dish it out but you can't take it?"

"I can take it."

"I sure hope so, because I've warned Brian, John, and Neil about you. They're ready."

"So am I."

I slid my eyes in the direction of the three friends—the three attractive guys who promised to show me a good time, if the laughter erupting from the bar was any indication. And I felt up to the task.

While Chris waited for me to decide whether I'd take the flame from his candle, I'd felt powerful, like I had the ability to surprise, to disappoint, and to make him want me even more. Back home my life rolled along smoothly, like I was a perfectly round ball without a single seam, unable to tell where I began or ended. But here I had edges, like a pair of dice, with each facet showing a side different from another, and instead of continuing along my well-worn path I could change direction at any moment.

Me and three of Chris's cute friends. I wasn't only up to the task, I relished it—after all, the ratio didn't sound so bad.

"Good. I'd better get over there before he starts telling stories." Chris pointed to Neil, who had three women huddled around him, listening raptly. "No one really needs to know about the time . . . Well, let's just say some things are better left unsaid."

As I watched Chris join the group clustered around the piano, I couldn't help smiling. Even surveying Holly's attempt to latch herself onto Chris's arm like a nicotine patch didn't bother me. My date had been all I thought it was. Everything was perfect, almost. I had only one little niggling problem to resolve: With my skewer-the-Stag idea dead in the water, so was my article. Now what would I deliver to Suzanne?

The red message light was still blinking like a lone Christmas light in my dark room. I flipped on the light and started peeling my clothes off, figuring I'd waited this long to pick up Suzanne's message; a few more minutes wouldn't matter. After I washed my face and wrapped myself in a freshly laundered Ritz robe, I pulled out the desk chair and took out my notebook, prepared to take notes from her call. But when I retrieved the message it wasn't Suzanne's voice on the recording. Instead I listened to the short message and felt a pang in my chest. Not because I missed home so much. But because it hadn't occurred to me to call Jack first.

His message said he'd just gotten home from work, which meant he must have left early to get home to Katie—it had been only around five o'clock in Chicago. First he was giving her baths; then he was leaving work early. In just over two weeks Jack had turned into Super Dad—able to file legal motions and bathe a dirty child in a single bound.

I couldn't picture Jack bent over the tub, the starched white sleeves of his dress shirt rolled up past his elbows, cleaning Katie's fanny with her ladybug sponge. Maybe a few years ago I could have imagined it, before he started to take his serious profession so seriously. But he'd just become too *lawyerly* for a task that involved bubbles and shampoo with an Elmo head for its cap.

It hadn't always been like that. During her first year Jack gave Katie baths, read her stories at bedtime, and could cook up a mean grilled cheese for lunch. I'd always observe skeptically, mentally noting that the bathwater wasn't warm enough or he'd messed up a line in Katie's favorite story. Eventually I started pointing out the way those tasks should be done, and eventually Jack stopped doing them altogether. And at the time, I didn't mind. After I quit my job at the agency, being a mother became my job. Katie and I had our daily schedule, a set way of doing things honed from our months at home together, while Jack went into the city for work every day. The house had become my domain, displacing my corner office. I figured Jack already had a job, and besides, we had already agreed on the plan.

When Jack considered quitting law school it wasn't the absence of a law career that bothered me so much. It was Jack's indecision. I'd seen Jack as stable, not exactly predictable as much as reliable. And that appealed to me at a time when I didn't know where I'd be or what I'd be doing when I graduated. It had been nice to be sure of one thing—I'd found someone who'd be there with me.

Once the tremors passed and he'd decided to stick it out, I felt like I was on solid ground again. On a well-planned course, a well-thought-out path.

I'd been on that path now for eight years, and, sure, it was stable and reliable, but it wasn't exactly exciting. In the past weeks I'd had more uncertainty than in the past three years. Every day was unexpected, waking up and not knowing what would happen, where last-minute decisions created anxiety and I was always a little off balance. For once I didn't know what to expect. And I was loving it.

So maybe writing the article wasn't my only problem. Maybe the fact that I was more concerned about the Stag's hot-tubbing habits than finding out how Jack's day was could be considered slightly alarming. But I was writing an article—I was being paid to get inside the head of the Stag. I'd let Chris get under my skin more than I'd intended, but didn't I have to in order to get my story?

It felt too good. I was having too much fun. So what if I was attracted to Chris? It was innocent flirtation. I could still stare at myself in the mirror and like who looked back—as a matter of fact, I was liking her more and more every day.

I glanced at the clock on my night table and was almost relieved that the numbers confirmed it was too late to call Jack. I deleted his message and put down the phone. Tomorrow morning a van was picking us up and taking us to the new bungalow, and my closet was still stuffed with outfits that needed to be packed.

As I took my clothes off their sturdy wooden hangers, I realized that in a few short weeks I'd become quite accustomed to the services of a luxury hotel. The fresh soap every morning and the ability to toss your dirty underwear in a bag and find them washed and pressed on your bed at the end of the day was nothing to sneeze at. Starting tomorrow there'd be no more room service, no more Ritz robe, no more electric lemonades. I'd miss this place.

I placed my notebook in the suitcase last. There'd be no writing tonight. Suzanne probably couldn't find a photographer on such short notice and hadn't even bothered to call back. Which was just as well. I hadn't come up with another angle for the article. If I wasn't going to write about the hens or the Stag, there wasn't much left.

I surveyed my room, looking for forgotten shoes or a shirt thrown carelessly over a chair. But I'd packed everything. The room looked almost as pristine as when I'd arrived. My fingers were on the bag's zipper when I noticed something hanging over the bathroom door. I grabbed the absorbent material and folded it over my arms, trying without success to make it smaller. Finally I gave up and threw the Ritz robe on top of my notebook and zipped the bag. What the hell. I would be back to reality soon enough.

# 14

While I waited for the bellboy to collect my bags the next morning, I dialed Jack's office number. His secretary put me right through.

"I tried you last night. Where were you?" he demanded before I'd even had a chance to say hello.

"We had a candle ceremony."

"Since you're still there, I'm assuming you made it through another week." He didn't sound happy for me, as he had after the first candle ceremony. "Katie keeps asking for you."

"Are you trying to make me feel guilty?" The bellboy knocked and I opened the door, directing him to my luggage.

"No."

"Because you're doing a pretty good job for someone who isn't trying."

"It's going on three weeks. Who'd have guessed you'd really end up staying this long?"

"Yeah, who'd have guessed," I repeated.

"I thought the goal of your writing was that you wouldn't have to travel."

Funny, I thought the goal of my writing career was to give me something of my own to feel good about besides my status as Jack's wife and Katie's mom.

"Jack, you knew this could happen. It's the first time I've been away in over a year. Is that asking so much?"

Jack didn't bother answering.

"I've got to go; they're probably waiting for me downstairs."

"Okay, you go and do your single-girl imitation for the Snot."

"It's the Stag."

"Fine."

"I'll call you later. I love you," I added out of habit.

"Love you, too," he automatically answered back.

After Jack and I had been dating almost a month, I knew I loved him. I thought he loved me, too. Although I wanted to tell him, to give voice to the feelings I had, I didn't. Not right away. I saved up that word like a child saves pennies, hoarding them until their purchasing power takes on mythical proportions. The word *love* had value to us back then, like currency you save up greedily and handed over only when you knew that what you were getting in return was worth it. When I finally told him and he said it back, I felt like I'd won the lottery.

Over the years our currency had become devalued as we started to hand out *I love you*s like tips, carelessly tossing them at each other because we knew it was expected. Our loving declarations had followed economic principles until supply seemingly overtook demand simply because the word was so plentiful. Until we'd forgotten that telling each other "I love you" had ever had value, and the meaning had become devalued, gone the way of the Russian ruble.

As I hung up the phone and reached for my purse, preparing to meet the other women in the lobby, Jack's words had already evaporated. He hadn't told me he loved me because, at that moment, he really believed it to his core. He'd probably had a call on the other line or a meeting to get to, and the words tripped off his tongue before he'd even been aware of what he'd said.

I looked around the quiet lobby for the other girls and realized I was the first one downstairs. The bellboy had already taken all my luggage out to the van, including my suitcase with my notebook. A quick visit to the hotel's store produced the most recent issue of *Femme* and a pack of Double Mint to keep me busy while I waited.

I was sitting in an overstuffed armchair in one of the intimate seating areas of the lobby, chewing my gum and reading Suzanne's most recent editorial ideas, when I heard two familiar voices heading in my direction.

"That lunch film was bullshit. They were like a bunch of no-brain zombies." Sloane's voice stopped on the other side of the towering, leafy plant acting as a divider between the seating area and the main hall of the lobby.

"Deadly fucking bullshit. I saw my career passing before my eyes." The pungent smell of Arnie's cigar smoke wafted through the plant's large, paddlelike leaves and settled on me.

"If I heard one more 'Pass the salt, please' or a polite little titter after some bland attempt at wit I was going to slit my wrists."

"Hey, we took care of the situation," Arnie said between clenched teeth, which I assumed were clamped down on his Cuban.

"Thank God. Otherwise there wouldn't have been one honest word out of their mouths. With the cameras there they were a bunch of frigging Stepford-wife wanna-bes."

We were not! There were six cameras on us, focused on every move we made, highlighting all the imperfections we'd hoped to keep hidden. We were uncomfortable and nervous, not plasticky-perfect imitation women. Sloane wasn't just being critical; she sounded downright contemptuous. No wonder last season's crew of hens looked so silly—Sloane Silverman was picking the footage!

By now I knew Arnie was a prick, but even Sloane was exactly like Suzanne pictured her—the bitchy aging producer jealous of the pretty young things who got all the media attention while she toiled behind the scenes.

"You can bet your ass we won't be showing that footage to any prospective advertisers, unless we want to be giving away airtime. Will you put out that damn cigar? It's giving me a headache."

I heard Arnie obeying, rubbing his Cuban out in the sand of the ashtray.

What a team. They never gave me any warm and fuzzies, but I had had no idea how much Sloane and Arnie disliked the hens. Arnie at least tried to mask his contempt, but then again, I guess he had to if he wanted to have happy hens willing to put on a show for advertisers. Besides, he was a guy. What was Sloane's excuse? You'd think that being a woman would have instilled some level of understanding and empathy for our situation. Instead she and Arnie were able to callously put a price tag on a woman's search for love—in fifteen-, thirty-, and sixty-second commercial increments.

But Sloane's lack of scruples didn't just give me the willies; it gave me an article. If I wasn't going to write about the women, and I couldn't write about the Stag, I could at least expose the show's opportunistic producers.

"Hi, Arnie. Hi, Sloane." A Southern twang was making its way down the hall toward us.

"Hello, Holly. All set to move to the bungalow?" Arnie asked.

"You bet. Hey, is that Sarah back there? Sarah!" Holly called my name and pulled some branches back to get a better look at me.

I dropped my head down and pretended to be engrossed in an article, which turned out to be just an ad for Tampax.

"Sarah?" Holly had come around to my side of the plant.

I glanced up, hoping my furrowed brow and narrowed eyes could substitute for genuine concentration. "Oh, hi, Holly. Sorry, I didn't see you."

"Sloane and Arnie are right over there. We're going to head outside to the van. Are you coming?"

"Yep." I closed the magazine and stood up. "Want a piece of gum?"

I held out the Double Mint, waiting for her to slide a piece from the pack.

"No, thanks, my dentist says I shouldn't. I just had porcelain veneers put on my teeth last month and I don't want to ruin them."

Even Holly's brilliant white smile was fake. It figured.

"This place is amazing!" Rose kicked her feet up on the table and leaned back in a deck chair. "I love this place. I'm never leaving."

Rose was right. The hens' bungalow was absolutely incredible. Although it wasn't as large and rambling as the Stag's house, it was cozy and comfortable and perched high above the beach. From the wooden deck off the back of the house we could hear the waves crashing below and see for miles out to the horizon. We didn't have a pool—or a hot tub—and there were only four bedrooms, so just one hen would get her own room while the rest of us doubled up, but it was perfect. From the bougainvillea climbing haphazardly over the deck railing to the skylights in practically every room, the house was way more charming than the Stag's tastefully decorated lair.

"Where'd they put your bags?" Rose asked, sipping a lemonade.

"Second room on the right. I'm bunking with Dorothy."

"That will be fun. Who'd they give the single to?"

"Samantha."

Rose sat up and grinned. "Are you telling me that—"

"Yep."

Rose let out a laugh and shook her head. "I hope Arnie and Sloane know what they're doing."

"Oh, I'm sure they know exactly what they're doing."

As if on cue, Holly tore back the sliding glass door and joined us. "I can't believe they put me with Claudia." She dropped a bowl of salsa on the table and let a full bag of chips fall out from under her arm. "I found these in the kitchen cabinet and the salsa in the fridge. Hope they weren't leftovers from the previous tenants. And how come Samantha gets the single room?"

Holly ripped open the bag of chips and passed it to Rose, who happily took a handful and started scooping salsa.

"Apparently a very scientific decision process," I explained, ready to repeat what my writer's eavesdropping had uncovered. "A focus group."

"A what?" Holly demanded.

"A focus group. They got together viewers in the show's demographic and showed them pictures of all of us. Samantha tested the best."

"The best in what sense?" Holly demanded, a scowl fixed on her face.

I shrugged. "Something about being the most likeable hen."

Actually, the words Arnie had used were *least likely to enter conflict and easiest to get along with*. Apparently Samantha would be too enjoyable to room with, whereas the rest of us had the potential to drive each other crazy.

"She's not the most likeable. She's just got a hot body, and that's all those focus group morons care about."

Funny, the morons Holly was referring to were exactly like her—single women twenty to thirty-five who loved to watch the show and hated to admit it.

"I thought I was going to miss the Ritz, but this place is wonderful," Claudia yelled to us through the kitchen screen door before poking her head out. "Need anything? There's a bunch of food in here."

"The guacamole in the door of the refrigerator," Holly called back, not bothering to add a *please*.

"And two glasses of lemonade," I added. "Please."

After the audible slamming of drawers, Claudia came out carrying a pitcher of lemonade and the container of guacamole. "Dig in, girls."

"So where did Vanessa go with Chris's friends today?" Holly asked.

"Rollerblading, I think," Claudia answered, dipping chips into the guacamole, which Holly had yet to touch.

"Better her than me."

"I'm sure they feel the same way," Claudia mumbled under her breath, cracking Rose up and causing her to choke briefly on a Tostito.

We'd been in the house only an hour and already Holly and Claudia were at each other's throats. The next week promised to be interesting, to say the least.

"Hey, guys." Joe waved at us as he came through the sliding door with a few of the crew. "Ignore us. We've just got to test some of the equipment, your conversation keeps cutting out."

Joe and the three other camera guys went to work tapping microphones strategically located in potted geraniums and under the lids of the hurricane lamps scattered along the deck's railing.

"Hey, Joe. Did you know about Iris?" Rose asked.

Joe didn't offer any answer, but Holly took the opportunity to let us in on her powers of perception.

"I could tell something was up with that girl," she told us. "She was just too weird, always avoiding my questions and giving illusive answers. I should have known she was a dangerous felon."

Claudia shook her head. "She was in jail for insider trading, Holly, not chopping off someone's head. I wouldn't exactly call her dangerous."

"Arnie had to have known," Rose continued, watching for Joe's reaction. "Makes you wonder what else he's capable of doing, doesn't it?"

Joe kept his head down and ignored Rose's prodding, but her question silenced the rest of us as we thought about our own secrets.

I'd tried to be careful with my phone calls home, but was it possible my conversations had been recorded by a hidden mike? I was sure Arnie and Sloane would kick me off if they found out, but maybe they were planning to expose me in front of everyone, like they did Iris.

I made a mental note to be extra diligent in the future.

"I don't know about the rest of you." Holly gave Claudia a sidelong glance. "But I've got nothing to hide."

"Are you so sure about that, Holly?" Rose asked.

We all fell silent again and diverted our eyes to the camera crew, quietly wondering what had yet to be revealed.

# 15

$\mathcal{I}$ was meeting John, Brian, and Neil at the Corner Pocket for some pool. A car picked me up at our bungalow and dropped me off at a plain brick storefront that could have been mistaken for an abandoned building if it weren't for the neon OPEN sign hanging on the dirty glass in the front door. The inside of the bar was a stark contrast to the sunshine and brilliant California colors on the other side of the faded wooden door with its curling paint and smoky glass. The cavelike atmosphere was barely helped by the stained-glass Budweiser lights hanging over the pool tables. As I looked around for the guys, I was hit by the smell of stale beer and disinfectant, the latter of which from the looks of the scuffed linoleum floor, and the fact that my shoes were sticking with every step, was probably a good idea.

I thought I saw three guys at a pool table in the back of the room, already drinking beers and picking cues off the rack on the wall.

Brian saw me and waved. "Sarah, over here."

I passed the empty tables and made my way toward them. They obviously hadn't felt any pressure to dress for the cameras, and looked more like they were ready for a fraternity party than prime-time TV. Neil was the most conservatively dressed in faded, wrinkled khakis and an untucked navy blue polo shirt. Brian, on the other hand, appeared to have gotten dressed in the dark, with a pair of the oddest green-and-orange plaid shorts, a mismatched yellow-and-white-striped T-shirt, and flip-flops. But it was John who stood out in a pair of faded Levi's and a plain white T-shirt. He looked perfectly all-American with his sandy blond hair just grazing the collar of his shirt and jeans that did his perfect ass justice.

"Hi, guys."

"Hi," they all chimed in unison.

"Care to choose your weapon?" John asked, sweeping his hand in front of the rack's remaining cues.

I reached over and slid out a cue that looked about right for my size.

"So Chris tells us you're an amazing tennis player," Brian said, putting quarters into the table.

"He did?"

"Kinda. He told us you kicked his ass on the court, which means he was pretty impressed with you." John started racking the balls, giving me a perfect rear view as he bent over the table. Could the cameras tell I was ogling?

"So do you know your way around a pool table as well as you know your way around a tennis court?" Neil asked.

"Not even close."

"Good." John cracked a smile. "It'd be really embarrassing if you beat us—not that we'd actually tell Chris."

"So where're you from, Sarah?" Brian asked, handing me a beer. "Beer's okay, isn't it?"

"Beer's great, thanks. I live in Chicago. But I went to school outside Boston."

"Where'd you go?" Neil twisted his cue in the chalk, making the tips of his fingers blue.

"Wellesley."

"No way, when'd you graduate? I dated a girl from Wellesley when I was at Brown." Neil stopped twisting his cue and waited for my answer.

You'd think I would have already done the math. Sooner or later I was bound to run into this question, I'd just hoped it would be later.

Let's see. If I was supposed to be twenty-six, that would make me eight years younger.

"In 'ninety-eight." I mentally crossed my fingers and hoped Neil's ex-girlfriend wasn't in that class.

"The girl I dated graduated in 'ninety-seven. Did you know Vicki Deane?"

I shook my head.

"Yeah, well, we only dated for a few months anyway. She was nuts. So what do you think of our Chris?"

Ah, back on familiar ground.

"He's great."

"He thinks you're pretty cool, too."

Pretty cool.

"And you're not scared off by that incident a few years ago?" Brian asked, lining up to break the balls.

"Incident?"

Brian leaned down and rested his fingers on the green felt, forming a cradle for his cue.

"Yeah, that homosexual period he had a while ago," Brian explained as the white ball crashed into the others and scattered them around the table in colorful chaos. "The gay thing."

The gay thing? The cue slipped through my hand and bounced off my sandal, leaving a perfectly round blue chalk mark on my foot. It wasn't possible. Chris was too perfect—or maybe that explained why he was so perfect. My hot Stag had a thing for guys.

Brian moved away from the table and nudged John, who was waiting his turn, and they all broke out into laughter.

"I'm just kidding, Sarah," he confessed, seeming pleased that he'd had me going.

Very funny. I gripped my cue again, snapped my fingers, and frowned. "That's too bad. I was hoping for a threesome."

Their three heads whipped around, taking new notice of the *Penthouse* "Forum" fantasy that stood not more than five feet from them.

"A threesome?" John practically stammered. God, he was gorgeous.

"I'm just kidding, John."

The three of them put their tongues back in their mouths and turned their attention to the table as Brian prepared to take another shot.

"Chris warned us about you," he said, bending over the table.

"What did he say?" I hoped they didn't think I was fishing for compliments. I just wanted to hear what Chris said about me—only the good things, of course.

"Oh, all sorts of things," John told me, raising his eyebrows at Neil.

Had Chris told them about our kiss on the rocks? Maybe he said I looked fat in a bathing suit. What if they knew about the hot-tub kisses? Did he say I was easy?

"Okay, forget it. I'd rather not know."

"You're up," Brian told me. "And don't listen to John. Chris had nothing but nice things to say about you."

Nice? I didn't want Chris telling them bad things, but I wasn't sure *nice* things were that great either. Like Vanessa said, nice is what you say about a visit to your grandmother's house—not a woman you're supposed to want to see naked. He did want to see me naked, didn't he?

I handed John my beer and stepped up to the table. I tried to look like I knew what I was doing, mimicking the position I'd seen Brian take. As I leaned over the table I wondered if they were sizing up my ass. I drew my cue back slowly and then scuffed the felt before cracking my cue forcefully into the white ball and sending it flying off the table. We all watched as the ball rolled under two other tables and stopped in front of the flashing jukebox.

"Now I know why tennis is your game," Brian said with a smile.

"You may know your way around a tennis court, but you suck at pool," John added. "How about something else? Darts?"

I nodded. I'd had plenty of practice playing darts. Jack and I used to play in bars while we waited for his band to go on.

"Darts it is."

After I'd retrieved the white ball from across the room, our foursome moved to the far wall, where dartboards were nailed to cracked plaster.

I removed the six darts stuck haphazardly around the red-and-black board, handed three to Neil, and took my place behind the faded white line on the linoleum floor.

"Step aside, boys; unlike a cue ball these things can draw blood," John joked.

I ignored him, aimed for the center bull's-eye, and let the deadly instrument fly. After two more throws landed mere millimeters from the bull's-eye, I stepped aside.

"Not bad," Neil commented, pulling my darts from the center of the board while Brian wrote my score on a dusty chalkboard.

"Thanks." I took a sip of my beer and turned to John. "So why's Chris on the show?"

"It started out as a bet." John leaned against the wall and watched as Neil's dart landed on the outermost circle. "When it came time, we all bagged except Chris. We owe him some big bucks."

"Couldn't he find a girl?"

"Sure, he had a serious girlfriend for, what, like two years."

"What happened?"

"I don't know; it didn't work out. He hasn't really dated anyone seriously since."

"What do you think about him coming on the show?"

The three of them looked at one another, waiting to see who'd answer first.

"Hello, anyone?" I prompted.

"If that's what he wants to do, that's cool," Brian finally answered.

"Does he really want to get married?"

"I think he'd like to meet someone who he *could* marry," Neil explained, filling in his score on the board next to mine. "We're all getting to that age where *wife* doesn't sound like a four letter word anymore."

"What does that mean?" I asked, wondering if Jack ever thought that.

"You know, the way a woman changes once she's sporting two months of your salary on her left hand."

I hadn't changed.

"No, I don't know."

"A friend of ours in New York married this girl who was lots of fun, loved going to Knicks games, went Rollerblading in the park, got a share in the Hamptons for the summer with twelve other people—she was great." John finished his beer, preparing to tell me all the horrible ways that his friend's girlfriend changed. "Now she's got him antiquing in Connecticut on weekends, made him ditch this really great beanbag chair he's had since he was, like, eight, and has the poor guy drinking soy milk."

The three guys quietly looked down at their feet, as if mourning a lost friend.

"Not every woman changes," I pointed out, thinking of myself. Their theory about women bothered me because it meant that Jack wasn't the only one who'd changed. I'd changed, too. And if that was the case, then I was just as much a stereotype as the hens and the Stag.

Screw that. I wasn't a wife here. I was Sarah Divine, single girl—a hen who'd made it through three candle ceremonies.

I drained the last of my beer and turned to the guys.

"More beers?" I asked, walking toward the bar. "Maybe a few shots?"

The rest of the afternoon I was Sarah Divine, the antiwife. I laughed at their lewd jokes, even offering a few of my own, matched them beer for beer, and I never complained, not once. Not even when the women's room was out of order and I had to use the only toilet in the men's room, which was just a sniff away from a row of urinals and a condom machine.

After several more beers and two rounds of Jägermeister shots, we'd stopped caring about where the darts landed, and perched ourselves on stools at the bar, where we shared round after round of amusing stories. When the car finally picked me up at four o'clock we were laughing so hard I had to cross my legs. Damn Kegels!

On my way back to the bungalow, as the mountains and palm trees passed by the car window in an alcohol-induced blur, I melted into the cool leather seat and closed my eyes. The air-conditioning blew against my face, drying out the toothy smile pasted across my lips. What a great day. What great guys. Even though they didn't know it, I'd shown them that not all wives are killjoys. It was exactly what I'd needed. It was exactly what *Jack* needed—to lighten up a little, to remember what it was like to relax and have fun. To remember what it was like before he married his wife.

"You played pool?"

"Yep. I sucked."

"I've seen you play. I know you suck," Jack snapped at me. He'd been glad to hear my voice when I called, but as I started to tell him about my day with Chris's friends he'd clammed up.

"What's your problem?"

"What's my problem?" As Jack's voice rose there was no question about it: He was pissed at me for something. "My wife is out playing pool with three frat boys while I'm home steaming carrots for our daughter's dinner. My wife is hanging out at a tropical resort getting loaded and then going to some wax ceremony, hoping a guy takes her out on a date."

Funny how when Jack went out drinking with frat boys masquerading in three-piece suits while I sat at home making Katie dinner, it wasn't a big deal. Apparently he didn't like the waiting game any more than I did.

"Don't you trust me?" I put him on the defensive and held my breath. I knew Jack trusted me; I'd never given him any reason not to. Until now.

"Of course I trust you. I don't trust the Scab."

"It's Stag, and his name is Chris."

"I don't care what his name is; I don't want him getting too friendly." Jack ran some water in the background.

"You know, I asked if this was okay with you, and you said it was fine," I pointed out, getting irritated. "You said it was a great opportunity."

"I know. It just sounds like you're doing more drinking and dating than writing."

He had me there. I glanced over at the dresser drawer where I'd stashed my notebook when we moved into the bungalow two days ago and hadn't bothered to take it out again.

"Jack, I have to do what the other girls are doing."

"I just wish you weren't enjoying it so much."

There was an awkward silence while he waited for me to assure him that I wasn't enjoying myself. I didn't offer any such consolation.

"Katie's pasta is ready. Can I call you back?"

"Not really. We're not at the hotel anymore; they moved us into a bungalow."

"What, the chosen few?"

"There are seven of us."

"Do you have pillow fights and panty raids all night?"

"You know, I don't need this."

"I'm sorry. What's the place like?" he asked, the edge in his voice softened.

"It's nice. On the water. I'm sharing a room with a woman named Dorothy."

"How's she?"

"Great."

"Good." Katie let out a scream and Jack covered the mouthpiece while he tried to quiet her down. "I'd better get going, Katie's going to start eating her fist in a minute."

"Sure. Give her kisses for me. I don't know when I'll be able to call again, being in the bungalow and all."

"Well, you know where to find us." He held the phone out to Katie. "Say bye-bye to Mommy."

"Bye-bye," her soft voice echoed, but before I had a chance to say anything back, they hung up.

I headed out to the deck to find the other girls; at least they understood. But just my luck—nobody was seated around the table throwing back margaritas, as I'd hoped. I was about to go back into the house and grab myself a cold beer when I spotted Joe in the corner filming Claudia asleep in the hammock.

"Leave her alone; she's sleeping," I reprimanded, thinking he was acting like kind of a pervert.

"She's not sleeping," he told me.

Claudia's eyes remained closed.

"Then what's she doing?"

"Dying," Claudia practically groaned.

I walked over and looked down at her ashen face. She did not look good.

"What happened?"

Claudia opened her eyes and looked right at me. "That bitch poisoned me."

"What?"

"I'm sick as a dog. It was that guacamole Holly asked me to get and then never touched. Now I know why."

It wasn't possible, was it?

"Where is she?"

"She went into town with everyone else. They should be back any minute."

I didn't know if Holly had it in her to sink that low, but I was going to find out.

When Holly arrived back at the bungalow with Samantha and Vanessa and Rose, I was waiting on the front steps.

Before she had a chance to drop her shopping bags on the foyer table, I pulled Holly into the living room and prepared to put her in her place once and for all.

"What's your problem?" she asked, shaking my hand off her arm.

"What'd you do to Claudia?" I demanded.

"Claudia? I didn't do anything. What are you talking about?"

"She's sick as a dog from food poisoning."

"So?" she asked coldly.

"So it's your fault."

"Me? I didn't do anything—it wasn't even my fucking food!" Holly started to storm away and then spun around, her eyes big. "I know what's going on. She's acting sick so I don't tell anyone."

"Tell anyone what?" I considered myself a reasonably intelligent woman, but even I was beginning to get confused with all the accusations being thrown around.

"She's pregnant!"

The force of Holly's revelation propelled me backward onto the couch, where I let myself get swallowed up in a mound of downy cushions. She had to be making that up. There was no way Claudia was pregnant.

"Claudia's pregnant?" I repeated.

"She has to be." Holly sat down next to me and rushed on. "Yesterday I was looking through the bathroom garbage can—"

"You were looking through the bathroom garbage can?"

"Anyway, I found a box buried among some tissues. A pregnancy test."

"And it was positive?"

"I don't know. There was no stick. Just the packaging."

"Then how do you know it's Claudia? It could have been left over from the last people who stayed here. It could have been anyone, Holly. There are only two freaking bathrooms in this house." There was no way any of the hens were pregnant.

"Food poisoning? Morning sickness? Put it together. She doesn't want anyone to know."

Was it true? Could Claudia be pregnant? Or was this just Holly's way of creating trouble for Claudia—or even a trick by Arnie?

I grabbed a pillow from beside me, buried my face in it, and screamed. This was just a little more than even I could handle.

"Sarah, stop!" Arnie came running into the room and lunged for me, grabbing the pillow out of my hand. His cheeks were flushed with excitement. "That was super! Can you do that scream over? Our mike couldn't pick it up with the pillow covering your face."

# 16

"Hey, Sarah, what's up?" Dorothy dropped a nylon backpack on her bed and kicked off her Keds.

"You don't even want to know." There was no way I was going to repeat what Holly told me. If what she said was true, then it was Claudia's business. If it wasn't true, I'd be as bad as Holly for repeating it. "How was your day with the guys?"

"You wouldn't believe it."

I flipped my notebook over so only the plain cardboard back showed. "After the pool hall, I'd believe anything. There wasn't a spot in the place that wasn't sticky—every time I'd get off my stool it'd sound like I had Velcro on my butt."

"We played miniature golf."

"That sounds cool. Did you win?"

"Are you kidding me? You'd have thought it was the U.S. Open, not Mutt's Putt-Putt next to the Tire Emporium."

As much as I didn't want to compare my day playing pool with Dorothy's day on the AstroTurf links, I couldn't help it. She'd lost at miniature golf and I'd won at darts. That had to put me ahead somehow—even as it made me feel small for caring.

"They're funny guys, aren't they?"

"Yeah, they were nice guys." Dorothy fluffed up her pillows and climbed onto her bed, reclining against the plumped-up mound.

"Did you get any dirt on Chris?" I asked, wondering if Brian tried the whole gay thing on her, too.

"Not really. I talked to John most of the day. Neil and Brian spent half the time arguing about whether the wrinkles in the artificial grass were man-made impediments or a natural condition."

"John's cute."

"He's gorgeous," Dorothy blurted.

I raised my eyebrows knowingly. "Am I sensing interest in the Stag's best friend?"

Dorothy took my *Femme* magazine off the night table and started flipping through the pages.

"I'd be interested, but he's not the one on the show," Dorothy answered, not taking her eyes off the magazine.

"Are you saying you liked him more than you like Chris?"

Dorothy closed the magazine and looked up at me, preparing to confide something in a friend.

"Remember when I said that Chris's hot-tub line didn't matter to me? It did. I just didn't want to admit it. But it didn't bother me that Chris recycled a line; it bothered me that he made me jealous of two people I didn't even know—that I automatically assumed he would have a better time with you and Rose than he would with me. Now that I know you and Rose better, it bugs me that I was so insecure—it wasn't Chris that made me feel that way; it was me."

I nodded to let her know I was following along.

"I was willing to come on the show because I figured it would be easier to let the Stag choose me than to choose someone first and have him say no. Then I went out with John and Neil and Brian and I held my own. We had fun. When we were out, I felt safe letting John know I was attracted to him because there was no risk. Then he acted interested in me, and I realized I couldn't just be the one waiting anymore."

"Are you saying you want to pursue something with John?"

"All I'm saying is, I wish it was this easy to find good-looking, smart, funny guys in Atlanta. Maybe I should ask Chris if he has any friends down there."

"You say that like you're not going to make it past the next ceremony."

Dorothy shrugged. "You never know."

Dorothy turned her attention back to *Femme*. She'd made it through three candle ceremonies, one date, and an afternoon with Chris's best friends. You'd think at this point she'd be a little less ambivalent about the guy.

But she wasn't giddy with teenage hormones at the thought of being with Chris. If anything, her round of miniature golf seemed to have cooled her enthusiasm.

The notebook on my lap contained an almost-completed article that was conspicuously devoid of hen stories. Good thing I wasn't writing about the women anymore. How could I explain one of the hens falling for the Stag's best friend? I'd been working on my article all morning, and I needed only another three hundred words, which I could easily finish this afternoon.

"I'm heading down to the beach to read." I slid my feet into a pair of sandals and tucked my notebook under my arm. "See you for dinner?"

Dorothy nodded without taking her eyes off the glossy pages of glamorous women.

I grabbed my cell phone off the dresser and slipped it into my beach bag. I could call Suzanne from the beach when I finished. She'd love me. In less than three weeks I was able to show the depth of the producers' complete disdain for the women they were selling to America as Cinderellas.

Down on the beach, the afternoon sun was still high in the clear blue sky. I wanted to finish the article in time to call Suzanne at *Femme* and let her know about my new idea. But every time I started to put my pen on the page I thought about Dorothy and the roller coaster of emotions she'd been on the past few weeks. And how this week, more than any other, was a test of how we fit with Chris. Because it wasn't just the Stag we were getting to know; it was his friends and his life outside the picture-perfect beachside villa.

It was one thing to turn on the charm for the Stag, but it was another to get along with a bunch of guys who would go back to him with their blunt opinions. I could imagine Holly oozing her sappy-sweet molasses drawl. I hoped they weren't that easily fooled. Holly in a pool hall or playing miniature golf? The snack shack at Mutt's Putt-Putt with Sno-Kones and greasy hot dogs shimmering on a rotating stainless-steel grill wasn't exactly the clubhouse atmosphere Holly was working toward.

I almost wanted to write about how the hens weren't just comprised of the snippets we saw on TV, that the show went out of its way to use the most embarrassing or titillating clips possible, which were a very small part of what actually went on during the five weeks. Most important, the times when the women were at their most natural, like my elevator ride with a drunken Dorothy and my bathroom conversation with Vanessa, were completely missed, or seemingly so unsensational that they would be left on the cutting-room floor.

But I had my marching orders from Suzanne. *Femme* wanted an article that would sell magazines, and that wouldn't happen with an article about the women I'd gotten to know personally. Suzanne wanted the same thing producers were after—to capitalize on *The Stag*.

The sun was getting lower, and my article wasn't any closer to being finished. I had only about an hour to call Suzanne before she'd leave the office. I gripped my pen firmly and started writing.

In less than half an hour, I had my completed article—a scathing behind-the-scenes look at a show that fed on women's insecurities.

I laid my notebook on the towel next to me and took the cell phone out of my beach bag, thankful that my time alone on the beach was deemed too mundane to warrant the company of a cameraman. Suzanne picked up on the first ring.

"I have a new angle on the story, something with a little more punch than a piece on the hens," I began.

"I'm listening."

I explained my idea for an article that showed how the network was taking advantage of—and profiting from—women's desire to be adored. How the producers held the hens in such low regard, and saw them merely as a means to the end—the price of commercial airtime.

"Hmm . . . the business of love . . . the commercialization of female frailty . . . the feminization of prime-time profit." Suzanne paused, letting the idea settle in. "It's fantastic! Is it finished?"

I glanced down at the lined pages that held my completed story, and hesitated. Suzanne would want to see the piece as soon as it was done, probably right after the next candle ceremony tomorrow night. And that meant she'd expect me to blow out my candle if I were picked, and head home.

"Not yet."

"Well, get on it! I want this piece ASAP. When can you get it finished?"

"I still have some holes in the story, and I'd like to get some good quotes. . . ." I trailed off, without committing to a date.

"Get what you need and get back here." It wasn't an editor's request. It was an order.

"I will."

When the show started we were surrounded by twenty-three strangers. But what used to be a room-sized circle had been reduced to a small arc of seven women who'd become friends. And you found yourself both rooting for them and realizing that if they all won, you lost.

"By now you've all had a chance to spend some time with

Chris's friends," Pierre began. "We hope you've learned a little bit more about him. I know he's learned more about you." He glanced over at Chris as if they were keeping a secret, and Chris looked away, embarrassed. "As you know, tonight two more of you will be leaving us. And so, without further ado, here's Chris."

"Thanks."

Chris moved into position as Pierre slapped him on the back with the familiarity of an old buddy.

"Well, where do I begin?" Chris clapped his hands and held them together, taking a deep breath. "My friends thought you were all great. Some of them even expressed an interest in stealing you away from me—as if they had a chance." Chris let out a laugh, and I thought I caught him deliberately looking in Dorothy's direction.

The women smiled furtively at Chris's attempt to lighten the mood, as if each one thought he was talking about her. Every woman, that is, except Dorothy.

Pierre handed Chris his candle and stepped back, hanging by the director's side.

Chris watched the flame grow in his hand before looking up at us.

"Here we go."

This time I wasn't first, which made me wonder where I'd gone wrong. We'd had a blast playing darts and drinking beers. It couldn't matter that much that I sucked at pool, could it?

As Chris walked away from Vanessa's bright candle, she kept her eyes straight ahead, looking bored.

Next, Chris lingered in front of Dorothy, bending his candle toward hers.

Dorothy stared at the flickering flame and inhaled deeply. As she exhaled, her lips came together as if she was going to kiss Chris, and with one quick blow, she snuffed out her candle.

The room was quiet except for the sound of shuffling equip-

ment as the director ordered more cameras to get into the scene and
shoot it from every angle.

Pierre looked around nervously, his head jerking to his left
and right as if trying to find someone to tell him how to handle this
unexpected situation. He probably anticipated that someone would re-
ject Chris in the beginning, but someone who'd made it this far had to
buy into the whole thing and be in it to win, didn't they?

Chris took a step back, putting some space between him and
Dorothy. She still hadn't taken her eyes off the smoking wick.

Finally Dorothy looked up at Chris, a smile on her face, and
shrugged.

"Thanks, but no, thanks."

Chris stood there speechless, not even noticing the red candle
wax dripping slowly toward his knuckles.

"You're out?" Chris asked, keeping his voice low.

The director motioned for the boom operator to move in
closer.

"I'm out," Dorothy confirmed.

"Was it . . ." Chris looked around the room as if realizing for
the first time that we were all watching him. "John?" he practically
whispered.

"No. It's me." Dorothy turned toward the host. "What do I do
with this?" She waved her candle in the air.

Pierre hung back, waving his hand for Dorothy to step back
into the circle and wait until the ceremony was over.

Chris backed away from Dorothy and ran his hand through
his hair, taking a minute to collect himself, as if he had to rethink his
strategy. With Dorothy taking herself out of the running, there'd be
only one person at the end of the ceremony holding a gloomy candle.
And that meant that somebody whom Chris didn't plan to pick was
going to get to stay. And we wouldn't know who that was.

Finally Chris squared his shoulders and continued toward me.

After Dorothy's daring move I felt like a wimp accepting Chris's candle. But the idea of not accepting it never even crossed my mind.

Three minutes later it came down to Holly and Claudia—Claudia, who was possibly pregnant and wanted to share her life with someone, and Holly, who was simply looking for someone to share his last name.

Claudia didn't deserve to be put up against the same woman who'd warned everyone about her that first night. And if she was pregnant, well, she'd have to tell Chris eventually, and that would truly test his commitment. Chris shouldn't even have to think twice when choosing between them; it was obvious who deserved to stay and who deserved to be handed her bags and a one-way ticket on the way out the door.

I looked over at Vanessa and Samantha and Rose, whose own eyes were riveted to Chris as he took one carefully planned step after another, as if in slow motion. I joined their visual vigil, hoping that together we could mentally will him in Claudia's direction.

As Chris lit the fifth and final candle for the evening, Holly glowed brighter than the flame she held, and Claudia was left with a tight smile on her face, the corners of her mouth making every effort not to turn down in disappointment.

Chris took Claudia's hand and led her out the front door. Dorothy had walked herself out as soon as Holly's candle was lit.

With Chris out of the room, Pierre took control of the situation, carrying a crystal punch bowl that reflected prisms of light around the room.

"Ladies, I have a bowl here with five slips of paper indicating five different dates. They range from an extravagant overnight trip to Napa Valley, to a no-frills pizza-and-beer dinner at Chris's house."

Pierre called us up one by one.

"Please don't look at your paper until everyone has had an opportunity to pick," he instructed us.

Once we were all back in position along our increasingly intimate half circle, Holly burst into a huge smile and could barely keep
herself from levitating. She was obviously on her way to wine country.
And me? Extra cheese, hold the pepperoni.

When we got back to the bungalow a bright light shone in my
bedroom window, but Claudia's room was dark. A production assistant was loading Claudia's luggage into the trunk of the car as she
came down the front steps. Holly brushed by her without even saying
good-bye.

Claudia stopped next to the rest of us and shook her head.

"Are you okay?" I asked, putting an arm over her shoulder.

"I'll be fine."

I hoped she was right.

One by one we gave her good-bye hugs and wished her good
luck.

"We're going to miss you," Vanessa told her.

"I'll miss you guys, too," Claudia replied, and continued down
the walk to the car, where the driver opened her door and gently helped
her inside.

I went to find Dorothy.

"Hey, can I come in?" I asked, pushing the bedroom door
open.

"Sure, it's your room, too," Dorothy answered with a smile.

"You sure seem happy to be leaving."

"I am. It was time." She picked up a wrinkled linen dress that
was in desperate need of an iron. "Besides, I was starting to run out of
clothes."

I knew she expected me to laugh, but all I could manage was a
weak smile. I was surprised when Dorothy blew out her candle, although, looking back, I guess I should have seen it coming. But what
surprised me more was how much I'd miss her.

"Besides, I never even thought I'd make it this far."

I knew what that felt like.

"But he liked you. Is it because of John?"

"It was John; it was Joe—it could have been any guy, really. It could have been anyone who made me see that there are people out there if you have the time to find them and you're willing to risk getting hurt. And Chris liked me, so what? I've liked lots of guys in my twenty-six years. Is the Stag worth uprooting my life for? He lives in Seattle and I'm from Atlanta." She shook her head. "I mean, would you really give up your life for a guy?"

My first reaction was to tell Dorothy, "Of course not." What woman these days would? But how could I tell her that when the truth of the matter was, I'd been feeling like that was exactly what I did? And it wasn't easy. The agency threw me a going-away party, complete with balloons and a good-natured roast. At the end of the night the agency's president pulled me aside and told me there'd always be a spot for me, if I changed my mind. In the first few months I must have stood by the phone ten times, tempted to dial the agency's familiar number and take him up on his offer. But in the end, I stuck with the plan.

"I don't know. Maybe, if I thought it was worth it."

"Well, when my parents divorced, my mom didn't know what to do. She had no education, no skills. She was stuck trying to figure out how to pay the bills and raise three kids. I don't want that to happen to me." She stopped packing and sat down on the bed. "I've worked hard to get where I am. Giving that up to follow some guy just because he might be 'the one' doesn't feel right. Not after only a few weeks. Besides." She stood up again and started folding a shirt. "If he really wanted me that badly, he'd be willing to give up everything and move to Atlanta, right?"

I reached for the pile of clothes and grabbed some shorts that needed folding.

How ironic that in order to gain something you had to give something up—and that even in the revered realm of love it was no different. As if a relationship required sacrificing something, some part of yourself, in order to truly mean anything.

At first Dorothy's words made me think of myself, how I'd put aside so much of who I was to give Jack the wife and family he wanted. But then I realized that Jack may have made sacrifices as well, even though they weren't as obvious as settling down somewhere or quitting a job. When he continued on in law school after I'd told him quitting was crazy, I didn't think he was sacrificing anything, but maybe he'd given up pursuing something he would have loved even more.

Dorothy didn't see anything wrong with expecting someone else to make just as big a sacrifice as he asked her to make. Any disillusionment with love she'd had that first night we met was gone. When she arrived on the show, Dorothy had accepted that she was the one who had to do all the work. Now she realized she deserved to receive as much as she was willing to give. And she'd figured out that it was worth waiting for.

"Are you sure you won't change your mind?" I was going to miss her.

"Nope. There's got to be one normal guy in Atlanta. I'm not willing to give up yet. If it's worth having, it's worth waiting for."

I sat there silently, watching Dorothy prepare to leave, and I wanted her to know the truth. I didn't want her to find out in a few months from the pages of *Femme* magazine.

"Dorothy, there's something I'd like you to know before you go," I started. "I'm really—"

"Hi, there, can I come in?" Vanessa peered around the bedroom door.

"Sure, Sarah and I were just talking." Dorothy stopped folding a shirt and looked over at me. "What were you saying, Sarah?"

I bit my lip and shrugged, letting my moment of revelation pass. "Oh, just that I'm really going to miss you."

Dorothy smiled and went to the bathroom to collect her makeup and shampoo. "You can keep the papaya shampoo; I know you love it," she offered, putting the bottles into a plastic bag.

"Thanks. I'll think of you every time I wash my hair."

I left Vanessa and Dorothy alone and went to join the rest of the women outside on the deck, where a hurricane lantern sat on the teak table in a feeble attempt to shed some light on the darkness. It was quiet except for the far-off echoes of waves crashing on the beach below the bungalow. No one had a drink or attempted to make conversation. It was as if we hoped the presence of other people would make the fact that Claudia and Dorothy were leaving easier to take.

"Thank God Claudia's out," Holly declared into the dark, to no one in particular.

"You know, Holly, that's a really shitty thing to say." Rose stood up and walked inside, slamming the door behind her.

"Geez, that's gratitude for you. I did her a favor."

"What do you mean, you did her a favor?" I asked, sure that Holly never did anybody a favor if it didn't end up helping her in the process.

"I told Chris what a bitch Claudia was when he wasn't around, and shared a little secret with him that I thought he'd find interesting." She turned toward Samantha, looking for an ally. "Rose should be thanking me for enlightening Chris about Claudia. I mean, she's way prettier than Rose, Chris definitely would have picked her over Rose."

"Holly, I can't believe you did that. Claudia was just kidding about that Elvis crack." Samantha glared at Holly in the dark.

"Maybe." Holly shrugged, a triumphant smirk on her lips. "But who's laughing now?"

Samantha let out an aggravated groan, pushed back her chair abruptly, and stormed into the house, leaving me alone with Holly.

Holly stretched her arms above her head, as if she didn't even notice.

"Well, I'd better be heading to bed. I have an early flight tomorrow to Napa." Holly stretched her long legs out in front of her. "Do you think I should bring a burgundy thong and panties or an emerald-green merry widow to go along with the whole vineyard theme?"

The only merry widow I knew was Anna Nicole Smith, but Holly didn't bother waiting for me to answer. She raised herself out of the low Adirondack chair and disappeared into the house.

# 17

"*H*ey, guys. Hi, Joe." I bent down and brushed the sand off my bare feet.

"Hi, Sarah." Joe had a camera on his shoulder, filming the card game taking place on the deck. "Looks like you enjoyed the beach."

"Have you seen Holly?" Samantha asked me, not taking her eyes off the cards fanned out in her hand.

"She's back?"

"Is she ever." Vanessa looked up from a run of five spades.

"What happened? Did they just have the most incredibly romantic date ever?" I'd rather hear it from Vanessa than sit through Holly's play-by-play account of an embellished fairy tale.

"Not exactly. We tried to talk to her, but she just stomped straight to her room." Vanessa laid her cards on the table. "I win, right Joe?" She looked up at him. "Joe taught us a great new game. Wanna play?"

I shook my head. "No, thanks. I think I'll go inside."

Every time Chris even looked in Holly's direction, she made sure we were aware of the secret messages hidden in his smoldering gaze. If she wouldn't talk about the trip to Napa, it had to be really bad.

I deliberately passed by Holly's room. Inside a run of jagged sobs was interrupted only by sniffling and the blowing of her nose. As irritating as she was, I wanted to hear her story—she was the car wreck I just couldn't ignore as I walked by.

"Holly?" I knocked softly on her closed door. "Holly? Can I come in?"

After a long sniffle I heard her eke out something that sounded like a yes, and I opened the door.

Holly was sprawled out on her bed facedown, looking like she'd fallen down and not bothered to move.

"Holly?"

She rolled over slowly, trying to see me through the mass of red curls that were matted to her face.

"Hi, Sarah," she said painfully, staring up at the ceiling as if looking to the gods for answers. The small rosebuds on her Victoria's Secret pajamas were the only attractive things about her. Her face was blotchy and swollen, making her eyes seem disproportionately small. She smelled vaguely like sour grapes, and her makeup had slid down her cheeks, leaving muddy tracks over her freckles.

"So how was it?" I asked, as if finding her hibernating in her bedroom at two in the afternoon were the most normal thing in the world.

"Mortifying." Holly put her hand to her mouth, stifling a burp that turned her face an even greener shade of gray.

"Tell me what happened."

"It started out great. We flew up there in our own chartered jet. We toured vineyards, had our own personal wine tastings." Holly's recollection of the events faded along with her voice.

"Anything good?" I prompted, sitting on a corner of her bed.

"Of course! Merlot, cabernet, chardonnay—you name it, we drank it."

"Then what was so bad?"

"Well, we must have spent two hours drinking wine, glass after glass. Then we were going to take a hot-air-balloon ride into the hills and have a sunset picnic. Sounds perfect, right? It was, except that we hadn't had anything to eat all day but wine and cheese. I was feeling a little drunk, but I figured we were going to be eating soon, so I'd be fine. So we're floating up, and the fire is flaring, sending the air into the balloon, making this horrible loud hissing noise." Holly closed her eyes and rubbed her temples with her fingers. "And we were going up and up and all of a sudden I didn't feel well. My stomach started turning, and that noise was driving me crazy, and . . . I don't know, I just lost it."

"Lost it?"

"Yeah, you know." She waited for me to say it, but I didn't offer any help. "I puked! I threw up, right over the side, all over the edge of the basket, on the camera crew; it was just awful."

Holly buried her head in her hands.

"I was so embarrassed."

"So what happened?"

Holly looked up at me with pink eyes, blinking back tears. "The guy operating the balloon took us down immediately. Chris put me in the limo, holding his breath and turning away from me like I was some gutter lush, and we drove to the hotel—this beautifully elegant place that looked like a European château."

"And you felt better?"

"I wish! I went straight to our room, where I threw up on the rug all the way to the bathroom, and spent the night on the floor dry-heaving into the toilet." Holly paused and bit her bottom lip to stop it from quivering. "Oh, my God, what have I done?"

Holly was in bad shape. This wasn't just a girl who'd had a bad date; it was someone who saw her future go up in smoke—or down in chunks, so to speak. The idea of consoling Holly wasn't something I felt up to, but she looked so pathetic, her nose all red and raw from the tissues, I had to do something. I wasn't heartless.

"Look, everything was fine up until the balloon ride, right?" I patted her foot for reassurance.

Holly sat up straighter, looking hopeful. "Yes, it was. It was perfect."

"Well, then, Chris knows you don't make a habit out of drinking wine all day. He's gotta know it was just a mistake."

"It *was* a mistake, a horrible, horrible mistake."

"He'll forget about it. Don't worry. He won't hold it against you."

"You don't think so? Because, really, up until I started throwing up wine and crackers and lumps of Brie, it was just amazing."

"Sure. And if he does, well, then you don't want anything to do with him anyway."

"Yes, I do!" Holly practically wailed.

"Come on, Holly. You're not the first woman to get drunk and throw up on a date."

"Oh, yeah? I'm the first one to do it on *The Stag*."

"I wouldn't want a guy who'd drop me because I made a little mistake."

"That's because you're not even in love with him," Holly accused, as if that were the greatest sin. "You don't get butterflies in your stomach when you see him. You don't have the urge to be with him every minute of the day, the way he makes you feel like you're the most special person in the world when he looks in your eyes."

She took a deep breath and looked down her nose at me. "Unlike the rest of you, I love him, and I know that we were meant to be together. I mean, come on, Sarah. Isn't he just a little out of your league?"

I slid off the bed and stood up. I'd had enough of Holly. Being nice was one thing. Being insulted was another.

Holly was wrong. I might not be in love with Chris, but I knew what it was like to stand next to him and want to reach out and pull him closer. And I knew what it was like when he held my stare. And listened to me. And made me feel like I was interesting and important. Like I used to feel before I traded in Sarah Divine for some wifely and motherly ideal. And at least I could hold my liquor.

"Holly, you're not the only one Chris spends time with. If I were you, I'd watch my words. What goes around comes around."

"Well, the only thing going around here is that you're all jealous of me and you can't wait for me to go."

I threw up my hands and left Holly alone.

Samantha and Vanessa were still on the deck.

"So what'd you find out? Is it true she puked all over him?" Samantha asked, shuffling the deck.

"She didn't puke on him; she just got sick in the balloon. And in their hotel room. And on the bathroom floor."

"She's outta here." Vanessa leaned back in her chair, waiting for Samantha to deal.

I shrugged. I might not subscribe to Holly's theory on men, or her insipid aspirations, but I wasn't sure I wanted her to get booted off the show just because she had too much to drink. If that were the criteria for lasting relationships, then Jack and I wouldn't have lasted past our first month.

A part of me wanted Chris to keep her on the show just to prove he could handle the unpredictably ugly moments that inevitably happen when you're with someone long enough. Then again, she was such a pill, how she made it this far was beyond me.

The next afternoon I found Samantha outside after her date with Chris. "What are you doing out here?" I asked Samantha, who was sitting Indian-style on the deck in just a jogging bra and Lycra shorts.

"Meditating."

"With him around?" I pointed to a cameraman filming her silence.

She opened one eye and frowned. "I know. I can't even get a little peace in peace." She unfolded her legs and sprang up, turning her back to the camera.

"How was your day on Catalina?" I was asleep when Samantha had returned home last night from her date on Catalina Island. Although I doubted it was as exciting, or messy, as Holly's trip to Napa, I was curious.

"It was nice," she began slowly, glancing over her shoulder at the camera before continuing. "We went snorkeling in Lover's Cove and stuff. . . ." Her voice faded away without elaborating.

"That sounds like fun."

Samantha put her hand on my arm and leaned into me. "Love the earrings." She moved her face close to my ear and whispered softly, "Meet me in the back bathroom."

She pulled away, smiled, and walked inside the house. I followed shortly behind.

When I reached the bathroom it was empty. I was about to leave when I heard Samantha whisper my name from behind the shower curtain. "Sarah, in here."

She pulled the curtain back, and pointed to the sink. "Turn the faucet on, just in case."

I turned the knobs until a steady stream of water flowed into the sink.

"What's going on?" I tried to avoid knocking over the array of shampoos, conditioners, and face scrubs lining the tub, as I climbed in next to her.

"I wanted to talk with you about something, but I didn't want the cameras around. This is the only safe place."

I nodded. On *The Stag* there was only one place off-limits to public viewing; the shower.

"I think I went too far," Samantha started, looking down at her feet. "With Chris. On Catalina."

"Sam, after his date with Holly I don't think anything could faze him."

"Even if I got too carried away?"

"How carried away?" There were always cameras everywhere;

how carried away could a hen get before she realized she was being zoomed in on?

"Well, we were in the water snorkeling for over an hour and the crew needed a break, so they went back to the beach while we stayed out in the water." She took a breath before going on. "We were only, like, twenty yards out, but we knew they couldn't see us, and we were kissing and then we started doing stuff."

"Stuff?"

"You know. *Stuff.*"

"Stuff that couldn't be shown on TV?"

Samantha bit her lip. "Only on cable."

I mulled this over before responding. "You'd better hope there were no hidden cameras in his bathing suit or anything."

She cringed. "It wouldn't matter. It wasn't on him."

"What were you thinking?" I practically scolded. "You can't trust the crew, and you certainly can't trust Arnie and Sloane. They live for moments like that."

"I know!" she cried, and then buried her face in her hands. "And now Chris is going to think I'm a slut or something—and I really like him."

She truly looked mortified.

"They probably didn't get anything on camera. I mean, you were underwater, right?"

She nodded.

"Then don't worry about it."

"Do you think I'm awful?"

I shook my head. "No, I don't think you're awful."

Someone was pounding on the bathroom door to get in.

"We'd better get out of here before Arnie starts thinking we're showering together." I pulled the curtain back and stepped out onto the bathroom tile.

"He'd love that, wouldn't he?"

I gripped the door handle, ready to leave. "At this point, it's the only scandalous thing missing around here."

When I swung the bathroom door open I didn't find Arnie trying to sneak a peak at what was going on between me and Samantha. I found Vanessa hopping impatiently from foot to foot.

She was as surprised to see us as I was to see her back from her spa date already.

"What are you two doing in there? Move. Holly's giving herself a facial in the other bathroom and I've got to pee. Then we're going down to the beach to talk." She bolted inside the bathroom and emerged a minute later.

"So the spa was fun?" I asked Vanessa, as we made our way slowly down the beach. Samantha stayed in the bungalow to take a nap, and I was trying not to think of her underwater escapades as I kicked dried pieces of seaweed out of my path.

Somehow knowing Vanessa was on the show only to placate her mom made me feel better. I didn't mind hearing about the day she spent with Chris as long as I knew she wasn't really interested in him—that she was only going through the motions.

"If you can call lying naked on a table with a washcloth covering the crack of your ass, while a cameraman practically uses his lens as a speculum, fun."

Vanessa stopped walking and threw down her beach mat.

"They filmed you getting massages?"

"Yep." Vanessa smacked her lips together and sat down.

I knelt next to her.

"At least you can skip your annual exam this year," I joked.

Vanessa didn't crack a smile. "It was the least relaxing spa experience you can imagine."

"What about Chris? What'd he think?"

Vanessa bit her lip and didn't answer right away. "The guy's great. Don't get me wrong," she started, "but he just acts like it's no big deal. I'm not a prude, but kissing in front of a camera crew doesn't exactly make for the most intimate moment in the world. There we were, getting this brown, slimy mud mask spread over our bodies, and there's Joe with his camera watching us. Chris would lean over to kiss me, and there was Joe. Every fucking move we made was recorded. I couldn't stop wondering what Joe thought of the whole thing—was he viewing the scene as camera angles and close-ups, or did he see a naked woman covered in mud kissing a guy who'd kissed another girl just yesterday?"

The fact that we were filmed every time we were with Chris did take away from the illusion that we were participating in what was supposed to be a romantic encounter. It was like finding yourself in a canopied bed with scarlet rose petals scattered along the silky bedspread like kisses—and then discovering the vibrating motor and a slot for quarters on the headboard.

"Does that make any sense? I don't know; maybe it's different for Chris." Vanessa dug up a stick that had been buried in the sand.

"So that's what bothered you? What Joe was thinking?"

"No, that's not it. It's something else," Vanessa told me, writing her name in the sand with the stick. "You want kids?"

I pictured Katie snuggled up with me in her rocking chair.

"Yeah."

"Me, too. And I just can't imagine one day telling my kids that I met Daddy on *The Stag.* That when I recount the story of my husband's proposal I'll have to preface it with, 'You see, it came down to me and this other girl. . . .' "

"I don't blame you." For all its promotion as a show filled with romance and heartfelt emotion, the proposal scenario was definitely designed more for season-finale impact than nostalgic memories.

"I thought I was, once—pregnant, I mean. Just over a year ago, before I even met the Geritol prick."

"What happened?"

"I was dating this guy and I was late. At first I was freaked out. I didn't want to marry the guy, but once I started to think about having a baby I kind of wanted it to happen." Vanessa's voice became wistful as she picked up a shell and held it in her hand. "I didn't want to be a single mom, but I've always wanted kids, and Mr. Right didn't seem to be anywhere in sight. Having a baby by myself wasn't exactly the ideal family I'd always envisioned, yet a part of me hoped it wasn't just a false alarm. So I took the test and waited for the little pink plus sign to show up. It didn't. And I wasn't."

Vanessa looked up at me and cleared her throat.

"If it happened today, I'd have no doubts. I'm not putting everything on hold while I wait for Mr. Right."

I reached for a handful of sand, watching the grains slowly filter through my fingers, the formerly pale, fleshy ring mark now as naturally tanned from the California sun as the rest of my body. I couldn't even tell where I'd had to rub the self-tanner; it blended in seamlessly.

"It would be hard. Having a child with two parents is hard." It probably sounded like trite advice coming from a twenty-six-year-old PR associate, but I was speaking from experience. I also couldn't help but think of the possibly pregnant, but certainly single, Claudia.

"You know what's hard? Pretending you don't want something you want. Pretending it's okay to do what everyone expects you to do, whether or not it's what makes you happy."

Now I wasn't sure whether Vanessa was talking about having a baby or vying for the Stag.

"So does that mean you want to leave the show?" I asked tentatively.

"No, it means I didn't want to come here in the first place," Vanessa said resolutely. "But we already knew that. It also means that while Chris may seem like the ideal guy, I already know that I'm ideal without him."

Was I the only one—besides Holly, I'm loath to add—who'd fallen under Chris's spell? Between Dorothy's abrupt exit and Vanessa's newfound resolve, Chris's potential love interests were dropping like flies while I was furiously flapping my wings and diving straight toward the flame.

I stood up, grabbing my sandals.

"I've got to get ready. The car's picking me up in an hour for my pizza party."

"An hour to get ready for a pizza party? Are you sure that's all you're expecting?" Vanessa's voice was no longer serious as she raised her eyebrows and grinned at me, insinuating something more illicit than a pepperoni pie.

"Well, I'm not expecting him to lather me up in mud, I can tell you that!"

"You sound disappointed," Vanessa added, laughing.

I brushed the sand off my shorts. "Not as disappointed as I'll be if he orders anchovies."

Back in my room I was rinsing sudsy papaya-scented shampoo out of my hair, remembering Jack's proposal. It was a week after he graduated from law school, right before he started his new job at the firm. I'd already accepted my position at the PR agency and was excited about beginning my new career and becoming the *Cosmo* girl I'd always known was inside dying to get out—from the fashionable suits and power meetings to the neatly upswept hairstyle and tortoiseshell glasses feeding every guy's librarian-in-garters-and-a-push-up-bra fantasy.

On the show the proposal was like standing on a stage and having Burt Parks crown you the most desirable woman in the world. It was the culmination of weeks of competition, where only the winner was left standing next to the Stag. In real life, I felt like it was just the beginning of the talent competition. Between working my butt off to establish myself at the agency, planning the wedding, and trying to play adoring fiancée who could spend all day at the office and still have crème brûlée waiting for dessert when Jack arrived home after twelve hours in the law library, I became a slave to my day planner and the life I thought I should have.

The baby, the house in the suburbs—I expected those things.

What I didn't expect was that seven years later I'd be showering with glistening moisturizer-infused bath gel and making sure my hair smelled like a tropical-fruit drink for a guy other than my husband.

And I hadn't even spoken to my husband in just over a week. After our last fruitless conversation, I'd started calling home during the day, when I was sure Jack wouldn't be there, and I could talk to Katie without having to listen to the growing anger that laced every sentence. My assignment had become yet another obstacle thrown up between us, another element of real life that sprang up to get in the way of us simply loving each other. It had begun to feel like a strange version of those old and grainy romantic movies—I see Jack, the object of my affection, across a meadow and run to him in slow motion with open arms. Only as I make my way toward him, I have to step over prickly weeds and rocks hidden under muddy soil like land mines, so that by the time I reach him, I'm too damned tired to do anything more than tell him to get out of my way so I can wash off and clean myself up—and then curse him for picking such a crappy meadow in the first place.

# 18

"*H*ere, I figured the least I could do was offer you a frosty mug."

I took the icy glass from Chris's hand and placed it on the coffee table next to the open pizza box. Of all the time I'd spent with Chris, our informal pizza dinner was most like my non-*Stag* life, as were the faded jeans and Gap tank top I was wearing.

Chris sat down on the rug next to me. The living room seemed different without the host and the director and all the girls waiting anxiously for a ceremony. The nicest thing of all was the absence of vanilla-scented candles. I didn't know if I'd ever be able to smell anything vanilla again without lining up around a room and holding my breath in anticipation.

"Here you go." Chris handed me a slice of pizza. "Careful, it's still hot."

I held the slice gingerly in my hands, blowing on the glistening cheese.

"Sorry you picked the worst date," he apologized.

"From what Holly told me, you already had your worst date."

"No comment."

"Well, don't be sorry about the date. This is great. I can't remember the last time I got to hang out at home eating pizza out of the box. There's usually so many interruptions that by the time I sit down, the pizza's cold."

"Your job must keep you really busy."

Actually, I'd been talking about trying to eat with Katie around, but his guess was close enough.

I nodded and lifted my slice to my mouth.

"Mmm." I reached for a napkin on the table as some oil slid down my wrist. "That's good."

"It is, isn't it? I love pizza. We used to have pizza every Sunday night growing up. We used to order five large pies, one for me and each of my brothers, and one for my parents."

"You have three brothers?"

"Yep. I'm the youngest."

Holly would be disappointed. Chris was last in line for the Masters family throne.

"Your mom must be a saint—or crazy."

"It wasn't so bad. We all stayed in line."

"Four boys? I don't know, no matter how good you were, that's a handful."

Chris washed down his pizza with some beer.

"Do you want me to put on some music? Maybe some Jimmy James and the Blue Flames?" he asked, winking at me.

The idea of listening to one of Jack's favorite bands made the pizza crust stick in my throat.

"Could we not? I kinda had a headache earlier," I lied.

"That's fine." Chris lifted another slice out of the box and placed it on his plate. "So what do you want to be when you grow up, Sarah Divine?"

Good question, if you're asking a twenty-six-year-old. But a little disconcerting for a thirty-four-year-old who's supposed to have it all figured out.

Chris chewed his pizza and waited for my answer.

"Happy?" My answer sounded more like a question than a goal.

"Let me help," he offered. "Do you want a family?"

I nodded.

Chris tipped his head to the side like he was sizing me up.

"You strike me as someone who'd be a great mom."

"I don't know about that."

"Why?"

"Being a mom isn't as easy as it looks—and it doesn't even look that easy. It can probably be frustrating at times, especially if you grew up believing you'd have some supersuccessful career. I'm not sure you can have both."

"You sound like someone talking from experience."

I paused, taking a sip of cold beer from my mug. "I have a niece."

"Yeah, well, I want to be able to be there for my kids. I work hard, but I'm not on the road a lot, and I can pretty much control my schedule."

"It probably helps that your family owns the company." I'd meant to be funny, but it didn't come out that way. I'd sounded like I was making fun of him.

Chris took the sharp kitchen knife and slipped it between two slices that had melted together.

He placed a slice on my plate and took a bite of the remaining slice before reacting to my words.

"I can't quite figure you out," he finally said.

"What do you mean?" I asked, even though I was pretty sure I knew exactly what he meant.

"On the one hand you're like the other girls—fun to talk to, you want me to get to know you, that sort of thing." He took his eyes off the slices and looked up at me. "But I also get the feeling that you're not sure you like me."

"I like you."

"Not the way the others like me."

I was tempted to break the news to him, that not every hen was exactly tap dancing at the idea of being Mrs. Stag.

"Don't be confusing obsession with genuine interest," I told him, thinking of Holly. "And if you can't figure me out, why am I still here?"

"Because you intrigue me."

"I could say the same thing."

"And I think even if we'd met under different circumstances I'd feel the same way."

I was sure *different circumstances* didn't include bumping into me at the grocery store with Katie perched on my hip and Jack throwing Cheerios into the cart. And if Chris did happen to bump into me with my ponytail, sweatpants, and au naturel, un-made-up face, I doubt he would have felt the same way.

"Then why even go on the show?"

"First of all, it wasn't my idea. My friends and I did it on a lark, and I was the only one who didn't drop out before the second round. I figured I had nothing to lose. There are worse ways to meet women, and these women all supposedly have what I'm looking for."

"And what is it you're looking for?"

"Someone to hang out with and have fun. Someone who's intelligent, independent, a little challenging."

"And beautiful with a great body?"

"Hey, I'm only human. I want someone I'm attracted to."

"Do you really think you'll propose to someone at the end of the show?"

"Why, are you worried it won't be you?" Chris smiled and looked at me through the fringe of his eyelashes. "Who knows, anything's possible. I have friends who met their wives at bars, in third grade, at a Mariners game—why is this any worse?"

"Before coming here I thought that any woman who'd do this was desperate."

"You want to see desperate? Ever been in a bar for last call? Everyone looking around for someone to hook up with. At least here the women are honest about what they're looking for."

Some of them, anyway.

"I'm full." Chris patted his flat stomach.

"Me, too."

"Want to go outside? Sit around the pool?"

"No hot tub?"

Chris threw his hands up in surrender. "And risk the wrath of Sarah? I don't think so."

We left the almost-finished pizza in its box on the coffee table, but we took our beers.

The cameras followed us out onto the patio, tagging along like a litter of puppies.

"Hey, guys? Think we could have some privacy?" Chris asked hopefully.

Joe shrugged. "Sorry, you know the rules."

Chris frowned but he didn't argue with Joe.

Chris pulled two cushioned lounges so close together their wooden frames rubbed together and squeaked as we sat down. He reached for my hand and I willingly let him fold his large fingers over mine.

"Are many of your friends married?" he asked, rubbing his thumb along my palm.

"Enough of them." In fact, almost all my friends were married with children.

"All of a sudden it feels like all my friends are getting serious with the women they're dating. I figure I'll be getting intimately familiar with the on-line Williams-Sonoma bridal registry very soon."

When I got engaged, registering over the Internet didn't even exist. As Holly pointed out, the entire mating process was becoming much more efficient.

"What do you think marriage should be like?" he asked, turning to me.

My hand leaped from his, and I almost jumped off the lounge, thinking he'd asked me what marriage was like—as if he knew I had personal knowledge of the institution. But then I realized he was asking me to *imagine* what marriage was like. As if how I anticipated it would be would have any bearing on reality.

"I think it should be fun."

"Fun how?"

"I don't know exactly; I just know it shouldn't feel like that movie where it's Groundhog Day over and over. I don't want to wake up every day knowing what to expect, knowing my husband's every move, and what I'll be doing every moment of the day."

"I think that's called dating, not marriage."

"Do we have to talk about marriage?" I shifted onto my side so I could get a better look at him.

"Isn't that why we're here?"

"I thought we were here to have fun."

"I thought you said marriage was supposed to be fun."

Chris turned toward the camera silently recording our conversation as Joe slowly worked his way out from behind my back and toward the foot of our lounges.

"Are we done yet?"

Joe took his face out from behind the dilated lens and considered us for a minute.

"You know the rules." Joe shrugged and went back to filming.

Chris turned on his side and faced me, his shoulder casting a shadow on our faces as he blocked the crew's lights. "That's a little better. You look beautiful tonight."

"In these old things?"

"These old things suit you better than some uptight dressy thing. You look more comfortable."

He leaned over his lounge's low armrest. Chris cradled my chin in his hand and leaned into me, the weight of his body pulling me closer. Our lips brushed lightly at first, a touch so imperceptible it almost tickled. Gradually our lips parted and the tentative kiss became two tongues exploring each other with abandon.

And then, abruptly, Chris pulled away. He stood up without

bothering to explain what he was doing, and arranged his warm body on my lounge next to me, pressing up against me with a firmness that left little to the imagination.

As his arm reached behind me and pulled me into him, our kisses grew more urgent and Chris worked his way on top of me. A hand easily slipped under my top, his cool fingertips lightly teasing my skin with featherlike gentleness.

"Do you want to take this inside?" he asked, his breath warm on my face.

I didn't respond, afraid to speak my answer out loud, as if it could be used against me in the future. There was a big difference between having a camera capture me going along with the Stag, and coming right out and saying I wanted to go along with him. But would Jack be that discerning?

Chris took my hand and led me back into the house.

He guided me over to the familiar leather couch and drew me toward him, never letting go of my hand. Chris lifted my hair off my shoulders and held it back, giving his tongue access to the exposed skin on my neck. I closed my eyes, letting the sensation of his hot tongue trickle down my neck.

"You feel so amazing." I groaned, sliding down the cushions until I was flat on my back.

"Mmm . . ."

The crunch of gravel fractured the room's silence, heralding in the sober bluish-white beams of the limo's halogen headlights.

"Why don't we tell the driver to come back in a few hours?" Chris whispered, not taking his lips off my neck.

I pushed him off me and quickly scrambled to my feet, thankful the limo arrived before I could do something stupid. And it's not like up until that point I'd been the picture of wise decision making.

Chris watched, grinning.

"What?" I asked, tucking my shirt into my jeans and smoothing out my hair.

"Nothing. It's just that you look like some disheveled teenager hurrying to get dressed before Mom and Dad catch her making out on the couch."

It wasn't my mom I was worried about. It was Katie's.

"I don't want to keep the driver waiting."

"God forbid we keep the driver waiting," Chris mimicked, making fun of me. "It's not like you need your beauty sleep for tomorrow's ceremony."

"Yeah, well, while you get to walk ten feet to bed, I've got a twenty-minute ride." I grabbed my purse off the end table. "And some beauty sleep wouldn't hurt."

"Well, the driver can wait until I kiss you good-night, can't he?" Chris walked over to me and put his hands on my waist. "He'll be fine. No reason for you to feel guilty."

I wrapped my arms around Chris's neck and reached up to kiss him good-night. And as he took me in his arms, the only thing I felt guilty about was not wanting to leave.

"What's up with Pinky Tuscadero over there?" Rose asked, pointing across the room to where Holly stood checking out her reflection in the grand piano's glossy surface.

Holly had decided that the best way to repent for puking her guts out on her date was to sport a lacy bustier and black leather pants to the fifth candle ceremony. As if coming across as a dominatrix would somehow put her right back into first place.

"I think you mean her cousin, Leather," I corrected, wondering how someone as young as Rose even knew who Pinky Tuscadero was— probably Nick at Nite reruns.

"It's Holly's attempt to make Chris forget what she looked like with Brie conditioner in her hair." Vanessa pinched her nose just in case we couldn't imagine what regurgitated Brie would smell like. We all laughed.

Chris and Pierre entered the room from the infamous tiled

hallway—a fifteen-yard walk that had come to be as mystifying as the rotating tunnel used to transport Steve Austin and Sasquatch in *The Six Million Dollar Man.*

The butter-yellow cashmere sweater from the last ceremony had been replaced with a French-blue oxford and navy blazer—no tie. Chris's hand was buried in the pocket of his silky khaki pants, adding to the casual country club look.

The host came over to where Samantha, Rose, Vanessa, and I were standing and asked us to get ready.

We all lined up against the fireplace while Holly took her sweet time, making sure the cameras and Chris got a view from every angle.

"Tonight two more of you will leave us," Pierre began. "I know that Chris had a very, um, *interesting* experience on his dates with you all this week. And so, with this week's dates behind you, Chris will begin the candle ceremony."

"What can I say? I had a great time this week, and now that I've been able to spend more time with you this has become even more difficult. I hope that the two of you who are not chosen tonight will go away knowing that this wasn't easy."

Pierre handed Chris his candle.

Five candles waited for him to approach. After lighting Rose's candle first, Chris came over to me. Which meant that of the three women standing beside me, only one of them was going back to the bungalow in our limo.

Even though I knew Vanessa didn't want to marry the Stag, a part of me hoped Chris would pick her—not because she needed him to, but because I couldn't imagine being on the show without her.

But as Chris moved to my right I saw him smile at Samantha—a warm smile that said she was his next choice.

After he lit Samantha's candle, Chris took a deep breath and walked back to the host.

As I turned my eyes toward Vanessa, I saw Holly. And she was pissed. Thank God she didn't pair a crop with the leather-and-lace ensemble or I would have feared she'd whip the shit out of Chris.

Vanessa walked across the room and handed her candle to the host. She said good-bye to Chris and headed for the door, her head held high. Holly didn't have the good grace to follow Vanessa's lead, and instead practically stabbed Pierre in the stomach with her candle and didn't even bother acknowledging Chris.

Chris hadn't risen to the occasion and decided that drinking too much and getting sick was something he could overlook. Or maybe he just realized that Holly was the shiftless bitch we had all had to live with the past weeks. Some small part of me, a very tiny piece, felt bad for Holly.

Did I feel bad enough to trade places with her? Not on your life.

"Samantha. Sarah. Rose." Pierre nodded at each of us as he said our names. "This week each of you will go away with Chris on an overnight trip. We've booked you separate rooms at three romantic destinations—whether you choose to use both those rooms or spend the night together is up to you."

The host raised his eyebrows at us as if trying to figure out who the slut would be, and then looked at Chris, psychically high-fiving him.

When Samantha, Rose, and I arrived back at the bungalow, Holly was recklessly dragging her luggage down the hall, the metal feet scraping against the flagstone floor with a shrill squeal.

"Hey, Holly, they'll help you with that, you know?" Samantha told her, stepping out of Holly's way like a matador fleeing a raging bull.

Holly sniffed at her and continued scratching her exit trail along the floor.

Rose shrugged.

"We're really going to miss you guys." Rose reached a hand out and laid it cautiously on Holly's shoulder.

Well, we'd miss Vanessa, anyway.

"Fuck him," Holly spat with such malice that even I was surprised. "It's not like I can't get a guy. Give me six months—I'll be planning my wedding."

Holly gripped the doorknob with white knuckles, tore open the front entry, and kicked her bags onto the steps.

"See ya."

The three of us watched as Holly stormed to the limo and ordered the driver to get her bags.

Holly's Southern charm had turned as cold and dark as her waiting candle, but she certainly wasn't sad to be leaving Chris—she was mad she wasn't going home with a ring. I turned toward Vanessa's room and started down the hall.

I wasn't worried about Holly; she'd be okay. She'd find a guy who met her criteria and become the country club wife she always dreamed of being. Women like her always landed on their feet. Even if it required stepping on other people's toes along the way.

"You need help?" I watched Vanessa gather up six pairs of shoes and dump them into her luggage.

"Nah, I'm almost done."

"Are you okay?"

"You know what bothers me the most?" Vanessa looked up at me, dangling a black sling-back pump from her finger. "That she lasted as long as I did." Vanessa pointed next door to Holly's room.

"Don't even say that. You two couldn't be more different. I'm sure Holly acted sticky sweet around Chris. He probably had no idea what a bitch she is."

"You're probably right," Vanessa concluded, and took some steps in my direction until she was standing in front of me. "Even if I didn't win the Stag, I'd like to think I'm leaving here with a new friend."

I opened my arms and we shared a hug.

"Not just a friend, Vanessa. A fan."

I helped Vanessa out to the waiting limo, where Holly was already tucked deep inside, probably bitterly sucking down whatever libation they'd stocked in the crystal decanters.

We hugged again before the driver opened the door and told Vanessa they had to get going. As the limo pulled away she slid down her window and stuck her dark head out to call to me.

"Good luck, lover girl!" she shouted, holding up her fingers, which were tightly crossed. As the car pulled away I waved good-bye with my right hand, keeping my left hand and my own crossed fingers hidden behind my back, hidden from the cameras.

An overnight trip with Chris. A man. Not my husband. I wasn't just holding a candle anymore. Now I was playing with fire.

# 19

"Okay, you've proved your point. Come home."

"Come home?" I sorted through the hangers in my closet looking for outfits appropriate for my trip to Sedona. I figured I had to tell Jack I was going away in case something happened with Katie and he had to call me. "What do you mean, come home?"

"Don't even tell me you were planning to go away with the little stud." Jack's voice was cold and hard.

"It's Stag. And his name is Chris," I reminded him. Again.

"I don't give a shit what his name is. The game is over, Sarah. I've tried to be the supportive husband, but you're making me feel like a chump while you flounce around California pretending to be someone you're not."

I wasn't pretending to be someone I'm not—for once I was acting like the person I was! Didn't Jack get it? I wasn't just some writer wanna-be who stayed home all day taking care of his daughter. Had he forgotten that?

"And what am I supposed to do about my reason for being here?" I spun around and walked over to the window, where the wind was brushing a palm frond against the glass.

"Please. You've been there four weeks. You must have your story by now."

"But the show isn't over."

"It is for you."

"If you didn't want me to go through with this, why'd you tell me to take the trip?"

Jack hesitated. "I didn't think you'd actually make it this far."

"Your confidence in me is overwhelming."

"Well, your lack of respect for me is a little staggering as well."

"I have responsibilities," I said flatly, refusing to be bullied.

"You have responsibilities here at home, too."

"I'm not your employee, Jack. You can't order me to do something."

Jack exhaled noisily. "That's rich, Sarah. I didn't know being at home was such a sacrifice."

A sacrifice. My mind flashed back to Dorothy and what she was and wasn't willing to give up in a relationship.

The line was silent as we both waited for the other person to speak, as if whoever lasted longer won. I could hear Jack's breathing against the mouthpiece.

I couldn't leave. Not yet. The stakes had become too high.

"I have to stay, Jack," I said, blinking first.

"Fine. Stay."

The thud of a slamming phone reverberated in my ear until the only sound on the other end of the line was silence.

I snapped my cell phone shut and threw it onto the bed with such force it bounced twice before settling on a pillow. Who did Jack think he was, ordering me to come home? Had I become so impotent, ceding control over decisions that used to belong to me? Jack had made it clear that he viewed me as merely a household employee whose job it was to ensure that his life ran smoothly—while Chris saw me as the desirable, interesting woman I'd let wither away over the years. Whose version of me did I prefer? It was no contest.

I'd show Jack. He was in for a surprise—his smooth ride was about to become very bumpy.

"It's pretty, isn't it?" Chris pressed his nose up to the window next to mine.

"It is," I agreed, watching the mountains and rocks loom larger as we began our descent into Flagstaff. "It's like something out of an old Western."

Once our wheels touched the ground and we'd taxied toward the main building, the steps of our Gulfstream lowered onto the tarmac and a rush of dry Arizona air invaded the cabin.

"Remember, it's a dry heat." Chris ducked his head below the doorway, taking my hand and leading me through to the steep steps unfolding outside.

"Does it really matter once it's over a hundred degrees?"

"Hey, I'm just telling you what I heard on the Weather Channel. As far as I'm concerned, heat is heat."

"It's actually not that warm up here," Joe told us, trailing behind me as I descended the stairway. "This is more forest than cactus—you're thinking of Phoenix."

"You've been here before?"

"On a movie set a few years ago."

We were booked into a two-bedroom casita at the Enchantment Resort—a politically correct way for the show to put us within fucking distance of each other without demanding it. A Southwestern theme was celebrated throughout the casita, creating an atmosphere that was ruggedly grand—from rough woven rugs dotting the hardwood floor with jewel-toned colors and Indian symbols, to the softly rounded stucco ceilings and exposed timber beams. Our oversize living room centered around the hearth of an undulating fireplace, whose feminine curves held logs and a blazing fire in its belly.

As the bellboy carried our bags into our respective bedrooms, I investigated one of the three decks leading outside. The scenery was spectacular. Chiseled red rocks jutted from the earth like fingers reaching up to touch the sapphire sky.

"Wow," Chris marveled as he came up beside me, holding two glasses of red wine. "They say this place has all sorts of magical powers."

"It certainly has the power to captivate," I agreed, scanning centuries-old cliffs that were once home to Apaches.

"So does the company," Chris remarked, handing me a glass.

I let my fingers linger suggestively on his hand as I grasped the stem.

"Did you see the garden tub in the master bedroom? An entire wall of the bathroom is a sheet of glass so you feel like you're part of the landscape."

"What? No hot tub?"

"I think we've stepped it up a notch here," he told me.

Our accommodations weren't the only things that we'd stepped up. Although I'd told the bellboy to put my bags in the second bedroom, there was the unspoken possibility that we were going to spend the night together. Our other dates lent themselves to making out on the beach or the couch. This date suggested a prelude to sex.

"So what do you want to do?" he asked, draping his arm gently over my shoulder. "Horseback riding?"

"Are you kidding me? I'm still walking funny from that trail ride the first week. How about another game of tennis?"

"I'm sure you'd love that. Isn't the fact that our first humiliating match is already going to be played on TV for millions of people to watch enough for you?"

"Winning once is never enough. What about heading to the pool?"

"I never thought I'd say this, but I'm getting sick of pools."

"Are you telling me we've run out of things to do together already?"

"Nothing lasts forever. . . ."

"How about a bike ride?" I suggested.

"Perfect."

I rode behind Chris, following his lead along the narrow dirt path. The trail wound along a wooded mountain and at some perilous points required my focused concentration to keep from slipping down the incline acting as the path's natural border.

"The scenery is great up here," Chris called back to me, without turning around.

*It sure is,* I thought, taking advantage of my view of his perfect ass in a pair of shorts.

As Chris worked to power his bike uphill, his thighs became like a map in relief—well-defined muscles swelled under his effort, emphasized by an accompanying hollow that only seemed to make the next wave of muscle appear more powerful.

"Think we can lose them?" Chris asked, looking over his shoulder at the two cameramen attempting to film us without falling off their mountain bikes.

"I'm willing if you are." My voice wobbled as my tires bounced over rocks pimpling the trail.

"On the count of three . . . one . . . two . . . three!"

Our feet flew into motion, our tires turning the dry dirt into smoky powder as we pedaled madly up the hill.

"They gone?" he called out breathlessly.

I turned my head and saw nothing but the mossy-colored trees and red rocks behind us.

"They're gone."

"Good. Let's find a flat spot and take a rest."

About fifty yards up the mountain we came to a cluster of smooth, even rocks and gratefully jumped off our bikes. Chris collapsed onto one of the rocks and uncapped his water bottle, taking hungry gulps until he finally had to stop to take a breath.

I lowered my burning legs down onto the rock next to him and chugged from my own bottle. My chest was freckled with beads of sweat, and Chris's thin cotton T-shirt was damp against his body. I took a deep breath and could smell the musky sweat seeping through his skin. He smelled masculine, strong, raw.

Chris held up his bottle and poured the rest of his water over his head, shaking his soaked hair like a waterlogged dog. "That felt good."

I tipped my face up toward the blistering sun, letting its heat spread down through my tingling muscles. The warm energy renewed me, heightening awareness of my throbbing legs and arms and churning up a lust inside me like nothing I'd felt before—a longing to be in control.

I turned to Chris, placed my hands on his chest, and pushed him back forcefully onto the rock. My body followed his, my hands landing on the cool, hard surface of the rock as I straddled him between my arms. I lowered myself onto him, our sweat mingling until I couldn't tell where he started and I began, and brought my lips to his.

Chris responded tenderly, his hand cradling the back of my head, holding us together as our lips parted and our tongues touched. I let the full weight of my body fall onto him and led his hand up inside my top, placing his palm on my breast. I arched my back and let my breast grow full under the strokes of his fingertips, my nipple puckering as it rose to meet his touch.

The last four weeks had peeled away the layers of marriage and motherhood like an onion, leaving only a sensitive core that was raw to the touch. Every nerve in my body had been brought to the surface, heightening sensations and thrilling me in ways I hadn't experienced since Jack and I first tentatively explored each other's naked bodies.

"Hey, cut it out, the cameras aren't even on," Joe huffed breathlessly, pushing his bike up the trail as another cameraman followed behind, the rolling camera already hiked up onto his shoulder ready to film us. "Arnie's going to go fucking ballistic if we miss anything."

I turned my head to face Joe, my hair falling in pieces against Chris's cheeks.

"That wasn't funny, you know. Your few moments of peace mean we get to listen to Arnie and Sloane rip us new ones for letting you give us the slip." Joe let his bike fall to the ground as the other camera guy moved in closer.

I quickly rolled off Chris and we both sat up.

"Can we head down now?" the other cameraman pleaded. "My arms are killing me."

We hopped off the rock and grabbed our bikes.

The red-faced cameraman let out a sigh and nudged Joe. "Remind me to tell Arnie no mountain biking next season."

"What was up with that?" Chris asked in a low voice, his back to the crew.

"Why? Did I surprise you?"

"You could say that."

I swung my leg over the bike frame and settled down onto the seat, ready to race Chris down the mountain.

"Good."


I sized up the full-length reflection of a tan, relaxed blonde in the mirror on the back of the bathroom door, taking mental inventory of my powder-pink La Perla bra and thong—a far cry from the cotton Hanes waiting for me at home. I took a deep, cleansing breath, hoping I could inhale the courage I'd need to get through the night. I watched my rib cage rise and fall, my boobs become full and then recede back to their normal post-breast-feeding weariness.

Courage. Was that what it took to cheat on your husband? Or did it take something that couldn't be so easily defined by a word, more of an absence than the presence of something? I needed to take charge, to command someone's undivided attention and prove I could hold it, even if gaining that control resulted in something reckless.

The confident, aggressive, vibrant woman I became as I pursued the Stag made me feel alive, like a bear coming out of hibernation and discovering senses that had been lying dormant—the sights of brilliant lights and colors, sounds that both excited and frightened ears that were still getting accustomed to unfamiliar noises, and smells that awakened memories warehoused for future use.

When I thought about this afternoon's bike ride, I could barely remember what it felt like kissing Chris, but I could recall vividly how it felt to seduce the Stag. The kiss hadn't been about an overwhelming need to feel Chris. It had been about an overpowering desire to feel like the Sarah I'd lost.

I slid the silky slip dress over my head and let its flouncy hem fall to my knees. There was no sign of the pink lace underneath the dress's coppery-brown shimmer. I bent over, shook my hair out, then flipped it back, letting the chunky highlights fall randomly down my back. I took one more glance in the mirror before opening the bathroom door and knocking on the wooden door frame twice for luck.

"That was an amazing dinner. I've never had quail before." I squinted up at the dark sky dotted with stars, making the shining white specks blend together into fuzzy, shapeless splotches. After we'd shared a bottle of wine and two more drinks after our meal, making things go fuzzy wasn't exactly a stretch. I wasn't Holly-drunk, but I was definitely toasted around the edges.

"I was saving my appetite for dessert," Chris mumbled, nuzzling his mouth against my neck from behind.

His line sounded vaguely familiar. I'd used something like it my last night with Jack.

Jack. The dreaded four-letter word I'd locked away for the past twenty-four hours shot through my heart, almost taking my breath away. I squeezed my eyes shut and shook my head, hoping to dislodge him. I didn't want to go there. Jack was thousands of miles away. Chris was here.

"Sit down by the fire and relax. I'll be right back with some more wine."

The terra-cotta bulb-shaped fireplace cast a warm glow on the deck as the tangy smell of mesquite drifted up and dissipated in the cool night air.

"I see you've found your spot on the lounge chair." Chris held out a glass of wine and sat on the lounge next to mine.

"I've never done so much lounging in my life, unless you count the summer after eighth grade when I was a substitute lifeguard." I took the glass and brought it straight to my lips.

"I know what you mean. All this dating and vacationing . . . I'm afraid I won't know how to function when I return to work."

"Work? What's that?" I asked, feigning ignorance.

Chris laughed. " 'Happiness depends on leisure.' Aristotle said that."

Of course he did. But he forgot to mention that the amount of leisure time you have is inversely proportional to how many other people are depending on you.

"Did he bother to explain how to find that leisure time?"

" 'Fraid not. Back then I guess it wasn't that hard to find. Remember what it was like when you were a kid, always complaining that you were bored even though you had a closet stacked with games and toys?" Chris reached for the wine bottle and refilled our glasses. "I'd love to have nothing but time to do what I wanted to do. Maybe that's why kids are always so happy—all that leisure time."

I ran my finger slowly around the rim of my glass, thinking about the last time I felt happy. Truly happy, where you stop yourself for a minute and close your eyes, trying to commit to memory exactly what you're feeling so you won't forget. It was probably a month after Katie was born, a Sunday morning in March. Jack and I had woken up to a blanket of snow covering the frostbitten ground. He'd opened the front door to get the newspaper and discovered close to five inches of wet snow already beginning to show signs of melting in the early spring sun. We'd decided to throw on our jackets and hats and gloves and take Katie for a walk. I bundled Katie up, packed into her Snuggly so she'd be warm against my chest, put on an old ski jacket of Jack's, and zipped us up. The snowplows hadn't yet been out to dingy up the unspoiled whiteness, and you could hardly tell the street from the front yards. The three of us walked along, the fresh snow buffering any sound like cotton, creating a silence that almost seemed to echo. Jack and I held hands and talked as Katie drifted off to sleep inside my coat, sucking her balled-up fist. I remember looking over at Jack and noticing how rosy his cheeks were, how clear his eyes seemed, and how adorable he looked with his flannel pajama bottoms tucked into a pair of Timberland boots. There was nobody outside, just me, my husband, and our sleeping baby. A happiness welled up in me from so deep I stopped walking and stood there until Jack's hand tugged on my glove and pulled me close to him. And we hugged—the three of us warming each other with our bodies and breath while our backs faced the stark coldness of winter.

"Earth to Sarah." Chris's voice snapped me back to Sedona. "You know, I thought the resort was taking creative license a little too far with its name, but this place really does feel enchanted."

"It's almost too good to be true. I half expect the mountains and sky to move aside, pulled by a truck like a movie set—revealing a one-dimensional board that some set designer created to fool unsuspecting viewers."

That morning in March was as beautiful as any snowy scene a set designer could have created, but it was anything but one-dimensional. In the moment that Jack and Katie and I were wrapped up in each other I felt a surge of emotions—fear, joy, gratitude, disbelief, elation, love. And in that breadth of sensations I'd felt a happiness that was more profound than any single emotion.

"Joe said he was on a movie set here. I wonder which one?" Chris asked lazily, bringing his hand to his mouth and stifling a yawn.

"Whatever production it was, I'm sure it paled in comparison to the real thing."

I tipped my heavy head back against the thin nylon cushion on the lounge and stared out at the sky, trying to find where it ended. There was no way a movie set could simulate the depth of that night sky. Just as no TV show could come close to replicating the series of events two people had to share in order to develop the depth and breadth of emotions one experienced in a true marriage. The range of feelings I'd had for Jack were as infinite as the desert sky—both as complex and as simple.

The foreign aroma of burning mesquite swam around my nostrils as I wondered what Jack was doing at that exact moment. Was he looking up at the Chicago sky? Did he see that star winking at us, letting us in on its secret—that no matter how far away we felt from each other, we could always find our way back if we remembered where we started from?

"I'm tired."

"Do you want to go inside?" Chris asked, reaching for my hand and turning to look at me. "My bedroom is just right through those glass doors."

I slid my hand out from his grasp and laid it on my stomach. "No. I'd rather not. You go ahead without me, okay?"

"If that's what you want." Chris stood up and waited a moment, as if he expected me to change my mind, and then walked away.

I closed my eyes, resting my heavy lids as I listened to my breaths gradually give way to sleep.

"Sarah," Chris spoke my name softly as he gently rocked my shoulder. "Sarah, get up."

I peeled my eyes open and saw golden embers glowing in the fireplace. The fire had long since burned itself out.

"It's almost seven o'clock in the morning. You fell asleep out here."

"I'm thirsty," I said, sitting up.

"Me, too. How about some breakfast. Should I order us some plain old juice and eggs, or do you want something more adventurous?"

"A plain old breakfast is fine. I think I've had my share of adventure."

# 20

*W*hen I opened the front door to the hens' bungalow, two voices echoed down from the living room.

"Holly? Jesus, Arnie, you really think we could fill up eight episodes with her?"

"Come on, she's the perfect hen—she looks good on film."

"It's not her looks I'm concerned with. I'm not sure she has what it takes to carry a show—mainly a brain and integrity."

Arnie sighed. "Okay. I'll go call the office and tell them to come up with someone else."

"What's going on?" I asked Sloane, putting my bags down in the front hall.

She spun around on the low heels of her wing-tip lace-ups, and faced me.

"Oh, nothing. Just an idea for a spin-off—*The Hen.*"

"And Arnie wants Holly to be the Hen?"

Sloane rolled her eyes at me before looking down at her clipboard and scribbling notes with her Montblanc. "That's not going to happen. I assure you."

The dismissive tone of her voice grated on me. The show had only one week left, and I'd had enough of Sloane Silverman.

"Sloane, why do you have such disdain for us?" Us? Had I really become one of them?

"I don't have disdain for you, Sarah."

"Then what's with all the snide remarks? The embarrassing hidden cameras? Calling us Stepford-wife wanna-bes and all that crap?"

Sloane looked up at me before continuing. "Sarah, I was referring to the way you were all afraid to show who you really were, all that polite conversation and fake smiling. This show is about women, not Barbie dolls."

"Then why do you act like you hate us?"

"I don't hate you. In a way I envy you."

"You envy us?"

"Sure. I envy your choices."

"What choices? There's only one Stag."

"I'm talking about more than just the show, Sarah. When I was in my twenties, more than thirty-five years ago, women didn't have that many choices. We didn't have careers. Few of us went to college, and even fewer went on to medical school or business school. We were expected to get married and spend the rest of our lives taking care of other people. And that's great, if that's what makes you happy. But at least you have the right to choose the life that makes you happy."

"But you have a great career."

"Let's be honest here, Sarah. I produce *The Stag*. I'm not exactly Sherry Lansing."

"But you've made it in an industry where few women succeeded before you."

"And I had Arnie. I was his wife, so people just put up with me at first, thinking how sweet it was that I wanted to tag along with him while he worked."

"But you weren't tagging along at all, were you?"

"Are you kidding me? Arnie had the aspirations, but I had brains. Don't get me wrong. He opened doors for me. I wouldn't be here without him, and I knew that going in. I needed him, but I didn't—"

"Then why are you doing a show like this?"

"It's not my place to judge you or the women on the show. At least they know what they want and have the nerve to go after it—even if the *it* is a husband. It may not be what I'd pursue, but at least it's their choice."

Arnie appeared in the doorway to the kitchen with a cell phone pressed against his ear. He waved a hand at Sloane, beckoning her to join him.

"I'd better go see what's happening."

"Hey, Sloane, ever consider using Joe as the next Stag?"

Sloane stopped and grinned at me. "That wouldn't be TV, Sarah. That'd be more like real life."

Sloane's words hung in the air long after she'd disappeared into the kitchen with Arnie. She was right. I had choices. I'd almost forgotten. Jack and I had come up with the grand plan of how our life was supposed to be way before I'd even figured out what I wanted to be. Or who I wanted to be. And a part of me had resented that—resented that I had to adhere to a plan I'd been only half-conscious of making. But I'd chosen to go along with that plan, and was every bit as responsible for the way things were. As much as I'd blamed Jack for the way I felt, he didn't take anything away from me that I hadn't willingly given away.

I was so busy revising my article I barely had time to remember that Chris was away on his overnights with Rose and Samantha. After my three previous article ideas fell flat, I had a lot of time to make up. My conversation with Sloane had given me a new idea, one that was completely different from anything Suzanne was looking for, but it had an angle that would still work for the magazine. At least I hoped it would.

By Sunday night I'd finished the final draft and put away my notebook for good. With *Femme*'s offices closed for the weekend, I couldn't tell Suzanne. Sure, I could probably have called her at home, but there wasn't really any point. I had nothing to lose by staying one more day; my only flight option was a red-eye back to Chicago, and this way Suzanne would think I'd gone the extra mile by going through with the fifth candle ceremony. Besides, there was no risk that Chris would pick me to stay. By not sleeping with him in Sedona I figured I'd sealed my fate.

Over our simple breakfast something had changed, almost imperceptibly. We took our cues from each other before talking and apologized when our hands accidentally touched as we both reached for the butter. Our interaction, once charged with electricity, lacked the sparks that had kept us attentive and alert to the signs that we were both still dancing the dance. On the trip back to California, Chris didn't act disappointed, but I had to wonder if he wished he'd gotten lucky instead of spending the night alone.

On Monday, Samantha, Rose, and I joined up for the first time all week as we waited on the front steps of our bungalow for the limo to bring us to the sixth candle ceremony.

"You guys have fun trips?" I asked them as we saw the familiar black stretch henmobile rolling down the driveway toward us.

Both of them looked beautiful, dressed in strappy sundresses—Rose in a dusty pink floral print and Samantha in pale tangerine.

"It was amazing—what a blast. I'd never been to Hawaii." Samantha reached over and pulled a loose thread off my skirt. "There, that's better."

"Our flight to Mexico was a nightmare. We hit all this turbulence, so we had to stay buckled in our seats while the plane bounced around. Even Joe looked green." Rose reached down and adjusted the strap of her shoe before continuing. "But once we got there it was great. The storm we'd flown through had already passed over, so the weather was perfect."

Samantha smiled at us as if remembering an especially nice moment with Chris that she wanted to keep to herself. "You know, I like to think of myself as a pretty positive person, but even I had my doubts about coming here. I figured I'd just come and have a good time—take advantage of the experience as long as it was on the network's tab. And then I found myself actually falling for Chris. I know this is probably a weird thing to say to both of you, considering the situation, but somehow knowing that two other women I like also fell for him makes me think that perhaps this isn't the weirdest thing in the world—that maybe it is possible Chris could be as great as he seems."

I smiled weakly at Samantha, feeling like an imposter.

"I kinda know what you mean," Rose agreed. "Even now, after four candle ceremonies, I sometimes wonder what I'm doing here. I'll be on a date with Chris and then I'll notice a camera sticking out of a bush or a boom floating over my head. It's bizarre. I'm glad I didn't have to go through this alone."

"Sure, but it would have made the candle ceremonies a lot less nerve-racking," Samantha joked.

I spent the twenty-minute ride to Chris's house listening quietly to Rose and Samantha take turns recalling their trips, each one discreetly skipping from dinner to breakfast as they glossed over the issue of where they'd spent the night. I couldn't help but wonder what other parts of the trips they were editing out to spare the other person's feelings, or if Samantha had a repeat performance of Catalina. They both smiled and laughed and worked hard to keep the conversation upbeat, practically accenting every other sentence with an exclamation point as they avoided the obvious—that no matter how great the trips sounded, one of us was leaving alone tonight. And I knew it would be me.

Chris was waiting for us when our car pulled up in front of his house. With a gentlemanly arm he held open the front door and brushed a soft kiss on our cheeks. He was as affable as always, neither his eyes nor his actions revealing any clues that would allow one of us to brace herself for the worst.

"This time I don't even know where to start," Chris began, his charcoal suit and red tie adding an oddly formal air to our intimate as-sembly. "You're all here because the past four weeks I've grown close to you. I hope that the person who leaves tonight knows that I agonized over this decision."

Chris took his candle from the host, avoided our eyes, and walked over to Rose.

She let out a nervous laugh and then put her hand to her mouth as if about to bite her nails, but must have realized what she'd done and let her hand drop to her side.

I glanced over at Samantha, a woman who always seemed to be in perpetual motion and seemed capable of turning any situation into a good time. She stood completely still, staring straight ahead at nothing.

I was so intent on watching Samantha's reaction to receiving Chris's candle that I didn't even notice that he'd moved in front of me until I heard him take a breath and tip his candle toward mine, where his single flame split into two like dividing cells.

Samantha's blue eyes grew large and round as they filled with water like fishbowls. She held them open as long as she could until her lids began to quiver. Finally Samantha gave in and let them fall, squeez-ing her eyes shut as two pregnant tears splashed against her cheeks.

How could I let Samantha leave when I knew that she had real feelings for Chris and all I had was an article? Damn Suzanne! It was easy for her to assign an article where I'd compete against the other woman—she didn't have to watch Samantha get her heart broken. But, as much as I wished I could blow out the candle, I knew I couldn't. After all, it was my job. It was what I'd come to California to do.

Chris took Samantha by the hand and led her from the living room, which signaled Pierre into action like a court jester lightening the mood after an execution.

"Okay, ladies, this is it. The final ceremony will take place Fri-day evening. This week you'll each have one last time to see Chris. Rose, you'll have dinner here at the house on Wednesday night, and Sarah, your dinner will be on Thursday."

*    *    *

"You're kidding me." Suzanne gasped on the other end of the phone. "You can't leave now."

"What?" What was she talking about? Of course I could—I had to!

"Sarah, you've made it to the final ceremony—think what that will do for interest in the article. Sure, hearing what goes on at *The Stag* is interesting, but hearing about it from someone who made it all the way to the final ceremony is, well..." She paused, trying to find the right word. "It's just fucking fantastic!"

"But I already got what I came for," I insisted.

"But it will be incomplete. You can't not see this thing through to the end."

Sure I could.

"Sarah. That's just unprofessional," Suzanne added, hitting me where it hurt.

"Fine, I'll stay. It's just a few more days."

"Super! I can't wait to tell Rolf and Suma and the twins. You just sent their fees skyrocketing, darling, and they were obscene to begin with."

I couldn't help but agree with her—this entire idea was obscene from the beginning.

"Here we are again." Chris looked at me across the dining room table, which was set with paper napkins and plastic plates.

"A small improvement over pizza and beer, but we haven't quite progressed past eating out of cardboard boxes." I passed the container of stir-fried chicken to Chris.

"Not exactly boneless breast of quail in cream wine sauce."

"Can you tell me something?" I asked abruptly, practically cutting Chris off midsentence.

"Sure."

"Did you nix Holly because she was a bad drunk?"

Chris laughed, and then realized I was serious.

"Is that what you think? No way. I'm sure you'll find this hard to believe, but I've been known to overindulge and make an idiot of myself now and then, too."

"Then how did she last so long?"

"You know, I can't explain it. Up until our trip she acted like a nice person, most of the time. Looking back I should have known something was wrong, because she'd say these things that I thought were nasty, but she said them with that Southern drawl and a Colgate smile, so I couldn't tell whether she'd meant to be rude or whether it was just my imagination."

"So what happened on the trip to change your mind, if it wasn't her getting sick?"

"When we were in the limo going to the hotel, she had these whitish cottage cheeselike curds all over her hair and down her shirt—I guess it was the Brie. Anyway, I asked the driver for some towels and I was trying to wipe her hair off, but she kept telling me to stop, that I was messing up her hair. I mean, here she was with a headful of curdling dairy, and she wouldn't even let me help her. She was so concerned with taking care of it herself, pushing me out of the way anytime I reached over. At that point I knew she had to go. She just wasn't a team player."

"And that's important?"

"Hell, yeah. I'd like to know that I could rely on her to wipe chunks off my head if the situation were reversed—even if she was gagging as she did it."

I hadn't meant the conversation to become an analysis of how to handle the remnants of vomit, but I couldn't let it go.

"Maybe she was afraid to admit she needed your help," I suggested, tapping the cellophaned fortune cookies with my chopsticks.

"Why would she be afraid?"

"Maybe she thinks she's not supposed to ask because you expected her to be perfect. That if she asked for what she wanted, she'd seem selfish."

"When you're married *not* asking for help is selfish. You're supposed to be able to lean on the other person—people like to feel needed. If you're both out there doing your own thing, afraid to act like you need each other, then what's the point? You may as well be roommates."

I took a bite of my egg roll and tried to swallow what Chris said. Even if he had zero experience in the marriage department, maybe he knew what he was talking about. I had seven years' experience and I sure as hell was no expert.

"So were you surprised when I picked you?" Chris asked, changing the subject.

*Surprised* wasn't exactly the word I'd use. Guilty. Fraudulent. Hypocritical. Undeserving. Those were more like it. I'd stood next to a tearing Samantha and become acutely aware that while she had genuine feelings for Chris—that while she'd been spending her time falling in love with a man—I'd been spending time with the Stag. Holly had been right: I didn't love Chris. I simply loved who I was when I was with him. And yet I was the one holding the candle. The woman who was more interested in the way the Stag made her feel than in the Stag.

I was as bad as Holly. After five weeks I hadn't even bothered to ask his favorite color.

"What's your favorite color?" I asked.

Chris looked up from his chow mein. "Blue."

Or his middle name. Or where the scar on his hand came from. I didn't know all the seemingly insignificant things that you discovered little by little when you were getting to know someone—someone you really cared about.

It never even occurred to me to ask Chris the things I'd loved discovering about Jack. Like when he had his first kiss and the first time he had his heart broken—by someone other than me.

"Are you nervous about tomorrow's ceremony?"

I glanced up at Chris, noticing the camera over his right shoulder as the red light waited for my answer.

"I'd think you'd be the nervous one. I'm not the one who has to make a decision."

"You never know. You may have more choices than you think."

Had Chris been talking to Sloane? Or was I having a serious case of déjà vu? All this talk about choices—if I knew seven years ago what I know now, would I have made the same choices?

I tried to imagine life without Katie and Jack, and I felt my chest tighten as if it were straining to contain the emotion welling up inside me.

I didn't wait for Jack because I had to or because he expected me to. I waited because I couldn't imagine not waiting. I still wanted to watch him walk through the door, to have him put his arms around me and smell his familiar smell. In those moments I could close my eyes and remember what it was like to anticipate his arrival at the library, eagerly looking for his faded Cubs baseball cap and navy windbreaker to be revealed to me one step at a time as he made his way up the stairs to our favorite spot between a row of West's Business Law texts and the microfiche machines.

There were nights when I could have gone to bed instead of staying up watching *Letterman* or *Cheers* reruns while I waited for Jack to pull in the driveway. There were days when Jack's schedule was so filled with pretrial hearings and depositions that squeezing in a phone call to me was nearly impossible, but he somehow managed to call, even if it was just to say hi. And it wasn't out of a sense of obligation, because after seven years of marriage we'd stopped feeling like we owed each other anything. It was that we still clung to those stolen moments like childhood memories.

As all good soldiers do, we'd taken our wedding vows and turned them into marching orders, never questioning the grand plan as we tucked our own needs away and hoped, in time, they'd stop screaming to be let out. But instead of rallying us together for a common cause, the plan had turned us against each other as we built up fences as incapable of penetration as barbed wire. And while Jack buried himself

in a bunker so deep I didn't know how to reach him anymore, I pretended not to need the things that the women on the show demanded as
their right.

"It's getting late," I told Chris, taking the napkin off my lap
and placing it on the table. "I'd better get going."

"Is everything all right, Sam?"

Did he just call me Samantha?

"Sam?" I repeated.

"I didn't call you Sam." He brushed away my question with his
hand. "Did I?"

I nodded.

"God, Sarah, I'm so sorry. You know I didn't really mean it.
It's just been a really tough week. It gets so confusing."

"It's fine. Don't worry about it," I assured him, not really bothered by the slipup.

"Are you mad?"

"Not at all." I smiled for what seemed like the first time all
night. "You said exactly what I needed to hear."

"Don't you want to see what your future holds?" he asked,
handing me a fortune cookie.

I let the cookie sit on the table untouched, its crescent shape
holding my prediction like a secret. "No, thanks. I think I'll just let my
future unfold."

Chris walked me outside to the waiting limo, keeping some
distance between us and never once reaching for my hand.

"Are you sure you're okay?" he asked, tucking some hair gently
behind my left ear.

I nodded. "See you tomorrow?" I asked, sliding onto the car's
cool leather seat.

"Not if I see you first," he teased, waving as the car drove away.

# 21

The next day I woke up late, savoring my last morning in California. After a glass of juice I walked barefoot down to the beach and wandered along the water's edge, letting the shallow water wash my sandy feet. Today wasn't just the last candle ceremony; it was the day Sarah Divine Holmes ripped a page out of the Sloane Silverman book of choices.

It was almost two o'clock by the time I got back to the house. Following a hot shower, during which I washed the last of my California experience out of my hair, I threw my Stag wardrobe into my suitcases, not bothering to fold the carefully selected clothes or keep the impeccably matched outfits together.

After I tucked my cosmetics bag and toiletries into the corners, I walked down the hallway to the kitchen. The camera crew was munching on sandwiches, taking a break before filming the final two women on their way to the last candle ceremony.

"Hey, Joe, can I see you for a minute?"

Joe grabbed a napkin and patted the side of his mouth before following me back down the hall to my room.

"What's up, Sarah?"

"Can you do me a favor?"

Joe nodded and listened as I explained how I needed his help.

"No problem, Sarah. I'll meet you out front."

When I was through packing, the room was as immaculate and unspoiled as when I'd arrived, the only sign that I'd been there a contraband Ritz robe hanging off the bathroom doorknob.

"Sarah?" Rose stood in my doorway wearing a pale periwinkle halter dress and high-heeled sandals that tied up her ankle. "My car's waiting out front, but I just wanted to say good luck before I left for Chris's house."

Rose and I were meeting separately with Chris. It was more romantic that way, as opposed to receiving a proposal in front of someone who wasn't chosen.

"Thanks, Rose. You look beautiful."

Rose glanced down at her dress and smiled. "You're not taking your robe?"

"Nope. I've got everything I need. Are you all packed?"

She nodded and looked almost sad for a moment.

"How are you feeling?" I asked.

"Weird. I knew that if I made it to the end it would come to this, but now it seems just a little too real."

"I know. I can't believe it's almost over."

"Yep. I guess this is it. I don't know if going first is a good thing or a bad thing, but in any case the driver is waiting for me." She reached over and gave me a hug. "I'm glad I got to know you, Sarah."

I returned her hug. "Me, too."

As I waited for the director's assistant to collect my luggage, I took one last look around. If I was going to go through with my plan, I didn't want to leave anything behind.

I zipped up my suitcases and brought them to the door just as the assistant arrived.

"Hold on a second." I held up my finger for him to wait, and grabbed my notebook out of my carry-on. I tore out a page and scribbled a few sentences. I had to explain that it wasn't his fault. It was only fair. My choice had nothing to do with him—and everything to do with me. The note was short but to the point—I was in love with someone else.

"Is this everything?" he asked, taking the two luggage handles in his hands.

I grabbed my purse and joined him in the doorway. "That's it."

When we reached the front foyer, I could see the limo waiting for me in the driveway, along with a taxi and the cameras.

"Here, I've got it," Joe offered, taking my luggage from the assistant, who didn't mind giving my two overstuffed bags to a willing replacement.

"Can you take care of this for me?" I held out the folded piece of notebook paper with Chris's name on the front.

Joe took it from my hand and stuffed it in the back pocket of his jeans.

"Thanks for the help," I said, smiling at the guy who'd chronicled my journey through a lens.

"No problem. The cab is waiting."

I followed Joe outside as he led me to a cab, and opened the rear passenger door.

I slid into the seat and leaned forward toward the driver.

"John Wayne Airport, please," I instructed.

The cab pulled away, gliding past the black stretch limo still waiting for its passenger. I didn't need to know whether or not Chris was going to pick me. It wasn't his decision that mattered anymore. It was mine. I didn't have to wait in front of him with a candle, wondering what his choice would be. I'd made mine, and that was all that mattered to me anymore.

I sat back and waved good-bye to Joe as the cameramen ran after the cab filming my exit scene. I was ready to go home.

"What the hell are you doing home?" Jack asked, coming into the foyer to meet me as soon as he heard the front door open. "A guy named

Arnie keeps calling here looking for you. He keeps asking if my sister's here. What happened?"

I put my bags down on the hardwood floor and looked at Jack. His hair was flattened on one side from lying on the couch, and there were pillow creases on his cheek. An ad for ESPN was playing on the TV in the family room.

"I came home early. It was the last day of the show anyway."

"Well, you've got this Arnie whipped into a frenzy. Didn't you tell anyone you were leaving?"

"No. It was kind of a last-minute thing. I just wanted to come home."

"We're glad to have you home." He reached out and pulled me into his arms, burying his face in my hair.

Jack's skin still held the fresh smell of Irish Spring and shaving cream. I wrapped my arms around his worn Chicago Cubs T-shirt and inhaled the familiar smell I'd been loving for years.

A shrill ringing interrupted us.

"That's probably Arnie again," Jack said. "Do you want me to answer it?"

"No, that's okay. I'll take it in my office."

Arnie barely waited until I finished saying hello before the questions flew. What the hell was I thinking? Didn't I know they were filming the final show? Why didn't I let him know, he could have had the cab miked? When the barrage finally died down I took a deep breath and started explaining.

"I wanted to come home."

"While I applaud your sense of drama, what about the show? And Chris? What if he was going to pick you? It was the final candle ceremony, for Christ's sake!"

"I know. I'm sorry." I thought about Joe and all the other crew whose jobs depended on *The Stag* getting picked up for another season. "I just couldn't go through with it."

"She couldn't go through with it," Arnie called to someone in the background, a someone who I assumed was Sloane.

"What is it with you girls?" he asked me, talking back into the receiver. "First you ditch the Stag, then Rose."

"Rose? She turned Chris down?"

"As if she had the chance! Chris was about to light her candle when this raving lunatic bursts through the front doors of the Stag's villa yelling something about buying the cow, or drinking the milk or something. Anyway, he runs toward Rose and falls on his knees, pulls out a ring, and proposes to her. The entire crew was looking at me like I'd planned it—as if this wack-job was a setup. Shit, I *wish* I was that good."

"Oh, my God. Rose's ex-boyfriend came to get her?"

"Apparently so. We got it all on film, so it'll make great drama, but how do we beat that next season? We had a police raid, a crazy ex-boyfriend . . . and here we thought it was Claudia who was pregnant."

"Rose is pregnant?" I gasped.

"Unfortunately, no. That would be too good—there could be a follow-up series capturing the birth or something—*The Chick* perhaps." Arnie mused for a minute before continuing. "We're going back through the hours of footage. She thought she was pregnant and called her ex-boyfriend. We got a terrific shot of her crying. But then she took a test and never called him back to let him know either way."

"Jesus, Arnie." I was speechless. Even Arnie couldn't have co-ordinated that kind of season-ending cliff-hanger. "Look, I'm sorry. I know I should have told you, but I just wanted to get out of there. It sounds like you had an exciting candle ceremony anyway."

There was silence on the other end of the line.

"Yeah, well." Arnie had calmed down and didn't seem to know what to say. "At least this season's final episode won't be predictable."

"Thanks for everything, Arnie, really. Tell Rose I said congrat-ulations. And tell Chris I'm sorry, too," I added.

As I laid the receiver on the cradle, I realized what Arnie had just told me. Chris was going to choose Rose. He wasn't going to pick me.

Jack's bare feet were padding softly down the stairs, and when I looked up he was standing in the doorway of my office. With our daughter.

"The phone woke her up," he told me quietly, holding Katie's sleepy little body in his arms. "Is everything all right?"

I watched him stroking Katie's head, trying to soothe her back to sleep. A man who five weeks ago worked too much, forgot plans, and probably didn't know where we kept the laundry detergent. And here he was, home with his wife and daughter, in an old T-shirt and sweatpants, cuddling our bleary-eyed toddler. Looking absolutely perfect.

"Everything's fine."

# 22

*J*ack turned around when he heard me shuffle into the kitchen in my fuzzy slippers.

"Hi, sleepyhead," he greeted, wielding a spatula. "Feel like some scrambled eggs?"

"Sure," I agreed, wondering when Jack had even discovered we owned a spatula.

Katie was in her high chair shoveling moist lumps of yellow-and-white egg into her mouth.

I bent down and kissed my daughter, who looked up and gave me an openmouthed smile and a mommy-bird's view of her breakfast.

"She's had enough. Why don't you guys go spend some time together in the living room and I'll call you when the eggs are ready?" Jack came over to us and snapped the high chair tray off. "I'll wash this."

"Hey, Hazel, if you see my husband anywhere around here, would you let him know his wife is looking for him?" I teased, un-buckling Katie from her safety strap and lifting her fleshy body into my arms.

I thought I heard Jack laughing as Katie and I walked out of the room.

I held Katie and wandered through the familiar rooms of my home. The dental molding around the fireplace still had traces of Katie's Barney stickers. And I was sure I'd find a sippy cup between the couch cushions if I searched hard enough.

Picture frames sat on tables and bookshelves, chronicling Katie's short eighteen months and my past with Jack. A prewedding ski weekend to Vail stood in a pale wooden frame next to a delicate glass oval holding our wedding picture. If the pictures represented our life together, you'd have thought we met, we got married, and we had Katie. As if between getting married and having a baby we forgot to stop and create new memories to sit beside our past and our future as a family.

"Barney." Katie pointed to her purple dinosaur propped up against the couch having tea with Pooh.

"Hey, that reminds me. Katie, stay here. Mommy will be right back."

I ran upstairs and took the stuffed Tigger out of my suitcase. It seemed like ages ago that I'd been wandering around Disneyland. My first real conversation with the Stag had already grown vague.

"Here you go, sweetie." I added Tigger to her collection of plush friends.

"Breakfast's ready," Jack called out.

I scooped up Katie and followed the smell of bacon back to the kitchen.

"What's your guitar doing in the living room?" I asked, sitting Katie on my lap at the table.

"Katie and I were playing a little music while you were gone."

" 'Twinkle, Twinkle, Little Star' or 'Foxy Lady'?"

He smiled sheepishly, found out. "A little of both."

"And why is there a dartboard on our fireplace mantel?"

"Well, weekends were getting a little boring around here with just me and Katie, so I asked some guys over to hang out with us. And after listening to you talk about playing pool and darts, I went downstairs and dug out my old dartboard."

"On the mantel? You must have been pretty confident in your abilities. I didn't see any holes in the wall."

"Yeah, well, just don't move the board. It's strategically placed to hide my mistakes."

Over breakfast Jack filled me in on what I'd missed at home, mainly silly little things Katie had learned in my absence.

"Why don't I put in a Pooh video for Katie and I'll help you clean up?" I offered, taking a last bite of my English muffin.

Once Katie was all settled down on the couch with her animals and a video, I joined Jack at the kitchen sink.

I watched as he dunked our breakfast plates into the soapy water and sponged off remnants of our morning meal.

"Here, I'll get that," I told him, reaching for a wet plate before he placed it into the dish rack to dry. I snatched the dish towel he had hanging over his shoulder and started rubbing away the remaining droplets.

"When did it stop being fun?" I asked softly, keeping my eyes on the plate.

Jack had his hand immersed in a juice glass, sponging off slivers of orange pulp. He didn't have to ask what I meant.

"Probably about the time following the plan became more important than figuring out what we wanted," he answered without taking his hand out of the soapy glass.

"Remember when you wanted to drop out of law school? Do you regret letting me convince you to stay?"

Jack handed me the dripping glass but didn't let go even after I reached for it. We stood there looking at each other, sharing our hold on the glass.

"Sarah, you didn't convince me to stay. I may not have wanted to be in law school at that moment, but I did want to practice law. I just had a crisis of confidence. That's not unusual when you're twenty-five."

True. What about when you're thirty-four?

"So you like what you're doing?"

"Yeah, I do." Jack turned back to the sink and started working on the silverware. "But I get the feeling I'm the only one."

"It's not that I don't like writing, or staying home with Katie. I just wish I felt like quitting my job was my choice, instead of doing what the master plan said I should."

"I sometimes think we mapped our lives out like we thought they should be instead of seeing where they led us." Jack handed me the forks. "Back then it was easier that way. It made an uncertain future less frightening."

"Well, the way things are scares me. The fact that I feel like we're strangers scares me."

"Me, too. It's like all you see is a lawyer and all I see is Katie's mom. We stopped looking for Jack and Sarah."

"I miss Jack."

"Well, you've found him. And while you were away I found him, too." Jack took a sudsy finger and placed it on the tip of my nose, leaving a cluster of bubbles. "Is there anything I should know about before the show airs?"

I wiped the suds from my nose and fell silent.

"I'm not going to like this, am I?" Jack pulled the plug out and we both watched as the water began spiraling down the drain.

"Why don't we sit down and I'll tell you everything," I offered, wanting to come clean to Jack.

We moved to the table and I told him. Everything. About the dates and the kisses and how I'd felt good about myself for the first time in ages. I explained the intoxicating feeling of being wanted and desired by someone, and how I remembered the last time I'd been truly happy—with him and Katie last winter.

"Anything more than that?" he asked, looking down at the table. "You didn't do more?" He looked up painfully at me, his eyes soft.

"No, I didn't. I contemplated what it would be like with another person and I couldn't imagine it. The only thing I could picture was being with you. I'm sorry, Jack. I realized I didn't have to lose you to find myself. I don't know what I was thinking." I reached out for his hand, which he let me take.

"I don't know what *we* were thinking." He squeezed my hand. "Somewhere along the line I just lost track of me, I guess."

"It wasn't just you. We got busy, life got busier. It was just easier to keep moving forward instead of stopping to remember what we were trying to do in the first place."

"It's no fun sitting at home waiting for someone to remember you, is it?"

"No, it's not."

I lifted his hand to my mouth and kissed it softly. "Why are you being so nice? I don't deserve it."

"No, you don't. But I'm sorry I didn't notice how unhappy you were."

"It wasn't just you; it was me. I let you forget me."

"I never forgot."

I got up from the table and moved over next to Jack, kneeling on the floor. "I love you, Jack."

He turned to me and took my face in his hands. "I love you, Sarah."

Our arms were wrapped around each other when Katie came toddling into the kitchen and found us kissing. She ran over and wormed her way into the middle of our hug until the three of us were squeezing so hard we could barely breathe, but none of us wanted to let go.

I spent the rest of the day typing up the final article, and then left Suzanne a message that I'd meet her in the office first thing Monday morning. I had some explaining to do.

"There she is, our hen!" Suzanne rushed toward me, her miniskirt rising along her fishnetted legs. "I can't wait to read it."

"Hey, Suzanne," I replied cautiously. I was already afraid to show her the final piece. Even though the show had paid for all my expenses, Suzanne did not take kindly to people wasting her time.

"You look great, all tan and relaxed. So tell me. How bad was it? Were the producers just horrid?"

"I had to change the direction of the piece again. The producer thing wasn't working." I started explaining, rushing on before she could get upset. Suzanne didn't like surprises. "I had another idea, but it's not exactly what you were expecting. Some things changed and I had to reflect those changes in the article in order to accurately depict what went on."

"Well, let me see it then."

I slid the typed, double-spaced pages across her desk.

"Love the title," she told me, pushing her glasses along the bridge of her nose with a single manicured finger.

I watched as she read the first few paragraphs, anticipating an uplifted brow or pursed lips—something that would indicate what she thought of the final product.

### Bachelorette Number One
### By Sarah D. Holmes

They arrive with a goal in mind, a mission to fall in love with the man of their dreams. They are dismissed regularly—nine here, two there—and return to their jobs, their friends, their lives. And, although they resemble the people they were weeks before, they're not the same women who left to take their chances on *The Stag.*

The media calls them losers, desperate women willing to put everything aside in their quest for a man. Male viewers pity them. Female viewers openly loathe them, and secretly

believe they could beat them if they were on
the show.

But as they walk out the door and leave
the limousines, champagne, and pink sunsets
behind, they know in their hearts that they've
won. They've won back their power to decide
what's right for them. They've reclaimed their
right to decide that they're happier alone
than with someone else. They leave knowing
that while the Stag may look perfect on the
cover of *People* magazine, he probably doesn't
remember to put the toilet seat down. Romance
fades, fairy tales end, and the harsh light of
day drowns out the candles' flickering flames.
It's what's left inside that they carry with
them.

All that matters is that, in their own
minds, they're bachelorette number one.
They're the catch. They're the ones who will
choose whether or not someone is right for
them and what they will compromise to make
love work. Because they haven't simply realized that they're number one—they've recognized that they're the only one. The only one
who can decide. The only one whose opinion really matters.

At last, her eyes stopped traveling across the page and she sank
back silently into her posh leather chair.

Suzanne pinched the frame of her glasses between her fingers
and carefully removed them without smudging the lenses.

"To say it's not what I expected is an understatement." She
started tapping the arm of her frames against her desk. "But it's good.

It's fresh. Empowering women to take charge of their destiny—
applauding the fact that they've taken responsibility for their choices.
It's exactly what our readers are all about, isn't it?"

"I'd like to think so."

"I'll need to read the entire article, of course, but so far it
sounds like you got to the heart of the story—even if it wasn't the story
we anticipated."

My shoulders fell a little as I relaxed. Suzanne was going to
approve the article.

"So what's going to happen when the piece is published? Will
they still run the show? Is the magazine going to get sued?"

"Do you reveal who gets picked in the end?"

I shook my head. "Actually, I don't even spend that much time
on the candle ceremonies. It's really about the women more than it is
about the competition."

"If we're not giving anything away, then they'll probably issue
a statement saying that we broke the rules, they're reviewing their legal
recourse, blah, blah, blah. But they'll secretly love the publicity, and it
will all blow over. We could even end up increasing the show's ratings—
who knows?"

"That's good." I wanted the article to run, but I didn't want to
hurt Chris or the show. "One more thing."

Suzanne stood up and came around to my side of her desk.
"Yes?"

"Do I get to keep the clothes?"

Back at home, I was on my stomach in the family room reading the
newspaper I'd picked up on my way through the train station. As I
leaned on my elbows trying to concentrate on the articles, Katie sat on
my back and yelled giddyap as she smacked my butt and pulled the
jump-rope reins we'd fashioned around my neck.

I couldn't help but remember that first trail ride in California, when a group of strangers were brought together under the most

bizarre of circumstances. Probably what surprised me the most about the entire experience wasn't that I'd made it to the end, but that I'd made friends along the way. Dorothy, Vanessa, Samantha . . . they were women I'd already labeled and filed away before I even met them. Looking at me they probably did the same thing. We probably ended up surprising each other.

I think once all the women turned their backs on the Stag and walked out the door, they realized that the experience wasn't a waste just because they didn't make it to the next round. The experience made them take a closer look at themselves. If anything, it made them better. In this case, the losers may even have gained more than the winner.

When Dorothy and I talked, I was wrong. I hadn't given up my life for a guy. I'd chosen to make my life with a guy. And I wasn't sacrificing anything to do so.

Maybe I'd thought that being the perfect wife and mother should take the place of being me—that it could be a replacement for all the other things I'd always wanted to do. And in the process of denying myself, I'd changed Jack and he'd let me. How weird to think that *The Stag* may have helped us grow closer, and that being apart for five weeks could actually make things better.

I was reading the "Happenings" section of the paper when the jingle of keys landed on the kitchen counter.

I grinned from ear to ear. Jack was home.

"No smile, Mommy. Horse," Katie ordered, jamming her heel in my side.

"We're in here," I called out to Jack, but he was already standing in the doorway watching us.

"Hey, you want to see if Marta can baby-sit Saturday night? Purple Haze is playing in the city. It says here they're the best Hendrix cover band around."

"You want to go see a Hendrix cover band?" Jack asked skeptically, kneeling on the floor next to me.

"Sure, why not?"

"Great. I'll call Marta tonight." He leaned over and planted a kiss on the cowgirl's chubby cheek. "Do you still have those lacy things Suzanne bought you for the show?"

I nodded.

"Think you could wear them under your outfit Saturday night?" he asked.

"I think that can be arranged; after all, I hear it's the latest in groupie fashion. Could you take Dale Evans here for a minute?"

Jack peeled Katie off my back as I hoisted myself up off the carpet.

"Welcome home, Jack." I took my husband and my daughter in my arms, making a Katie sandwich.

"Welcome back, Sarah."